WITH NO REMORSE is

"An edgy, sexy thrill ride you won't want to miss. I look forward to her every release."
—Christine Feehan, #1 *New York Times* bestselling author

More praise for CINDY GERARD and her *New York Times* bestselling BLACK OPS, INC. series

"Romantic suspense at its best!"
—Kay Hooper, *New York Times* bestselling author

"Gerard's deadly Black Ops series kicks romantic adventure into high gear."
—Allison Brennan, *New York Times* bestselling author

"Excellent . . . straightforward, immediately engaging writing style."
—Robert Browne, author of *The Paradise Prophecy*

"Gerard artfully reveals the secret previously known only to wives, girlfriends, and lovers of our military special-operations warriors: These men are as wildly passionate and loving as they are watchful and stealthy. Her stories are richly colored and textured, drawing you in from page one, and not simply behind the scenes of warrior life, but into its very heart and soul."
—William Dean A. Garner, former U.S. Army airborne ranger and *New York Times* bestselling ghostwriter and editor

RISK NO SECRETS

"Gerard dishes thrills, heartbreak, and sizzling love scenes in rapid-fire succession. . . . Brace for a hot, winding ride and a glorious ending."
—*Winter Haven News Chief* (FL)

Also by Cindy Gerard

CINDY GERARD

WITH NO REMORSE

Pocket Star Books
New York London Toronto Sydney

Pocket Star Books
A Division of Simon & Schuster, Inc.
1230 Avenue of the Americas
New York, NY 10020

This book is a work of fiction. Names, characters, places, and incidents either are products of the author's imagination or are used fictitiously. Any resemblance to actual events or locales or persons, living or dead, is entirely coincidental.

First Pocket Star Books paperback edition August 2011

POCKET STAR BOOKS and colophon are registered trademarks of Simon & Schuster, Inc.

For information about special discounts for bulk purchases, please contact Simon & Schuster Special Sales at 1-866-506-1949 or business@simonandschuster.com.

The Simon & Schuster Speakers Bureau can bring authors to your live event. For more information or to book an event contact the Simon & Schuster Speakers Bureau at 1-866-248-3049 or visit our website at www.simonspeakers.com.

Cover design by Lisa Litwack

Manufactured in the United States of America

10 9 8 7 6 5 4 3 2 1

ISBN 978-1-4516-0681-2
ISBN 978-1-4516-0685-0 (ebook)

There is no other choice. This book, like the books before it, first and foremost is dedicated to the brave and valiant men and women of the United States military. I am forever grateful for their unfailing dedication to duty, to country, to honor, and to defending the American way. You are a continuing source of inspiration for the characters I create.

Also to Micki Nuding—amazing editor—for making this story sing and dance! Thank you so much for the wonderful edit.

Finally, to my wonderful, loyal, enthusiastic readers who spend their hard-earned money on my books, who write to me and tell me how much they love them, and who fuel my fire to deliver stories worthy of their praise. Thank you so much!

Acknowledgments

It feels like we're heading into broken-record territory here, but I have to acknowledge some of the same very important and special people who have held my hand, critiqued, and supplied vital information in the writing of this book. Susan Connell, Joe Collins, Glenna McReynolds—I don't know how I could have done it without you. Gail Barrett, brilliant author, thank you so much for sharing photographs and information from your trip to Peru. Because of you, I almost felt like I had been there.

And Tommy—you are the bedrock that keeps my foundation solid. Without you, my world would fall apart around me. I love you, honey.

Author's Note:

I had so much fun researching this novel. Peru is a magical and mystical country and I fell in love with everything about it during the writing of this book. While I attempted to be as accurate as possible with geography, for the sake of the storyline I "enhanced" some of the topography and "created" a new railroad line with a midnight run to Cuzco. In my humble opinion, there should be one anyway. ☺

Whoever said the pen is mightier than the sword obviously never encountered automatic weapons.

—General Douglas MacArthur

1

Luke Colter's number one rule of self-preservation: Don't ignore the itch.

The last time he'd blown off the warning, he'd ended up gut-shot and on life support in a San Salvador hospital. So when he felt that first tickle of unease skitter along the back of his neck, he shot straight to attention.

Nothing looked out of sync inside the gently rocking train as it ate up the miles across the Peruvian Andes in the middle of the quiet June night. Still, his heart had kicked up like that of a marathon runner on his last leg, so he methodically scanned for signs of trouble from his seat in the middle of the dimly lit passenger car.

Everything looked status quo, a bunch of tired people making the best of the overnight ride on the hard, narrow seats. Everything smelled status quo, too: the damp wool of the Quechua farmers' ponchos, stale tobacco smoke, the faint aroma of llama dung on the bottom of someone's shoe, and the moldy, musty scent that always seemed to permeate enclosed spaces in the Andes.

Had he misread the sensation? At this elevation, the air was so thin that even the locals chewed coca leaves to keep light-headedness and a slew of other altitude sickness issues at bay. And God knew, at three a.m., after two weeks of lugging his medical kit through the mountains from one Quechua village to another, he could be a little off his game.

Face it, Colter. You've been off your game since El Salvador.

His hand moved involuntarily to his side. Close to a year later, he still felt the occasional twinge of pain. But it wasn't the pain that bothered him. More and more lately, he woke up in the night drenched in sweat, reliving the shooting yet again.

Enough, already. He was so not going there tonight, because too easily and way too often he let himself get dragged into that sucking pit of quicksand. A sure way to get killed in his line of work was to think about dying. About almost dying. About being so scared you were gonna die that you made promises you knew you could never keep. Promises to God. Promises to the devil.

Promises to your mom.

At what point is enough, enough, Luke?

Yeah. Quicksand.

He scrubbed a hand over his stubbled jaw and glanced around the train again. The half-full car held a few mestizos, a few misfits like himself, but most on board were Quechua, the indigenous people of Peru. And most of them were asleep, including the teenage boy curled up on the bench seat across the aisle.

The kid, who'd boarded the train several stops back, was out cold, using his backpack for a pillow and his poncho as a blanket. Mildly curious, because he was as bored as he as weary, Luke had been trying to figure the kid out. Nothing about him quite fit in a neat little package. Number one, even though a quick glimpse of the little he could see of the boy's face told Luke he clearly had Latino blood running through his veins, he was not mestizo. Couldn't be Quechua, either. He was too tall, too slim, and although his striped wool poncho looked like local goods, the cut and fit of his faded jeans screamed money and American made. Number two, he seemed a little young to be traveling alone in South America, especially this time of night. And number three, the way he wore his navy blue watch cap, so low over his brow that it met the ridiculously huge aviators parked over his eyes—in the dark, no less—smacked of hiding out, like maybe he was trying to conceal his identity.

Or maybe it was just the latest fashion statement of some rich man's kid who was on a great, indulgent adventure and one day he'd be hitting on girls at the tennis club, retelling tales of his travels through the wildness of Peru. Whatever. Luke was beyond trying to figure the logic of a teenager's mind, and didn't care enough to ask.

God, he was tired. Dog dead tired. He could use another week off, but tomorrow it was back to Buenos Aires. Back to the trenches. He swallowed the acid taste of dread.

Suck it up, nancy boy. It's not like you've got a lot of options.

The military and then Black Ops, Inc. had been his life for years. The life he'd always wanted. Yet since San Salvador . . . well. Since San Salvador, his backbone seemed to have gone the way of the dodo bird.

Was his mother right? Had he given enough? Had he *had* enough? Was that what this erosion of his nerve was trying to tell him?

Bleary-eyed, he stared at the large dust- and fingerprint-smeared windows and pushed back the memory of his mother's heart-wrenching tears.

Outside, the night scrolled by, star-studded and black. Iron wheels on iron rails rumbled and clacked in a rhythmic static of endless white noise. In front of him, someone snored. Other than that, it was all quiet on the western front.

So . . . back to the itch. False alarm? Short circuit? Too many celebratory pisco sours at the medical team's farewell party last night? Or was he merely feeling the tension as he headed back into bad-guy-and-bullet-look-out mode after his annual two-week leave from Black Ops, Inc.?

He could use some more time to get his shit back together. Time where his biggest fear wasn't of dying, but of causing a five-year-old Quechua girl to cry when she saw the needle and syringe containing the vaccine that could save her life.

On a huge yawn, he settled his stained, brown leather fedora lower over his forehead, determined to catch a few z's before the train hit Cuzco. That's where he'd catch his flight back to Buenos Aires and return to life in the kill zone. Crossing his arms over his chest and his battered boots at his ankles, he slumped further down on the hard bench seat and closed his eyes.

He was almost asleep when he felt the itch again.

His eyes snapped open.

Luke Colter's second rule of self-preservation: Don't second-guess rule number one.

A split second later, the interior lights blared on like strobes. The brakes engaged, metal screamed against metal, and one hundred fifty tons of iron on steroids waged immediate and full-scale war against the law of inertia.

The car erupted in a cacophony of startled shrieks and yelps as shocked passengers jerked awake, battling a g-force determined to wrench them out of their seats, and damn near tossed Luke off his own perch. He caught himself before he went airborne. The boy across the aisle wasn't as lucky. He rolled off the bench, slammed against the seat in front of him, and dropped with a thud to the floor.

Luke was about to lean across the aisle to help him up and check for broken bones, when the train ground to a screeching stop.

The screams rose even higher at the front of the car. When Luke glanced up he saw the reason why. Two rifle-wielding banditos had burst inside.

"*Manos arribas. Ahora!*" Hands in the air. Now!

The gunman's Spanish was lost on the Quechuas, but he got his point across by aiming a state-of-the-art assault rifle toward the ceiling and firing off several rounds.

"Well, hell." Luke's disbelief was outdistanced only by his disgust with these assholes, who were probably going to make him do something he didn't want to do. And disgust with himself because Mr. Cool-Under-Fire Colter was feeling a little too much like diving out an open window and letting someone else play hero.

At what point is enough, enough?

When there was world peace, he thought sourly. When guns didn't kill people, and he and Osama Bin Laden sat around a camp fire holding hands and singing "Kumbaya."

Shit. He'd morphed into Miss Frickin' America.

Get a fucking grip!

Pissed at himself for even thinking about bailing, pissed that his ears were going to be ringing for a week from the close-quarters rifle fire, and *royally* pissed that he was probably going to have to deal with these yahoos, he reached for the SIG Sauer P238 he always carried on his hip . . . and swore when he came up empty.

Luke Colter's third rule of self-preservation: Never, ever go anywhere without a gun.

Helluva time to break rule number three.

"Stay down," he ordered in a strained whisper when he saw that the kid had levered himself up off the floor.

"What . . . what's happening?" the frightened boy whispered back in English as he gripped the seat in front of him and peeked up over it.

"Nothin' good." Never taking his eyes off the action in the front of the car, Luke reached across the aisle, planted his hand on top of the kid's wool cap, and pushed him back down. "Stay the hell down."

Keeping his own profile low, Luke locked on to the gunmen as they systematically worked their way down the aisle demanding cash and jewelry. Slowly, so he wouldn't draw their attention, he unsnapped the sheath of the Leatherman multi-tool attached to his belt. His frickin' hand was shaking as he worked his way past the pliers, screwdriver, scissors, and bottle opener, finally locating the three-inch blade folded inside the housing.

Okay, fine. Adrenaline had kicked in, accounting for his unsteady hand. It didn't mean he couldn't get on top of this. Didn't mean he'd totally lost his nerve.

It *did* mean he had to get his act together. They had two damn big guns, he had a three-inch knife made to cut leather and rope. And since bullets trumped blades any day of the week, he had to figure out some kind of force equalizer.

He shot a scowl skyward, getting madder by the minute. *Really? Was it really too much to ask? A lousy two-week vacation? No bullets? No bad guys? Nobody's life on the line? Especially mine?*

Muttering under his breath, he slouched deeper into the seat and prepared to roll into combat mode just in case these guys got too frisky.

He hoped to hell they didn't.

Yeah, he'd turned into *that* man. Once upon a time, he'd have relished the thought of putting the hurt on these two cretins. Now he was looking for escape routes.

At what point is enough, enough?

Get out of my head, Mom!

The memory of her standing by his hospital bed in San Salvador, tears tracking down her cheeks as she took in all the tubes and machines keeping him alive, made his gut ache.

"You almost died this time, Luke. What do you have left to prove, son? And for God's sake, who are you trying to prove it to?"

Same person he'd always tried to prove himself to: his dad, who had never forgiven him for walking away from the family ranch. Old story. Old news.

He'd hated seeing his mom that way. Hated knowing that his parents had dipped into their meager rainy-day fund for the airfare to get to him, knowing even before he'd offered that his dad would be too proud to let Luke reimburse them. But he hated even worse that they'd had to see the horrors of his world.

You almost died this time.

Yeah, so what? Between his SEAL days, his stint with Task Force Mercy, and his current position with the Black Ops, Inc. team, he'd almost died a dozen times. So why had he let El Salvador get to him, turn him into someone he wasn't proud to be?

Who the hell knew? The only thing he *did* know was that there was a good chance he was going to die tonight if he didn't pull his head out of his ass and do what he was trained to do.

He slid the stainless steel housing of the Leatherman up into his sleeve and palmed the blade. Then he sized up the Bad-Ass twins and his odds of taking them out.

They were short and heavily muscled—possibly Peruvians, definitely Latino—and they knew exactly what they were doing as they worked the aisles with the precision of a well-oiled machine. Something about that precision rang alarm bells from here to Lima.

In the first place, this wasn't one of those jazzed-up sightseeing trains that hauled cash-laden *touristas* back and forth from Arequipa to Machu Picchu. This was a bare-bones transport train carrying mostly locals who barely scratched out a living raising potatoes and beans. They probably didn't have any cash, so why target this particular train? And who the hell robbed a train in the middle of the night when it was likely to be half empty?

Something else bothered him. While they dressed like run-of-the-mill thugs, both carried state-of-the-art HK416s dressed up with laser target designators and high-tech holograph scopes. The automatic rifles were souped-up versions of the U.S. military's M-4, tricked out like Cadillacs on a showroom floor. *Big*, big bucks. No low-rent bandito had access to that kind of firepower.

So if they weren't locals, then who the hell were they? He immediately ruled out the possibility of them being terrorists. The government had pretty much gotten *El Sendero Luminoso*—the Shining Path—under control in this area. Besides, there wasn't a damn thing of value in these mountains, tactical or otherwise. To top it off, they were speaking Spanish. The prevalent language here was Quechua or Aymara; most of the passengers wouldn't even understand Spanish, which the bad boys would have known if they were from around here.

Something was way off-kilter . . . not the least of which was the fact that they seemed to be more intent on searching the faces of the passengers than they were on robbing them. As they drew closer, Luke grew more and more certain that a search, not a robbery, was their main objective. When the kid popped his head up above the seat again and they spotted him, it got real clear, real fast, who was the object of their search.

Bad-ass number one nudged his partner in crime, pulled a photograph out of his pocket, consulted with the other man over it, and pointed in the boy's direction. Then both gunmen headed straight down the aisle toward him.

"I told you to stay down," Luke growled, sinking lower in the seat to avoid drawing their attention. "Wanna tell me why those nasty boys are looking for you?"

"*Me?*" Shock colored the boy's pinched voice. "They aren't looking for me. Why would men like that be looking for me?"

The two assholes were closing fast—until one of the passengers panicked. A older Quechua man wearing a bowler hat and sandals made from rubber tires jumped up out of his seat and started running down the aisle. The lead gunman instantly shot him in the back. No hesitation. No mercy. No remorse.

The railroad car erupted in more horrified screams and wails, which the shooter silenced with another blast of his rifle into the ceiling.

Now Luke was royally pissed. There had been no reason to shoot anyone. Yet a man lay dead or dying, shot without provocation.

At what point is enough, enough? When the world was free of scum like this.

A sudden calm washed over him, the combat calm that took him to the place he always went when he knew there was no other option, and where fear didn't factor in. A place where muscle memory and gut instinct ruled, to get him through the fight.

He glared at the shooter with hard, cool eyes. When the sonofabitch with the quick trigger finger shot that unarmed man, he'd sealed his own fate.

2

"This is going to get real ugly, real fast," Luke warned the kid. "So when I say move, you move."

A mix of confusion and paralyzing fear crossed the boy's face.

"Listen." Luke leaned lower and drilled him with a hard look. "We'll sort out the details later. In the meantime, denial's not gonna keep you alive. For whatever reason, they've targeted you. If you want to get out of here in one piece, I suggest you get on board with me and do it now. We clear?"

The kid gave him a sharp, clipped nod.

"Then make like a mole and burrow as far under that seat as you can get."

The boy moved like a bullet, dropped to all fours, and skittered under the wooden seat.

Luke's hands were steady, his head clear as he pulled his hat low over his brow and watched from beneath the narrow leather brim as the men approached. He figured they had to be just the tip of the spear. Someone else had to have stopped the train, and was most likely guarding the engineer so he couldn't call for help or try to take off before their ugly business was finished. So there was more than just these two bad boys to deal with.

One problem at a time.

"¿Qué pasa?" he mumbled, adopting the sluggish speech of a half-conscious drunk as the pair stopped between the seats.

"Silencio!" The shooter took a bead on Luke's chest when he faked a failed attempt to stand. He fell clumsily back into the seat, hands in the air, palms open, the picture of helpless submission.

The second gunman bent over and reached for the kid. To his credit, the boy scrapped like a street brawler, kicking and swinging and giving the bandito all he could handle when he started dragging him out from under the seat.

When the shooter glanced down to see how his partner was doing, Luke made his move.

He kicked the gun skyward, sprang to his feet, and hooked one arm around the guy's neck. With the same mercy the bastard had shown the unarmed Quechua man he'd just killed, Luke sliced the blade of the Leatherman across his carotid artery.

The man collapsed in Luke's arms. His rifle clattered to the floor as his hands scrabbled helplessly at his throat. He was already as good as dead; he'd bleed out in less than three minutes.

Before Luke could grab the rifle, the thug who'd gone after the kid reared upright.

"Run!" Luke yelled.

The boy crab-scrambled over the dying gunman, then stumbled toward the rear exit while his attacker came up swinging.

The butt of his rifle clipped Luke hard on the shoulder, knocking him back onto the seat. Luke gripped the seat frames on either side of him for leverage and kicked his boots hard in the guy's gut. When he doubled over with a *whomp* of pain, Luke flew to his feet again, grabbed the front of the guy's shirt, and slammed his head into the metal seatback. The would-be kidnapper dropped to the floor like a bag of sand.

Luke had just stomped his heel into the guy's throat and finished him off when two more men burst through the front doors of the car, rifles drawn. When they spotted their downed *compadres* they sprinted straight toward them.

It went against all his fighting instincts—and he was running on pure instinct now—but Luke knew he had to run. Odds were good that there were more bad guys waiting in the wings. There was no winning this battle. Not against these numbers. If he removed the kid from the mix—and despite the kid's denial, Luke was certain the boy was the main attraction—a lot of innocent people stayed alive. *He* might even stay alive.

He quickly slung his backpack on one shoulder. Grabbing a rifle and a handgun that he shoved into his waistband over his right hip in a Mexican carry, he sprinted down the aisle.

"Keep moving!" he ordered, catching up to the kid as a blast of automatic weapon fire missed them by inches.

He fired high over the passengers as he retreated, then jerked the rear door open. "Jump and roll!"

When the boy hesitated, Luke heaved the rifle out the open door in a sling toss, prayed for the best, then grabbed the kid's arm and launched them both out of the train.

Legs and arms flailing, they hit the ground hard, rolling together like a pair of runaway logs down the steep embankment flanking the railroad tracks.

When they finally slammed to a stop a good twenty yards away from the tracks, the kid had landed on his back beneath him. Like Luke, he was gasping in pain from the hard landing. But now wasn't the time to lick their wounds—the bad boys would be barreling out right behind them with a helluva lot more pain in store.

Luke started to push to his feet, but stopped abruptly when the moon broke through the heavy cloud cover and cast the boy's face in soft shadows.

The aviators had flown off in their wild plummet down the ravine. The watch cap was gone, too.

"What the—" He did a double take at the long black hair fanning over the ground, then took a quick, hard look at the kid's face.

The eyes that stared back him, glazed with pain and wide with fear, were decidedly familiar. And the boy wasn't a boy at all, but a woman.

Slender. Gorgeous. And very *much* a woman. A very *familiar* woman.

"Jesus H. Christ." Luke shot to his feet, grabbed his hat, slapped it against his thigh to bang out the dust, and resettled it on his head. Then he reached for her hand and dragged her up with him.

"Stay!" he ordered and sprinted back up the hill to retrieve the rifle.

He found it lying cockeyed against a rock. The pricey scope had been knocked off in the tumble down the ravine. He cursed the bad luck, then raced back to her side.

Grabbing the rest of his gear, he clutched her elbow and took off at a run. "You've got a lot of explaining to do."

But not right now. Right now, as the shouts of men grew closer, he needed to tend to a pressing little matter called running for their lives.

Rifle fire cracked through the crisp mountain air, echoing off the mountain peaks. The *pa-zing* of bullets slamming into the dirt at their feet, then glancing off a rock just behind them, had Luke moving fast, ducking low and pulling her close. The short head start and the cover of night were the only things they had going for them.

Now was not the time to make a stand, not when he didn't know how many guns they were up against. Two for now, but there could be others. Besides, he had no idea how much ammo he had in the guns he'd lifted from the dead men. Until he had time to take stock, he couldn't be shooting off rounds in the dark. Every bullet was going to count.

With his hand clasped tightly around hers, he ate up

the ground in a crouching run, hurrying down the steep, rocky slope in full retreat mode. If the shooters had night-vision goggles—and as well equipped as the rifles were, he had to figure they did—he and the woman were easy targets out in the open. He'd have given his left nut for a stand of trees to hide in, but had to settle for the thick clumps of tall, brittle grass dotted across the open ground. He darted from one to another, never staying put for long before taking off again, pulling her along with him as he worked his way toward his goal.

Fifty yards ahead, the barren ground gave way to one of the massive rock formations this area was known for. If they could make it there, they had a chance of losing those goons in the maze—or of getting trapped in a box canyon.

Since he didn't have a Plan B, he decided not to think about that prospect as more bullets zipped near their feet. He just ran, hoping he didn't die before he found out what this particular woman was doing in this particular place at this particular time.

Finally they reached the tall spires and gigantic boulders that made up the canyon, its walls towering as high as twenty feet in places, as little as five in others. He picked a meandering path, swearing when he slipped on the stone floor slick with scree and the beginnings of frost.

Fifteen minutes passed as they rushed down a winding path, dodging scrub brush and deadfall and fighting for breath. Then half an hour, then an hour as they threaded their way beneath a series of steeply pitched cliffs, following twisting trails cut by thousands of years of wind and rain and erosion. They didn't exchange a word, only stopped for brief moments to listen for pursuit as the wind whistled through the canyon walls, their lungs burning, backs pressed against the cold stone, eyes watchful. Then they ran again, tripping over rubble, skirting rock piles, hiding deeper in the murky darkness and tall slabs of stone until finally, the voices faded and eventually drifted away to nothing.

"I think we lost them," Luke whispered. He gulped in a serrated breath of air that smelled of damp earth, cold stone, and the winded woman at his side. "At least for now. Let's take a minute and catch our breath."

His sides ached; his lungs screamed for oxygen in the thin air, pressuring his heart so it pounded like a bass drum. Hers had to be doing the same as he steered her to a wide crevice cut into a wall. Above, a rocky overhang knotted with gnarled tree roots and the detritus of thousands of years provided some shelter.

They leaned back into it, then slid to the ground exhausted, sitting side by side, sucking in great gulps of air.

As he fought for a deep breath, Luke kept an ear out for the bad guys and took stock of their situation. The handgun was a Glock 19, a solid weapon. The fifteen-round magazine was only short one round and it was in the chamber.

He checked the broken scope mount on the rifle, cursed silently, and unclamped it from the barrel. The scope was useless; he'd make do with the iron sights.

Next he ejected the rifle's magazine and checked its ammo supply. Half full. Add the nine live rounds left in the clip to the one already chambered, and he had a total of ten shots. With the pistol, that made a total of twenty-five rounds. Twenty-five freakin' rounds between him and the guys with the working scopes and, no doubt, several extra mags.

That just meant he had to shoot better than they did — hard to do when his hands were shaking like a virgin's knees on her wedding night. Any SEAL worth his salt would call this a slam dunk. Hell, at his peak, he could have outgunned most bad guys armed with automatic weapons, with a slingshot. Even on an off day he should be able to outshoot these yahoos, because shooting was all about muscle memory, which was programmed into the reptile portion of the brain. It was time to channel his inner anaconda and get a goddamn grip.

He let out a deep breath and assessed the weather conditions. The sky was mostly cloudy and dark. That, at least, was good for them. It was also cold. Not so good for them. Sixty to sixty-five degrees Fahrenheit was the average daytime high in June, but it could drop into the twenties at night. It was heading that way now; the patches of frost underfoot told that tale. They weren't feeling the bitter cold yet, because adrenaline and exertion kept the blood pumping hot. But the chill would set in soon enough. He could take it, but he worried about her.

Luke set the rifle beside him, tucked the gun back in his waistband, and glanced at the woman panting for breath beside him. Even in the dark he could still make out her features, see the rise and fall of those famous breasts beneath her dark turtleneck shirt.

He still couldn't believe it.

"Valentina," he muttered and could tell by the way her shoulders sagged and the resignation on her face that she wasn't happy he knew who she was.

Keee-rist.

Valen-*freakin'*-tina.

The Valentina. Like Beyoncé or Madonna, one name was enough to tell the entire world who this woman was.

How in hell had he ended up on the run, in the Andes, with a woman whose face and body had inspired more wet dreams than a man his age should ever admit to?

He suppressed an incredulous laugh and slowly shook his head. The first time he'd seen her image, he'd been seventeen, stuck on the ranch in Montana, and at the height of his horny period. He'd been bored to death, running a ranch errand for his dad, cruising down the interstate in the pickup on the way to Billings. And there she was, only a teen herself, stretched out on her side on a fifteen-by-fifty-foot billboard along I-90, her long, dark hair blowing in the wind, seductive smile beckoning, the ripe curves of her young body artfully draped in a filmy piece of champagne-colored silk, all sex appeal, innocence, and original sin.

His teenage brain had shut down like a smashed clock; he'd damn near driven off the road. And though a lot of years and a lot of women had passed since then, the "Valentina mystique" had been rockin' a little corner of his world ever since.

He'd had it bad for the California-born model whose melting-pot heritage—a blend of Latino, African American, Irish, and Cherokee Indian—had created outrageously exotic beauty.

But now wasn't the time for a stroll down teen-memory lane. Now was the time for some answers.

He was fairly certain they'd ditched their pursuers, but caution kept his voice low. "Okay, time for Twenty Questions. And you know what's at the top of the list."

She gulped down a breath and let her head fall back against the rock wall. Her thick black hair trailed halfway down her back and Jesus, he had another flashback to those long-ago nights with a flashlight shining on a magazine spread featuring her angel face and sinner body, doing what teenage boys with runaway hormones did in the dark, in their beds.

"What's a nice girl like me doing in a place like this?" she suggested in a voice made husky by the effort to replenish her lungs with oxygen.

He was relieved she hadn't danced around the issue. "That'll work for starters."

She rolled her head to the side and glanced at him just as the clouds parted for the moon. The vulnerability on her astonishing face coupled with the moonlight that shadowed her perfect brow elevated his heart rate by at least a hundred beats per minute.

Down, boy.

"Just taking a little downtime." She looked sad. "Anyway, that was the plan."

Right—it all came back to him. A few months ago, he'd spotted her photo on the cover of a gossip magazine while waiting to catch a flight out of Buenos Aires. After checking to make certain the rest of the guys weren't watching, he'd been all over it. And, after reading the article, he understood why she would want to disappear from the spotlight these days.

Couldn't say he'd been brokenhearted to read about her very public divorce from Marcus "Irreconcilable Differences" Chamberlin, the golden-boy senator from California, but he had felt bad that the paparazzi's constant hounding over the "fairy-tale couple's" divorce had forced her into seclusion. Now he knew where that seclusion was—and it sure as hell wasn't a spa in Switzerland, as the tabloids had speculated.

No need to explain why she was traveling in disguise, either. There wasn't a corner of the globe remote enough for Valentina to hide in. Her legendary beauty had made her internationally famous.

Jesus—he was on the run with *Valentina*. Barely able to suppress a laugh, he wiped a hand over his face. *Of all the gin joints in all the world . . .*

"So," he whispered, after scanning the shadows again, "who were those guys?"

"I told you. I have no idea."

He raised a brow. "No. Seriously. Who were they?"

A hand flew to her chest. Eyes as dark as ebony narrowed in anger. "What did I just say?"

Hokay. The lady had a temper, and she clearly didn't like being questioned. "Well, they sure as hell knew who *you* were."

She hugged herself against a chill that he'd known adrenaline overload couldn't stave off forever. Unfortunately, she'd lost everything—her poncho, her hat, her bag were all back on the train with his jacket.

"They couldn't have been after me." She looked confused but committed. "No one even knows I'm down here."

"Darlin'," he said, exercising what he thought was a fair amount of patience in the face of the obvious, "they killed a man to get to you. They were willing to die to keep me from taking you away from them. They obviously knew *who* you were and exactly *where* you were."

3

Her look of mystified agony cut straight to Luke's heart. She shook her head. "No one knows I'm here," she insisted again.

"Seriously? You don't keep in touch with anyone? Not even your parents?"

"My father was a nonstarter. My mother is dead."

He'd forgotten. More tabloid journalism filled in those gaps. She'd never known her father. Her mother had died in a car accident several years ago. "What about a best friend, then? Or your manager?"

"If I stumble on an Internet café, I contact my manager to let her know I'm fine. As for telling her where I am, no. Even she doesn't know."

Well, someone knew. No one of her celebrity status dropped that far off the grid. And a simple tap on her office computer could back-trace those brief e-mail messages and provide a loose fix on her location. For now, though, he'd play it her way because *now* was all about getting out of here alive. If he managed to pull that off, he'd find out what she wasn't telling him later.

They probably should get moving again but, damn, he still couldn't catch his breath. The thin air at this altitude was a killer. She was having the same problem. Five more minutes—then they were out of here while their luck held.

"Why are you helping me?" she asked.

He couldn't stop a confused blink. "Are you for real?"

She blinked right back.

"Because you need help, for God's sake," he said when her silence demanded an answer. "Well, not *you*, as in Valentina, but *you*, as in a kid who looked scared to death. Was I supposed to just sit there and watch them do whatever they planned to do with you?"

"So, you're what . . . a natural-born hero?" The sarcasm in her tone was outdistanced only by her doubt.

He was surprised by the sarcasm; not so much by the doubt. Hell, he doubted himself. "Actually, I have to work at it these days," he admitted. Until those bastards had shot that defenseless man, he'd been determined to save his own ass and to hell with anyone else's.

But back to the sarcasm. WTF? Was there a raving shrew lurking beneath the goddess façade?

Please, God, no. Don't burst my bubble.

He studied her perfect angel face. No, he told himself decisively. No way. He couldn't have been wrong all these years. She was just scared; he got that.

"Who exactly are you?"

The last time Luke had been given the third degree, he'd been tied to a chair with a gun pressed against his temple. He hadn't liked it then. He didn't much like it now. But because she was scared, because she *should* be wary, because she was Valentina, he cut her some slack.

"Luke. Luke Colter. But my friends call me Doc. And I guess now's as good a time as any to confess that I'm a huge fan."

Crap. That had sounded *so* much better in his head. From the way she scooted a few inches away from him, it was pretty clear that not only had he sounded like a dumbass of epic proportions, but he'd also spooked her.

He raised his hands to show her he was absolutely no threat. "Let's take a little time out, okay?" he suggested, still keeping his voice to a whisper. "Don't interpret *fan* to mean *stalker*. I'm just aware of who you are. Thought it might reassure you. My bad."

Her gaze darted away, and he could see that she was thinking about running.

Yep, he'd spooked her good. Hell, she'd just been chased off a train at gunpoint. She'd seen him slit one man's throat and bash in another one's head. And in his grubby jeans and two-day beard, he looked more like a derelict than a Boy Scout.

She didn't know him from the Unibomber, so from her perspective, what was to say he *wasn't* the biggest danger in these mountains?

"Valentina," he said quietly, shifting to look her in the eye.

Her head went down, but not before he saw the full-out terror on her face.

Aww, hell.

"I know you're scared, but you have nothing to fear from me. I'm one of the good guys."

She still didn't look at him.

"Let's try this," he suggested. "What do you want to know about me? Just ask. I'm an open book." Sort of. Right now she probably couldn't handle the full truth about The Book of Luke.

She still didn't say a word, which meant that *spooked* didn't begin to cover it.

Man, he was blowing this.

"Okay. How 'bout I cover the basics for you? I'm an Aquarius. I love long walks on the beach, soft cuddly kittens, and my red Jimmy Choos. Fave movie—*The Sound of Music*. Favorite food—"

Her narrow-eyed glare was as good as a stop sign. Okay, humor wasn't going to work, either. So how the hell was he supposed to make her relax?

"I'm from Montana," he said, shifting into earnest mode as he swept another glance around them. "Grew up on a ranch, just like John Wayne. Cows. Horses. Big dumb dog who loved me."

He left out the part about being voted "most likely to kiss the girls and make them cry" his senior year.

"John Wayne didn't grow up on a ranch. He was born in Iowa," she said, sounding accusatory.

"I know that," he said, working for reasonable, but it came out sounding testy. "*You* weren't supposed to, though. Give me a break here; I was just trying to find some level ground. So. Seriously. What do you want to know?"

She looked away, then back, her eyes narrowed. "You're a doctor?" she asked, sounding doubtful.

"Doctor?" He rolled back the tape on his clumsy introduction. "Oh. No. Not a doc—a medic. Corpsman, if you want to pick nits. In the Navy. SEALs, actually."

"For real? You're a SEAL?" She didn't want to be impressed but he could see that she was, marginally—if she believed him.

"I *was* a SEAL."

"And now you do . . . what?"

How did he explain that he worked for a private contractor whose business was taking out terrorists, and not lose the little ground he'd gained?

"A little of this. A little of that." He flashed his brightest smile, a tactic that had distracted a helluva lot of women over the years.

He should have known it wouldn't work on her. "Your open book has a lot of blank pages."

Like a dog with a bone, this one.

"Okay, that's fair," Luke conceded and turned the floor back over to her. "Ask away."

It was as much a dare as an invitation. She hesitated only a moment before accepting.

"What's a Montana cowboy turned SEAL turned whatever doing in Peru?"

This, he could handle. "I'm on vacation. I was on

my way back . . . home. The past couple of weeks,
I've been working in the mountains with a medical
team."

That earned him another dubious look. "A medical
team?"

"Humanitarian aid," he said, relieved that she was
finally more curious than wary. "A bunch of us—doc-
tors, nurses, medics—hold clinics every year in the
Quechua villages between Arequipa and Machu Picchu."

She mulled that over, clearly trying to make up her
mind whether she was going to buy it. "How very altru-
istic of you."

Damn. She sure had snark mastered. He decided
to ignore the fact that she'd managed to make it sound
like an insult. "I had a SEAL buddy," he explained,
"who was born near Caylloma. Chewy was a five-year-
old orphan when a missionary family adopted him
and brought him to the States. He was the one who
brought me to Peru the first time. Introduced me to
his people, and to the sad state of their medical treatment."

While the sense of loss Luke still felt over losing
his Quechua SEAL team member several years ago
wasn't as acute now, it was still hard for him to think
about it.

He touched the brim of the hat his old friend had
given him and frowned, not wanting to walk that road
right now. "That was a lot of years ago. Now I'm in the
habit of coming back every year. My two weeks were

up so I was on my way to Cuzco to catch a plane or I wouldn't have been on that train."

Though she still appeared to be uneasy, at least she was watching him with more interest than trepidation now. He could tell that she wanted to believe he was a good guy; she just wasn't ready to take that final step.

"But you know all about humanitarian aid missions, right?" The press loved covering her visits to Sierra Leone, where she and her ex had made frequent trips over the past several years.

She blew off his mention of her charity work in Africa. "And you really were a SEAL?" Her tone was guardedly hopeful.

Due to the Iraq and Afghanistan conflicts and the media's hunger for breaking big stories, most of the world knew about the U.S. Spec Ops units. Along with the Marine Force Recon and the Army Rangers and Special Forces, the Navy SEALS got their fair share of ink and sound bites.

He smiled, upping the "trust me" ante, because he needed her to trust him if he was going to get any cooperation out of her. "Savior of God, country, and the American way."

He was pouring it on thick, but luckily, it worked.

Her shoulders relaxed the slightest bit, and she finally smiled. More of a grimace, actually, but it beat a stick in the eye.

"I guess I really don't have much choice but to believe you, do I?"

Resignation—he'd take it. It worked better for him than her doubt.

"You know, it'd be a lot easier to protect you if I knew who the baddies were."

She bristled right up again. "How many ways can I say this? They *couldn't* have been looking for me. Once they saw me, maybe they recognized me and figured they could hold me for ransom or something. Other than that, I haven't got a clue."

Once again, she was convincing. But if she kept looking at him with those ink-black eyes and beseeching him with that "kiss me, baby" mouth, she could probably convince him that Mahmoud Ahmadinejad was a front-runner for the Nobel Peace Prize.

"Maybe it's a stalker," she suggested in a frustrated tone. "I've had plenty of problems with overzealous fans. Or . . . I don't know . . . I recently fired my agent. Maybe he's gone off the deep end or something."

She was reaching, but he humored her. "Why'd you fire him?"

"Because he was trying to control me instead of work for me."

Luke shook his head. "If what you say is true, that no one knows where you are—"

"No one does," she insisted again.

"Then neither option computes. Stalkers and agents wouldn't have the kind of international connections to find you, let alone send out hit men to the end of the earth. There's gotta be something you're not seeing. Something you're not remembering. Just keep digging into your memory banks. It'll eventually surface."

Her frustration showed on her face. He hoped to hell that his fascination wasn't showing on his. He should probably stop staring at her and keep a keener eye out for the bad guys, but Jesus God, she was stunning. Even more striking now and in person than when he'd first laid eyes on that billboard damn near twenty years ago.

She'd been fifteen or sixteen when she was discovered by a Hollywood modeling agent, whose savvy marketing had used her knock-out beauty and wholesome sex appeal to launch a designer French perfume and catapulted her to international fame. In a world where beauty was generally fleeting and popularity fickle, she had built a career that spanned nearly two decades and was still going strong.

Even eighteen years later, she was still a major fox. Now, however, was not the time to get caught up in one of his all-time fave adolescent fantasies—stranded alone with Valentina and rescuing her from the bad guy of the day—that had bizarrely turned into reality. Just his freaking luck, he finally had her where he wanted her and his hero quotient had hit rock bottom.

He jerked his gaze away from her face. He had to get his shit together: They were a long way from being clear of trouble. It was the middle of the night. The temp had dropped below freezing in the last half hour and the adrenaline rush was letting down fast. If the boys with the guns and night-vision scopes didn't get them, the elements could.

He stood up abruptly, picked up his backpack, and settled the straps on his shoulders. "We'd better get moving. You ready?"

"Like I have a choice?"

She finally smiled, which showed him what he needed to know about her state of mind.

She had spunk. He liked that. She was going to need a lot of it if they were going to get out of these mountains alive.

4

"You are telling me that you have not yet secured the target?"

After excusing himself from the dinner table where his wife, Jin, and their three-year-old daughter, Cho, now awaited him, Ryang Wong Jeong pressed the phone tighter to his ear and closed his office door behind him.

The room smelled of new leather and lemon oil. The furnishings were so recently purchased Ryang wasn't yet comfortable with the placement of the antique black lacquered desk, and was uncertain whether he was pleased with the boldness of the pattern in the woven silk rug. The four-thousand-square-foot Macau high-rise apartment was his latest extravagance. His oasis. His most recent reward to himself—and to Jin and Cho, of course—for the success of his business endeavors.

Now his sanctuary had been compromised by this insult of a report.

"How difficult can it be to detain one woman—a pampered Western woman—and deliver her to me?"

He listened as his operative on the ground in Peru,

where they had tracked the woman via her Internet connections, related the deaths of two of Ryang's assets, killed by a man who had intervened on the woman's behalf.

"This man—he was accompanying her?"

"Unknown. We only saw a glimpse of him after he'd eliminated the men we had sent to remove her from the train."

"Tell me why you are not dead like the others."

A long pause. "We were securing the engineer, ensuring that he did not radio for assistance. By the time we arrived in the passenger car—"

"Two assets on my payroll were dead," Ryang broke in, "and the woman had escaped."

The ringing silence was telling.

"Find and secure her," he ordered with a deadly calm. "Find and dispense with this man who has cost me time and money. And be advised, I have no patience for another phone call advising me of failure."

He hung up, willed his breathing to a steady cadence, then rejoined his family with a smile in place. Jin and Cho were everything to him. He would never allow any of this aspect of his business to touch them.

"My apologies." He plucked his napkin from beside his plate and settled himself at the table. "The kimchi is delicious, do you not agree?"

Jin nodded but looked troubled.

"Now tell me, dear wife," he said in an attempt to allay her concerns, "about the linens you found in the market today."

• • •

They'd been on the move again for over an hour when panic finally caught up with Val. She'd staved it off until then with sheer will. One foot in front of the other. Didn't think about what had happened, what could happen, or why it was happening. She wasn't defenseless like she had been when she was ten years old. She could only be a victim if she let herself become one.

That didn't mean she wasn't entitled to be good and mad. *Why was this happening to her?* She'd been working things out. She'd been living a sequestered existence the past month, exploring and discovering this magical country, rediscovering herself, finally coming to terms with the divorce . . . and bam. On her way back home, ready to resume her obligations, she'd fallen into this nightmare of gunfire and death.

And no matter how vehemently she fought the idea, this stranger who had saved her life was right: It looked like she was a target. A chill eddied through her. Men with guns were chasing her.

She didn't know why. She didn't know who they were. But she was forced to accept that they were dead serious. As Luke Colter had so bluntly reminded her, they'd killed an innocent, unarmed man to get to her.

Her stomach rolled at the memory, which triggered another—a long-ago nightmare of a big man with hard hands, and a dark, creepy cellar. She couldn't let herself think about it; she'd succumb to a panic attack if she didn't keep it together.

So she moved. One step. Then another, and another.

It didn't matter that she was cold or that she'd lost everything—her ID, passport, money, even her poncho—when they'd jumped off the train. Didn't matter that it was dark. Or that she was confused and scared.

So what if her knee ached from her tumble down the hillside? So what if the high altitude made her slightly nauseated, and the air was so thin it felt brittle and raw in her lungs every time she drew a breath?

And so what if she was in a foreign country? On the run. With a stranger. Who had just killed two men.

Okay. Enough. No point dwelling on the bad stuff. On to the good.

Her stomach rolled again. Oh, wait—there *wasn't* any good stuff. Granted, she wasn't on her own, but the jury was still out on this tall, lethal stranger who said he was one of the good guys and tried to make her laugh with an image of him wobbling around in red Jimmy Choos.

She kept flashing back to the image of a knife in his hand, slicing across a man's neck, and blood pouring from the gaping wound.

Oh, God.

The world started spinning and she was that helpless little girl again, trapped in the dark with bugs and rats and . . . She stopped abruptly, planted her hands on her thighs and waited for the dizziness to pass.

"Hey, hey. You okay?"

He was right there to steady her. One strong hand tightened around her elbow, another gripped her waist.

She willed away the wooziness, and surrendered to a knee-jerk, self-protective instinct to pull out of his grasp.

She was suddenly and inexplicably angry. At her situation, at her own weakness, and at the resurrection of those old nightmares she'd thought she'd put to rest. She was even angry at him.

"You know what? I'm really not. I'm not one bit okay."

Hysteria bubbled just below the surface, threatening to suck her under. She was far too familiar with what full-blown hysteria and anxiety attacks felt like, and she was heading straight for a monumental meltdown.

Why did this have to happen on the heels of the debacle with Marcus? What was it with her and men? She'd been young and stupid and gave in to her one and only act of teenage rebellion with Sean Gun. Sean was a wild, reckless rock star with a self-destructive bent that had eventually included a herculean effort to drag her down with him. She'd made an equally herculean effort to deny he had a problem—until the night he'd hit her, then wrapped his car around a tree with her in it. Amazingly they'd both walked away with scratches, but it had been the wake-up call from hell.

Marcus was supposed to be the calm after the storm. With his quiet dignity, his warm brown eyes and surfer-blond hair, and gentle disposition, he was supposed to have been everything right. And for a very long time, she'd thought he was. Only everything had ended up wrong. So very, very wrong.

She couldn't think about that now. She could not

let herself rehash the divorce. And she would not let Marcus's actions turn her back into someone she hated: a weak-willed whiner who couldn't take care of herself.

Right now she had to concentrate on keeping herself alive. To do that, she had to be the woman she used to be.

"Let's rest for a few minutes, okay?" Luke suggested in a supportive, steady voice that begged her to believe he was everything he'd told her he was, with some Boy Scout tossed in to sweeten the pot.

Six months ago, she would have trusted him without a second thought—that's how far she'd moved beyond the horrors of her childhood abduction and how secure she'd been in her marriage. She would have looked into his kind brown eyes, been charmed by his dimpled smile and rugged good looks, and fallen for any line he'd thrown her.

Six months ago, she'd thought her life was perfect. She'd felt protected and pampered and loved. Turned out it was all a joke.

So now she didn't trust anything or anyone to be what they claimed to be. Not even this very competent, very capable stranger who had a little-too-perfect, cow-boy-warrior-Indiana Jones vibe going on.

It was the hat, she decided, straightening and glancing up at him. It wasn't a cowboy hat . . . it was closer to a fedora. Brown suede, well worn, and yeah, it looked like something Indy would wear, exactly the way Indy would wear it—pulled low on his brow, slanted at a rakish angle. And just like Indy he was sexy as ever-loving sin, especially with that heavy five o'clock shadow covering his jaw.

So the movies were old school. When she was in high school, Indiana Jones had been hot and so had Harrison Ford—for her money, he still was. Even though Colter put her in mind of both Ford and Jones with a little Jason Bourne thrown in, she could *not* let that sway her opinion of him.

She glanced up at him. Scowled. Could she really trust him? Or was he just pretending to help her, was in on the deal himself, and trying to win her trust so he could . . . what? What could he possibly want from her?

"Valentina? Hey . . . you still with me, Angelface?" Luke waved a hand in front of her eyes.

She batted it away, confused and unhappy.

"I'm fine," she grumbled, because damn it, she needed to be.

She walked over to a big rock, dusted it off, and plopped down. When she looked up, he was still standing a few feet away. He'd cocked a knee, propped one fist on a narrow hip; his head was tilted at a belligerent angle.

Well, well. Cute cowboy guy was finally fed up with her attitude. Couldn't say that she blamed him. She didn't much like it, either.

"Was it something I said?" he asked, sounding pissed.

She looked away, feeling guilty.

"Or is this rescue just not going the way you'd hoped?" Clearly out of patience with her, he shrugged out of his backpack and dropped it to the ground. "Sorry I haven't stumbled across a Hilton or a day spa for ya, Princess, but in case you haven't noticed, I've been a little preoccupied keeping you alive."

She remained stubbornly silent. She didn't even know why. Or why she was so angry at him.

"Not that you give a shit," he continued, removing his hat and dropping it on top of the backpack, "but can I remind you that I didn't ask for this gig? I could be happily on my way to Cuzco on the train by now." He exhaled a disgusted breath, then muttered to himself, "But no. I had to climb up on my white horse and save her sexy little ass."

That brought her head up. He moved closer, not exactly looming over her, but it was close enough. "What is with you? I don't expect you to fall all over me with gratitude, but couldn't you at least pretend—"

"I'm sorry," she snapped, then dug her most insincere smile out of her bag of tricks, because at least anger gave her some sense of control. "Thank you. I'm ever so grateful that you and your white horse saved my ass. Happy now?"

He snorted and forked a hand through his dark hair, shoving it back off his forehead. "Delirious."

She really looked at him then, wanting with everything in her to believe he was on the up-and-up. His sarcasm was genuine; so was his flare of temper. And oddly, the fact that he'd lost his cool finally convinced her he was for real.

"Look. I get it, okay?" he said, clearly working hard to settle himself down. "You're confused and you're scared and you're frustrated."

She propped an elbow on her thigh and lowered her head to her hand. "Ya think?"

He joined her on the rock, forcing her to scoot over.

"You don't know me," he continued in an understanding voice, "and apparently you have issues with trust."

It was her turn to snort. *Understatement of the year.*

Marcus had obliterated her trust. She'd come to Peru to move past it and to get over him, but it was more than that. She'd come to prove to herself that she could stand on her own two feet again. She'd been so stupid to let him become her life, to have relied on him for everything from dinner reservations to vacation getaways . . . to fidelity.

So this trip had also been about never again becoming that dependent on a man.

Wow. That had worked well.

She was right back where she'd started, relying on yet another man to keep her alive. It rubbed like sandpaper against a burn.

She sat up straight, dragged both hands through her hair, and made a decision. Bottom line, it was either trust him or drive herself crazy, and she already had enough going on in that area. "I'm sorry I've been such a bitch." She was done heaping Marcus's sins on this man's shoulders. "It's just that I'm not—" She stopped, at a loss where to start.

"Not used to being shot at?" he suggested. "Not used to seeing men die? Not accustomed to jumping off trains? How about not used to running through the mountains in the dark and the cold?"

"Yeah. That works.

"Look," she said, "I owe you. Thank you for helping me, okay?"

One corner of his mouth turned up in a charmingly crooked grin. "Okay. And thank you for trusting me."

"You're welcome."

My, weren't they being careful of hurt feelings all of a sudden? All seemed to be forgiven. How could she not like him for that alone?

He smiled at her then, a genuine, no-holds-barred, devastating smile. She let herself smile back before shifting her attention out over the shadowy landscape.

"So . . . do you think they'll give up looking?"

He followed her gaze. "They went to a helluva lot of trouble to find you. I doubt very much that they're going to give up the hunt now."

She shivered. From cold. From fear. From adrenaline overload. "You figure they're out there now?"

"'Fraid so."

Tears stung her eyes, unexpected and embarrassing. She quickly looked away from him, concentrating on measuring her breaths when her chest tightened in the familiar precursor to a panic attack.

"Hey . . . hey. It's okay," he said softly.

She realized just how scared she was when she let him settle an arm around her shoulders and she didn't pull away.

"It's okay," he repeated, and she let him provide the anchor she desperately needed to keep herself grounded.

And when he laid his cheek against the top of her

head and enfolded her with his big, strong body, it felt right to move into him, to wrap her arms around his waist, lay her head on his shoulder, and indulge in the strength of him, in the heat of him, in the steady beat of his heart pounding against her ear.

Safe haven. She hadn't known how badly she needed it. Or how much she'd missed the feel of a man's arms around her.

God, there she went again, needing a man.

So what? Right now, she was too beaten down to care. Now that she'd committed to trusting Luke Colter, she realized how desperately she needed to believe in something good again.

Ten minutes ago she was ready to believe he was with the gunmen. Now she'd declared him hero material.

It showed how much she needed a good guy in her life.

Wait. Whoa. In her life? This was exactly what she'd come down here to escape. She was *not* going there. It was going to be a long, long time before she invited the kind of heartache that came with strong arms and a handsome face.

"It's going to be okay," he promised, stroking her back. "Take all the time you need to get yourself together."

Since there wasn't enough time in the world to make that happen, and since she didn't want to get used to leaning on him, she finally made herself push away.

He let go with a gentle squeeze. "Better?"

She sniffed. "Yeah. I'm . . . good."

"I know you are," he said, smiling kindly.

"So." She squared her shoulders. "Now what?"

"Now we head for Cuzco."

She stared into the dark ahead of them. "How far is it, do you think?"

"See those shadows ahead?" He pointed to a break in the rock wall that opened up to a bank of shadows at the end of a gently sloping field. "That's a stand of trees. We haven't seen trees for a while, right?"

She'd been so busy trying to keep up with him and keep ahead of her panic that she hadn't noticed. Now that she thought about it, though, he was right.

"Most of the land along the train route and main roads has been badly deforested over the years," he added. "Until you get closer to Cuzco, it's pretty barren."

"So you think we're fairly close." Cuzco wasn't much of a city by U.S. standards, but she knew that it was big enough to support some industry and an airport. Like him, she'd been headed there to catch a flight.

"Not as close as I'd like. But if we can find a road and hitch a ride, we can lie low in the city until I figure something out or until they get tired of looking."

They. The bad men with the big guns. She shivered. "You don't think they'll quit, do you?"

"No," he said with a grim look. "But they're going to be damn sorry that they didn't."

5

Val suspected that Luke had meant to reassure her with his ominous statement, but she immediately flashed back to him slitting one gunman's throat, then making quick, brutal work of the other.

"If there had been any other way to get you off that train alive, I'd have taken it," he said quietly.

She nodded, wondering again what kind of man she was dealing with—a man who apparently read minds, among his many talents.

Talents that included the ability to kill without hesitation and then comfort her with uncommon gentleness.

"I really have no idea who they are," she said because suddenly it was important that he understood that. "Or why they're after me. I've sifted through it in my mind again and again but I just don't have a clue."

"It's all right. We'll figure it out. In the meantime, I'm not going to let anything happen to you."

She believed him. Didn't make a lick of sense, but she believed him—this stranger who had come to her rescue, and managed to make her trust him.

"We'd better get going."

She meant to say, "Okay," but her gaze involuntarily stalled on his mouth. His utterly sensual mouth.

A rush of sexual awareness shot hot and deep through her blood. So hot, so deep, she felt the shock of it like a burn.

Embarrassed and mystified by her intense physical reaction, she quickly looked away. Since she'd found out the truth about Marcus, her sex drive had plummeted to nonexistent.

And you pick here? Now? While you're on the run for your life with a total stranger, to unthaw your libido?

Still in shock, she chanced meeting his eyes . . . and realized he'd caught her staring.

Oh, God.

She pushed up off the rock, determined to diffuse this embarrassing turn of events. But when she put her weight on her right leg, a jolt of white-hot pain shot through her leg. She sucked in a breath and sank back down; her hands flew to her knee.

"You're hurt."

She bit her lip and tried to work through the pain.

"You should have told me," he grumbled, dropping to his knees in front of her. "Let me take a look at it."

"It'll be okay. It just stiffened up while we were sitting. It'll loosen up after I walk for a while."

"Could be, but I want to take a look anyway."

She braced her palms on the rock and clenched her teeth as he tried to work her pant leg up her calf.

"This isn't going to work. The legs are too tight. You're going to have to drop trou so I can get to it."

When she didn't move, he looked up at her.

"Yeah," she said with a slow shake of her head. "That's not happening." If she'd been embarrassed before, she was mortified at the thought of stripping in front of him.

He parked his butt back onto his boot heels. "Okay, modesty is not on the table here."

"*You're* not the one undressing," she pointed out. Or wearing only a thong beneath his jeans.

He laid a hand over his chest. "Medic, remember? If I wanted to do more than check out your knee, I'd have done it by now, don't you think?"

He had a point. And when he undid the buttons of his shirt, then whipped it off and handed it to her with a clipped "Cover up with this," her argument lost its steam.

That wasn't all she lost when she was suddenly face-to-face with the lean, muscled breadth of his chest. Her power of speech took a hike as she sat like a mute and stared.

His black T-shirt was as tight as a second skin and nicely showed off the trim, toned abs and the buff, tough body of a man who knew his way around a gym— or a minefield.

She was no stranger to beautiful men. She'd made a living posing with the hottest, most sought-after male models in the world. She'd married a man who routinely made *People* magazine's "100 Sexiest Men" list.

And she knew all too well that beauty was often merely a pretty package disguising an ugly truth.

So she should absolutely not have been affected by his stunning physique. Yet she was.

She was clearly bordering on certifiable.

"Now put it on, Angelface. Please," he prompted, with enough insistence in that she finally shoved an arm into the sleeve.

The dark blue shirt was a made of heavy fabric, almost like canvas but much softer. It still held his body heat when she reluctantly wrapped the shirt around her.

It smelled like him. Masculine and dangerous and a little bit spicy and, God, she had to focus.

The sleeves hung well over the ends of her fingertips; the tails hit her about mid-thigh. It was huge on her, which was oddly comforting. And he was, she admitted again, astonishingly sexy as he sat back on his heels, his biceps straining beneath the sleeves of his T-shirt, his thighs bulked up beneath his worn jeans and that lethal-looking gun tucked into the waistband near his hip.

Both disgusted and disturbed that she was still thinking about him that way while he was clearly all business, she reached up under the shirt while he reached for his backpack. Using his shirt like a cape, she stood with her weight on her good leg, undid her belt buckle and the snap on her jeans. Then she wiggled them down her hips, shoved them below her knees and, self-conscious, sat back down. The boulder was cold as ice beneath her bare cheeks even through the shirt, and for the first time in years she longed for a pair of granny panties.

She'd posed for hundreds of photo shoots in bikinis or lingerie that constituted little more than three wisps of fabric and some flimsy pieces of lace, yet she still felt overexposed in front of him.

Not that he seemed similarly affected; he was in pure medic mode as he gently probed her knee.

"It's a little puffy," he said, thoroughly examining her knee with the help of a flashlight he'd dug out of his pack. "Tell me if this hurts."

She bit back a yelp when he manipulated her knee-cap. "A little."

"You can go to hell for lying, you know." He shot her an admonishing glance. "We need to get you off of it."

"More than we need to make it to Cuzco?"

"Good point." He turned back to his pack and pulled out a large, well-worn nylon bag.

"You don't do things halfway, do you?" She recognized the mix of medical supplies inside the biggest first-aid kit she'd ever seen.

"Go big or go home," he said with a tight smile. "I've had this surgical kit since my Navy days. Any medical issues I need to know about? Diabetes? Heart issues?"

She shook her head.

"Any medications, or allergies?"

"No. Nothing."

Apparently satisfied with her answers, he uncapped a bottle and shook two tablets into his palm and held them out to her. "Grunt candy."

"What?"

"Ibuprofen," he clarified, handing them to her along

with a bottle of water. "They'll help with the pain and inflammation. I'd give you Toradol but we're short on water and I don't want to risk kidney damage. This bottle and one other are going to have to last us until we get out of here."

Wondering how long that might be, dreading the possibility that they might be here long after the water was gone, she sipped lightly and forced down the pills as he deftly wrapped a wide elastic bandage from mid-thigh to mid-calf.

"How's that feel?"

He held out a hand to steady her when she stood and then tested his handiwork by putting weight on her leg. "Better. Thanks."

"Best I can do for now. If it starts giving you too much trouble, I want to know, okay?"

She bent down, pulled up her jeans, and zipped up as he repacked his surgical kit and stowed it away in his backpack. "And you'll what? Carry me out of here?"

He shot her a look. "If I have to."

She believed him. The look in his eyes and the conviction in his voice assured her that he could do it. She'd read stories about Navy SEALs, knew what hell they had to endure to make the grade.

When he stood, she started to take off his shirt to return it to him.

"Keep it." He stopped her by tugging the placket back together over her breasts.

"You need it," she insisted, her mouth suddenly dry

when he shoved her hands away and started working the buttons through the holes.

She knew she should object but was totally distracted by his careful attention to his task. There was something oddly mesmerizing about his concentration and single-minded focus. Something graceful, yet endearingly awkward about his big fingers maneuvering those buttons through the holes.

Val was tall—five foot nine—but he was taller by at least a head. His shoulders were broad, his hands big and so very, very capable as he painstakingly worked one button after another through each buttonhole until she was tucked in tight from neck to knee.

"You'll get cold." She tried one more time, even though she understood she would not win this battle.

"I'm from Montana, remember? And you know what?" he asked after a quick glance around. "These mountains actually remind me a little of home. Big sky. Big peaks. High plains.

"Anyway, it's always cold in Montana," he added, almost as an afterthought. "The blood acclimates. I'm fine."

He stood where he was, inches away, holding her gaze for a moment that pulsed with anticipation of something she couldn't discount as anything but awareness on his part now, too.

Oh, my.

Her breath caught on a little hitch when he reached out and tucked a strand of hair behind her ear. His fingers lingered on her cheek before he let his hand drop away. And when his gaze continued to hold hers just a moment longer, she wished she could ascribe the shiver that coursed through her body to the chill in the air. Yet the cold didn't cool the burn where his fingers grazed her cheek. Or douse the heat he generated low in her belly with that long, probing look from his dark-brown eyes.

Then he took her hand in his and her breath caught. His palm was warm. His fingers calloused. Her gaze slid back to his mouth . . . full and soft and yet so firm as he lowered his head.

He was going to kiss her.

Her heart stampeded.

He was going to—

Oh.

He was going to roll up the shirt sleeves so they weren't hanging over her hands.

Oh. Well.

Good.

Good thinking.

"Ready?" he asked after adjusting the final fold on the cuff.

Yeah," she murmured, feeling a little bereft and wanting to slap herself for it. "I'm ready."

She'd lied. She wasn't ready for any of what was happening to her. She wasn't ready to accept that she was being chased by men who wanted her dead. She wasn't ready to accept that she might not get out of the Andes alive. And she really wasn't ready to dissect and process her hyper-acute awareness of this stranger who had her contemplating any number of reckless actions.

Like letting him kiss her.

She would have. If he'd tried to kiss her a moment ago, she would have let him. It was a very titillating yet depressing realization.

Was she really that desperate, was her ego really that deflated, her heart that broken, that she was ready, willing, and wanting to throw herself at a total stranger?

Not just any stranger, her pride protested. Not just any man.

He'd saved her life.

She glanced at him as he shrugged into his backpack and settled his hat on his head. He was all broad shoulders and narrow hips, this Indiana Jones clone, former Navy SEAL, former Montana cowboy, current all-American hero, expert medic, volunteer humanitarian aid provider, and giver of shirts.

Now? she asked herself again, on a burdened breath. Her bruised and battered libido had to pick this place, this time, this dangerous situation, to lurch to life like an accident victim awakening from a six-month coma?

Chemistry, the rational part of her brain reasoned. Sensory overload. Fear plus adrenaline plus confusion equaled arousal. Go figure.

At least now she knew how her system reacted to very real, very acute danger. Along with adrenaline, her body mass-produced pheromones.

Oh, joy.

"Let's move." He slung the rifle strap over his shoulder and headed away.

For one brief moment she considered turning and walking in the opposite direction, because deep in her gut she knew that no matter how this played out, that way lay danger. Bad guy danger. Good guy danger.

"Valentina?" He glanced over his shoulder, regarding her with concern from beneath that damn sexy hat brim. "Are you with me?"

"Yeah," she said, finally walking toward him. "I'm with you."

Before she had a chance to figure out just how "with him" she was, the sharp crack of a rifle shot shattered the silence.

She screamed and watched in horror as he dropped, face first, to the ground.

6

Luke spit dirt, then snapped his head around and looked over his shoulder.

Jesus. Valentina stood totally exposed in the open, frozen in fear.

"Get down!" he roared. To hell with playing dead. He pushed himself into a fast roll toward her, wrapped his arms around her thighs, and dragged her to the ground just as another bullet zipped into the dirt near his shoulder.

"I thought you were dead," she panted, scrambling alongside him on all fours toward the shelter of a boulder.

So had he, and for a second there it had almost seemed like a relief to think he'd dodged his last bullet.

"Apparently I don't die that easily." He made sure she was tucked out of the line of fire, then rose to his knees beside her. "These guys are really starting to piss me off," he muttered as another bullet ricocheted off the stone near their heads.

But he was even more pissed with himself. He hadn't

been paying attention to business and he'd almost gotten himself killed. Again. And almost gotten *her* killed! What the fuck was wrong with him?

He was on the run with the woman of his dreams—and yes, goddamn it, it was juvenile and he should have grown out of his crush years ago, but for God's sake would you look at her? He'd defend to the death his reaction to this woman. She'd always been the unattainable dream, and he'd just held her in his arms. Hell, he'd almost kissed her!

Well, he wasn't a eunuch, damn it, although he'd sure as hell done his best to act like one. When he wasn't acting too stupid to live.

Christ. He felt like he was watching himself in one of those old cartoons, with an angel sitting on his right shoulder praising his virtue and a devil perched on his left, egging him on to *do her, stupid. What are you waiting for?*

An invitation would have been nice. And for a moment there, he'd thought she was going to give him one.

But he was going to have to come to full terms with that later. Right now, they were in a boatload of trouble. She flinched and ducked lower when another bullet *pa-zinged* off the front of the boulder. He glanced to the east. A faint, thin halo of sunlight rimmed the horizon.

Perfect. They were under fire and about the only thing they had going for them, the cover of darkness, was about to give way to dawn.

"What are we going to do?"

Yeah, jackass, the devil prodded, *what are you going to do?*

He looked north. Nothing but shadows against the jagged line of stone monoliths. To the south were the bad guys. He couldn't see them but judging from the sound and the trajectory of the rifle fire, he had a pretty good idea where they were. And how many there were. He was guessing two. Even if there were more, they would have split up into pairs. And if there were more in the detail, the gunfire was sure to draw the rest of them like gnats to horseshit.

He had to make something happen before the odds tilted even more in the shooters' favor.

He looked west. Blinked. Then blinked again.

"What do you see?" He notched his chin in that direction.

She followed his gaze, squinted, then cocked her head. "Horses?" she ventured uncertainly.

She'd just given him corroboration that the silhouettes against the uneven terrain weren't figments of his very hopeful imagination.

"Close enough," he said, taking stock of the small herd of mules. "There are farms scattered all over this mountainside. We must be at the edge of a pasture. Come on." He gripped her elbow and, crouching low, scuttled toward the herd of a dozen or so animals. "If we move low along that rock wall, it'll take them a while to realize we're gone.

He dropped to all fours, then started belly crawling toward the herd. She hung tight right behind him. Her knee had to be killing her but she didn't make a sound. Tough cookie.

They managed to move within twenty yards of the mules, who stood in a loose circle, heads down, dozing. If the gunshots had bothered them they didn't show it, but he wasn't going to count on that lasting forever.

"So, where do you fall on the Annie Oakley scale?" he asked as she peeked at the mules from behind the wall.

She shot him a narrow-eyed look. "Annie Oakley? Wasn't she some kind of a cowgirl?"

"Some kind, yeah," he said with a grin reserved for those who were criminally uneducated in western folklore. "Let me rephrase. Do you ride, Angelface?"

Her eyes turned wary. "Cars. I ride cars."

"Well, get ready to broaden your horizons."

She stared at the mules, looking scared but resolved.

"Just like riding a rocking chair," he told her

Spunk, he thought again, unbuckling his belt and tugging it out of the loops. Guns and bullets and bad guys were as foreign to her as a week without a pedicure. She had more than enough reason to fall apart, but look at her now. Scared, yeah, but she was holding it together. And he admired the hell out of her for it.

"Let me have yours." He gave her more points when she removed her leather belt without asking why he wanted it and handed it to him.

"I don't suppose you've ever fired a gun?"

"I don't suppose so, no," she confirmed in a worried tone as he shrugged the rifle sling off his shoulder and hunkered down behind her.

He showed her how to hold the rifle, then gave her a quick point-and-shoot lesson. "Just in case," he added in warning and hoped, for both their sakes, she didn't have to use it.

"Stay here and stay down. Don't even think about pulling that trigger unless you see something to shoot at, and then don't even think about shooting unless you want what you're shooting at dead. Got it?"

Her nod told him that she did.

He squeezed her shoulder. "I'll be right back with your new ride."

As he started off toward the closest mule, he thought he heard a softly murmured "OhmyGod."

Luke moved in a crouching run, keeping his profile low, trying not to spook the mules. He had to make this fast. The bad guys had been quiet for too long, which meant they were trying to move into better firing positions.

"Good luck with that," he muttered under his breath. He planned to be long gone before that happened.

Knowing he had to relay a sense of calm so he didn't scatter the herd, he drew a deep breath, retooled, and stood, counting on the rise of the hill between him and the gunmen to provide cover. Forcing himself to walk slowly, he approached a tall, leggy bay that had come awake and was watching him with big, sleepy eyes. His chest was narrow, his backbone spiny. Luke cringed. His "boys" were never going to be the same after a ride on that bony back.

"Couldn't have been a herd of Pasos, could ya?" he crooned as he closed in on the rough-coated mule.

Peruvian Paso Finos were known not only for their long manes and flowing tails, but for their smooth gaits. If he'd been wishing, however, it would have been for a solid, dependable quarter horse like the ones he'd grown up with on the ranch.

Not that wishes counted for jack shit, he lamented as he neared the mule with a soft "Whoa now, fella" that he crooned in a sing-songy drover's voice he'd perfected over years of herding cattle as a kid.

Very near the now-wary animal, he kept his tone the same but switched to Spanish, and then to one of the few Quechua words he knew because he'd used it so often on the village children.

"Easy," he said over and over in Aymara, until he reached the mule's side, and then scratched the sweet spot under his jaw.

Before the big guy knew he'd been had, Luke had slipped a belt around his long neck and tugged the end through the buckle, making a loop for his improvised lead rope. Then, keeping the mule between him and the rest of the herd, he singled out another animal. His years of wrangling horses paid off and he quickly had another ride in tow—a little gray mare that he hoped was as docile as she looked.

"Valentina," he whispered, leading both mules back toward her.

When her head popped up from behind the rock wall, he motioned her over.

"I have managed to avoid sitting on an animal's back my entire life," she muttered as she reluctantly joined him.

He relieved her of the rifle and laid it at his feet. Then he patted the bay's neck to settle him. "Not an animal lover?"

"If they're bigger than me, I prefer to love them from a distance."

"So, just think of this little girl as a pussy cat."

The look she gave him told him that wasn't happening, but there was no time to ease her into this.

"Follow my lead, okay? Nice and easy." He showed her how to grip the gray mule's mane, then made a stirrup with his hands.

"Left foot," he coached and encouraged her to put her foot in his cupped hands. "Hurry. Up you go."

She swung her right leg over the mule's back and just that fast, was on board. She wanted to scream. He could see it written all over her gorgeous face, but she bit it back.

"A natural." He grinned even though she had a death grip on the mane and her eyes had widened to the size of dinner plates.

"Grip with your thighs," he whispered after he'd slung the rifle over his back. He swung up onto the bay and adjusted his seat to accommodate the boys. Keeping her mule close beside him with the belt rope, he clucked softly. His mule lumbered forward and, after a gentle tug, the gray fell in stride beside him.

"You're doing fine," he told her, though she still

looked terrified. "Just relax and let your body ride to the rhythm she sets. It's all about balance."

"As long as we don't go any faster than this, I think I can stay on," she said, a world of determination in her voice.

"Yeah, about that . . ." He looked over his shoulder. Two dark silhouettes materialized against the slowly rising sun about one hundred yards away. Their time had just run out.

"Hang on, Princess. We have to kick this up into racing gear."

He nudged his mount with his heels and added a firm "Git up!"

The mule gathered himself, reared up on his hind legs like he thought he was the damn Black Stallion, then burst forward at a full-out gallop. Beside him, Valentina let out a surprised yelp when her mule followed suit.

Luke had a bad moment when he thought she was going to take a tumble, but *goddamn*, she dug deep, leaned low over the mule's neck, and clung like a tick.

Problem was, the mare sensed her fear and it spooked her. She turned on the after burners and would have streaked out ahead of him if Luke hadn't had a good grip on the makeshift lead rope and reeled her back in. After he spent a few more heart-pounding moments grappling for control, the two mules finally found a compatible rhythm.

Luke took a moment to grieve for his balls, which were taking a hammering on the boniest backbone he'd ever had the misfortune to straddle. But when a barrage of automatic weapon fire cracked across the ground beside them, the state of his balls took a backseat to the danger to Valentina's life.

"Stay low!" he shouted as they raced over the hard-packed earth, clumps of grass and divots of dirt flying under the mule's thundering hooves.

The rifle fire kept coming in short, three-round bursts. These were no novices on the triggers. They were conserving ammo and making each shot count. And they kept hitting closer. One of these times, a bullet was going to hit the mark.

Luke glanced over his shoulder. Even though they were putting real estate between themselves and the shooters, he had to do something to increase their odds of survival. Returning fire from the back of a running mule was not the answer.

"Hang on!" he yelled and, applying pressure on his mule's left side with his knee and using his hand to push the big guy's head hard to the right, he managed to change their course.

Valentina's mare wasn't so keen on following his lead. The gray's sides were lathered up. Her chest heaved; her nostrils flared wide as she tossed her head wildly, fighting the belt rope, as scared now as Valentina. Hoping to hell she didn't blow and start bucking, Luke headed them toward the thick stand of trees about a quarter mile ahead.

If they could reach it, the cover it offered would buy them time to get good and gone before the gunmen caught up with them.

"He-yaw!" He slapped the bay on the rump and asked for more speed as the rifle fire picked up, bullets hitting dangerously close.

Another hundred yards. Seventy-five. Unless these guys were trained snipers or damn lucky, each yard decreased the chance of a direct hit.

As the sun grew higher, he could make out individual trees, not just a massive clump. Almost there . . .

"Oh, shit!"

A gaping gorge that he hadn't spotted earlier yawned directly between them and the trees.

The ravine was too wide to jump, too deep and steep to try to ride through. He needed to stop these mules and stop 'em fast. Without a bridle, that was going to be a damn tough trick.

He leaned back, stretched out his legs, hooked his boot heels over the bay's chest, and pulled like hell. All he got for his efforts was a banged-up tailbone as he bounced along that bony damn back.

Trying not to think about the ravine getting closer and closer, he shifted his weight forward again, leaned over the mule's withers, and transferred the end of the belt on Valentina's mule to his teeth. With both hands free, he loosened the belt he'd looped around the bay's neck, worked it up over his ears, and slid it down over his muzzle like a modified bridle.

He tugged once to tighten the loop, then knowing he had to control the mule's head to stop him, he jerked hard to the left. The big guy's head swung sideways into his own shoulder, effectively swinging his hindquarters around. The action turned him in a circle and finally slowed him down. Beside him, Valentina's little mare fought and fussed and jerked the leather belt out of Luke's mouth.

He caught the trailing end just in time, doubled it around his fist, and managed to keep her with him as the two animals gradually slowed in a helter-skelter dance of flying hoofs and confused braying.

Just when he thought they wouldn't get stopped in time, he somehow brought them to a jerking, bouncing trot that had his boys screaming for relief.

By the time the dust cleared and they slowed to a stop, both mules were trembling with exhaustion and fear, they were skirting the very edge of the ravine, and he was damn close to singing soprano.

"You okay?" he managed in a pinched voice as he leaned forward, bracing his palms on the mule's withers in an attempt to take the heat off his throbbing crotch.

"I . . . think so." Valentina sounded breathless and a little amazed that she was telling the truth.

He heaved a deep breath, was about to tell her, "Well done," when the bay decided he'd been hospitable for as long as he could tolerate.

Luke should have felt it coming. Might have, if 99.9 percent of his attention hadn't been fixed on his aching gonads and wondering if he'd ever father children. By the time he realized what came next, it was too late to do anything but warn Val to "Bail!" as the bay's muscles bunched into one huge, dynamite-driven knot.

The pissed-off mule arched his back, let go a bloodcurdling bray, then threw every ounce of strength left in his half-ton body into a series of bucks that would have made Bodacious, the all-time champion bucking bull, look like an amateur.

On the fourth buck, Luke went airborne like a kite in a stiff wind, his arms and legs flailing, before gravity— the greedy bitch—sucked him back to earth.

He hit the ground face first, right at the edge of the ravine. He tasted dirt, saw stars, and felt nothing but all-consuming pain.

7

When Luke yelled, "Bail!" Val shimmied sideways off the mule just before it charged off, running and bucking. Her feet hit the ground, then her butt when her knees buckled, and she landed with a bone-rattling *umph*. As she sat there catching her breath, Luke's mule blew sky-high and sent him sailing.

Her hand flew to her throat. "Oh, my God!"

It was like watching a train wreck in slow motion. One second, he was sitting astride that mule like he'd been born on his back. The next, he was soaring, stretched out like a pro wrestler taking a flying leap off the top rope in a ring. Then he lost altitude like a stalled jet and plowed into the unforgiving ground.

She gasped when he hit, flinching in sympathy at the pain he must be feeling. For a long, tense moment she just stared, frozen with fear as she waited for him to move. Then realized he wasn't going to.

She pushed to all fours and, ignoring the pain in her knee, scrambled over to his side.

"Luke."

Nothing.

She knelt by his shoulders, touched him with care. "Luke?"

He didn't move.

Oh, God. Please, please, please let him be alive. If he died, she probably wasn't going to make it out of here alive, either.

She shoved a jerky hand through her hair and glanced over her shoulder. All she saw was the backside of the mules and the flying clods of dirt as they ran back home like their tails were on fire. She didn't see the gunmen yet. Even though they'd put a substantial distance between them, she knew they'd catch up soon. All they had to do was follow the hoofprints.

Praying for a miracle, she glanced back down at Luke. Not so much as a groan.

He couldn't be dead. He was too strong, too vital, too . . . *Indy,* she thought, battling panic. She didn't want him to die. She was just getting used to him. She might even like him. And if he did die, it would be because of her.

Riddled with guilt, she placed a hand on his back, then slid it under the rifle and his pack. When she felt his ribs rise and fall, her breath whooshed out in a rush of relief. "Thank God."

When he groaned, she let out a little yelp of joy. "I thought you were dead."

He grunted. "I couldn't be . . . that lucky." He lifted his head and very gingerly tested his ability to turn it.

"And like I . . . told you earlier," he said around a wince of pain, "apparently, I'm not that . . . easy to kill."

"Do you think you can get up?"

He snorted. "Princess, I'm still working on . . . breathing."

"We really have to get out of here."

That got a muffled curse as he painstakingly pushed his upper body to his elbows, then hung his head in his hands. "I know. Just . . . give me a minute."

She glanced nervously over her shoulder again. Still no sign of the gunmen, but that could change any second. And the sun was climbing fast. Once it was up, they'd be easy targets. "We don't have a minute. Come on. Let me help you."

"Jesus, woman." He pushed himself painfully to his knees, swayed. "You ever hear the term *tender mercy*?"

"You think those guys are going to show any mercy?"

He heaved a pained breath that puffed out in a cloud in the freezing air. "Good point. Help me up."

She gave it her all, but when he tried to stand, he fell back on all fours. This was bad. This was really bad.

She had to do something. She relieved him of the rifle and his backpack, then nearly buckled under the weight when she settled both on her back.

"What's *in* here?" she muttered.

"Important things," he told her. "So don't even think about emptying it."

"Fine. Whatever. Now try again," she pleaded, and helped him upright.

It was a struggle but this time he made it to his feet—then swayed like a twig in a stout wind. "Whoa."

She caught his wrist and slung his arm over her shoulder, then wrapped her other arm around his waist to steady him.

And she'd thought the pack was heavy. He was tall and lean, but the weight on his frame was all muscle.

"Come on," she coaxed, her sense of urgency mounting by the second. "We've got to move."

"I hate to break this to you, Angelface—but my whole world is movin'."

"All I care about is this little part of it. One step. Come on."

"You do know that a lesser man would need life support, right? A morphine drip at the very least."

She hoped he was joking.

"Wait." He jerked them to a stop. "My hat."

"Forget about your hat," she sputtered, and would have plowed forward if his dead weight hadn't anchored them where they stood.

"I need the hat," he insisted. He looked like he meant to take root if he had to. "It was a gift," he said, as if it came from the Pope or something.

She scrunched her eyes shut and breathed deep in an attempt to get a handle on her frustration. "Fine."

She scanned the area and spotted the brown fedora about twenty feet behind them. "Can you stand by yourself?"

"Don't be long."

She ducked out from under his arm, made certain he was steady, then sprinted for the hat.

She snatched it up on the run, plopped it on top of her head, and scooted back to his side just as he started to list sideways.

"My hero," he said as she propped him against her again. "Lead the way, Angelface. I'll follow you anywhere."

She was stronger than she looked. Tougher too, Luke realized with admiration, and picked up his pace to match hers as she soldiered on toward the copse of trees less than fifty yards away.

He felt like he'd been hit by a train. Adrenaline expended, the damn cold had started to set into his bones and pound on his bruises. More bruised than his body was his pride. He was a cowboy, for God's sake. Had the big belt buckle he'd won on the youth rodeo circuit years ago to prove it. And he'd let a mangy mule take him down. Never should have happened.

He gritted his teeth and sucked it up. He should let her know he'd recovered enough to shuffle along on his own now. He was still dizzy, yeah, but he could probably even sprint if he had to. But they were making good time and the last time he'd glanced over his shoulder, they were still in the clear.

And there were perks to playing the walking wounded. The last time he'd been this close to a woman who turned him on this much had been so long ago, he couldn't pinpoint the date, the occasion, or the lady's face.

So he took advantage of the solid strength and warmth of her pressed against his side. And he thoroughly enjoyed the look of her wearing his hat. The old fedora had never looked so good.

"You doing okay?" she asked, sounding breathless as they skirted yet another rock pile. Despite the cold, her brow was damp with moisture from the exertion.

A better man would have felt guilty for contributing to the exhaustion in her voice. "I'm so good, I've got half a notion to burst into song. Any requests?" he added because he knew it would make her grumble and maybe smile.

She didn't disappoint him on either count. "I'll take a rain check on that, if you don't mind."

He didn't mind at all. He was just damn happy that she'd dropped her guard enough to banter back. She hadn't wanted to bend, but he was breaking her down with his stupid jokes. And it wasn't just about getting her to like him. It was about getting her mind off dead bodies, men with guns, and the mystery of who wanted her dead. *If* they wanted her dead.

He might have had his bell rung when he'd plowed into the ground, but he was still thinking straight. And what he'd been thinking was, if those guys had orders to kill her, she'd be dead by now. Their rifles were state of the art and top of the line. If they'd wanted to shoot her off the back of that gray mare, they'd had plenty of opportunities.

So he was pretty certain that they didn't want her dead. Their orders were to keep her alive. And yeah, he was certain someone else was calling the shots on this op. There was serious coin invested in this hunting expedition, which meant there was a puppetmaster somewhere pulling the strings.

If he had to die trying, he was going to find out who the sonofabitch was. Then he was going to feed him his own teeth after he shoved the bastard's head up his own ass. Somewhere along the way this had ceased being about Luke and his lack of backbone, and had become all about keeping Val safe and getting the bastards responsible for terrorizing her.

"Just a little farther," she said, encouraging him when he stumbled and almost dragged her down.

Just listen to her, playing protector. His heart got all squishy.

"Just so you know," he said when her arm tightened around his waist, "Superwoman's got nothin' on you, Angelface. You're one tough lingerie model, you know that?"

A puff of frosty air escaped when she laughed. "Yeah, all those years of wearing silk and lace make a woman mean."

He grinned, because, damn, she had a wicked sense of humor. And because laughing was better than belly-aching. But mostly because he still carried very vivid mental images of her wearing that silk and lace that never failed to make him smile. Or get hard.

"What now?" she asked when they reached the trees that had once seemed a million miles away.

He glanced behind them just as two dark silhouettes emerged against the great orange glow of the sun, the dark barrels of their automatic rifles silhouetted in stark relief. They were no more than a couple hundred yards away and closing fast.

"Now we find ourselves a nice little hidey-hole."

And we pray, he thought as they ducked into the thicket to search for a safe hiding place.

Hidey-hole.

Val tried not to think about that as they alternately jogged, skidded, and slid down the steep slopes.

She was not an outdoor, commune-with-nature kind of girl. She'd never even picnicked in the woods unless it was for a photo shoot. So she'd always thought of a forest floor as being covered with ferns and wildflowers. Not the case here. Lots of deadfall. Lots of rocks. Lots of ravines and sunlight filtering down through it all.

Still, it was actually very pretty. So she concentrated on that rather than the hidey-hole. But after they stumbled upon the trunk of a monster tree that had been uprooted and blown to its side, and he gave her a thumbs-up indicating he'd found something, she had to think about it—whether she wanted to or not. And what she thought of were those horrible days she'd been locked inside a dirt cellar. She'd been ten years old, crying for her mother. No light. No love. Nothing but dark and despair and terror. And rats. And snakes. And bugs. *Oh God.*

She'd made it a point to never get near a dark, tight space ever since and she was minutes away from doing exactly that. A violent shudder rippled through her body.

Don't think about bugs, or rats or spiders or snakes. It'll only give you bellyaches.

She remembered her mother's arms around her, rocking her, holding her, singing that silly little song. For years after she'd been rescued, she woke up screaming and sobbing, after dreaming she was locked in that cellar again.

"Hurry," Luke urged as he followed the length of the tree trunk down a steep grade to truck-sized roots caked with moss and dirt and reaching out of the ground like giant spider legs.

The root ball was a good ten feet in circumference; half of it was aboveground, the other half made a scooped-out hollow in the earth. At first Val hadn't even seen the hole, mostly hidden by rocks and moss and a handful of new growth of trees and shrubs.

"It's perfect. Just big enough to conceal the two of us and my pack," he stated with a triumphant smile.

Oh, God. It was perfect all right. Perfectly horrifying.

She watched as he crawled inside to clear out some of the debris. Then he dug a paper-thin silver survival blanket out of his pack and spead it out for them to lie on. He shimmied back out again. "Hold tight. I want to go cover our tracks."

She swallowed thickly, hardly aware of him leaving as she stared into the hole.

Don't go back there. This isn't the same. There's no lock. There's no force. There are no boogeymen waiting in the dark.

No, the boogeymen were chasing them in the daylight.

She wished she was like one of those kick-ass women

in her favorite books. The kind who not only held their own with the big, tough alpha males, but often saved the day themselves when faced with danger.

Her twice-a-year visits to Sierra Leone didn't count as dangerous, despite the lingering violence still associated with the region. Though the civil war and the atrocities committed by the Revolutionary United Front—RUF—had ended almost a decade ago, the undercurrent of violence still existed. And for the women and children who had survived the brutal rapes and mutilations, their lives remained a constant struggle. Especially the "bush wives," the young girls and women who had been kidnapped and raped and forced to "marry" the RUF soldiers who had brutalized them.

Even now, years after the war had ended, those women remained ostracized by their families, by society. While Valentina went to help them, those trips were also healing; they nourished her soul and renewed her spirit. Those trips, and the medical, shelter, food, and school supplies that made the journey with her, were essential. There was no bravery involved. Only necessity.

So no, kick-ass didn't seem to be a card in her deck. She was scared spitless. And as she stared at the gaping black hole in the ground, all she could think of was how she could avoid crawling into it.

If she'd had any breakfast, she would have lost it right then. She wanted to vaporize and be magically transported to another time continuum.

Don't think about bugs, or rats or spiders or snakes. It'll only give you bellyaches.

Eyes closed, she repeated her mantra—then yelped when a twig snapped behind her.

She spun around, fists clenched, and sagged in relief when she saw Luke. He was out of breath but looked much better than he had earlier.

"In you go, Angelface. We don't have any time to waste."

"Are you sure we shouldn't try to outrun them? We've been doing a pretty good job so far."

"And we've been damn lucky. This is our best option."

"Why don't you go in first?" she suggested, feeling the blood drain from her head.

"Because I want to make sure I can't see you once you're inside. Now scoot."

When she hesitated, he cupped her shoulders and ducked down to look in her eyes. "Hey. What's happening? Are you claustrophobic or something?"

Or something, she thought, heart hammering.

Don't think about bugs, or rats or spiders or snakes. Don't think about it. Don't think about it. Don't think about it.

She repeated the mantra in rapid succession and, gathering all of her courage, crawled slowly inside.

8

Taking great pains not to brush her shoulder on the earth wall or ceiling, Val maneuvered into the opening on all fours. Inside, she cautiously stretched out on her side on the survival blanket. When she laid her head down on her upraised arm, she realized she was still wearing Luke's hat.

Her hand was trembling when she reached up and removed the fedora, then set it on the blanket beyond her head. And then she waited. Eyes closed, her chest tight, her mantra ringing through her mind while her thundering heartbeat tried to drown it out.

She gasped and jumped involuntarily when the small trees surrounding the hole rustled and a little shower of dirt dusted her shoulder. Eyes wide now, she saw that it was Luke tossing brush over the exposed cavity. Then his pack landed down by her feet, then the rifle, and finally he crawled in, dragging more brush behind him to cover the last of the breach.

"If they can spot us in here then they've got X-ray

vision," he said as he shimmied up until his head was even with hers.

Light filtered in between the leafy tree and bush branches, casting their hiding place in shadows yet still allowing them to see out. The floor of their cave was lumpy and hard beneath the thin blanket, and every bit as damp as she'd thought it would be. Every bit as terrifying.

"Not bad," Luke said settling himself in. "Comfy, even."

Not even a little bit, she thought, fighting a chest-tightening knot of claustrophobia.

You're not locked in, she reminded herself, concentrating on deep, even breaths. *And there's plenty of room.* At least a foot on either side of them, another two feet above their heads, even more at their feet. They could lie stacked on top of each other if they had to and still have plenty of clearance. That was good. That was all good.

Still, she couldn't stop the shivers wracking her body.

"Damn, babe," he whispered with concern, and maneuvered his arm around her shoulders, pulling her snug against him. "Body heat," he explained when she stiffened. "We can use it to warm each other up."

After a few seconds of some very guarded breaths while she got used to the fit of their thighs and hips and of her left breast pressing against his chest, she realized that he was right. His big, tough body generated megawatts of heat.

And cocooned in the strength of his arms, she gradually stopped thinking about bugs and rats and snakes.

She thought instead about the intimacy of their positions. About how, if she tipped her head just an inch, maybe two, the tip of her nose would brush the stubble on his jaw. About how, if she moved her hand just the tiniest bit, it would rest on his muscled chest. If she bent her knee, just so . . .

"Um." His voice startled her out of her thoughts as he turned his head and whispered against her cheek. "I never in my life expected to hear this coming out of *my* mouth, but . . . is that a flashlight in your pocket, or are you just very glad to see me?"

She jerked back so she could look at him.

"What?"

His eyes were sparkling with amusement, and he was grinning.

Then it dawned on her, and damn if she didn't have to muffle a laugh. Very carefully, she reached between their hips, fished into her jeans pocket, and pulled out the source of his confusion. "Potato," she said quietly, holding it up for him to see.

"Oh." Long pause. "Right." Longer pause, then, "Huh?"

She let out a soft puff of laughter because . . . oh, who knew why? Because she was warm for the first time in hours? Because if she didn't laugh she might cry? Because of the puzzled expression on his face?

"I picked it up in the field when I was waiting for you to bring back the mules. They were lying all over the ground. And I thought that if we got hungry, maybe we could eat it."

Amused bafflement transitioned to a soft smile. "I just luvs me a resourceful woman."

Instead of buoying her spirits, his comment leveled her again. She set the potato above her head by his hat. "At least I'm good for something."

He tucked his chin so he could see her face better. "What are you talking about?"

"About me being a wimp," she said, matching his whisper. "And don't start with the Superwoman bull again. The closest I've ever come to filling her boots was for a costume party years ago. I suck at this."

To add to her self-disgust, now she also felt stupid for unloading with that little outburst.

"Jesus." He sounded genuinely perplexed. "Where did that come from? You've been a brick. We wouldn't have made it this far if you hadn't picked me up out of the dirt and hauled me out of the line of fire."

"That had nothing to do with being brave or tough. That was about being scared. Like I've been scared since this whole thing started."

With the same gentleness he'd shown her back in the canyon he folded her closer. "You think *I'm* not scared?"

"No," she said, feeling miserable. "I do *not* think you're scared."

"Well, think again, Angelface."

The hollow ache in his voice made her wonder if he actually meant it. She quickly dismissed the notion. This man had nerves of steel. She doubted he was afraid of anything.

She turned her head away, but he curled a finger beneath her chin and tipped her face back up to his.

"Listen to me." Even in a whisper, his tone demanded her attention. "It's how you react to fear that says who you are. And it's keeping your head that tells me what you're made of. You haven't bitched once about that bum knee, and I know it's giving you fits. You climbed on that mule's back and stuck like a burr even though you were terrified. And don't think I couldn't see how afraid you were of crawling into this hole."

His eyes were clear and gentle as they searched hers. "I know what happened to you." When her breath caught, he repeated, "I know what happened when you were a little girl. That's what this is about, isn't it? You *are* claustrophobic."

She lowered her gaze. Of course he knew. The whole world knew about the abduction. When you were a celebrity, your life was an open book—even your life before you became famous. The tabloids had been merciless when they'd uncovered the story of her abduction by her mother's ex-boyfriend. Mario had thought he could win her mother back by staging a kidnapping, then playing hero by rescuing her child from the "kidnappers."

He'd thrown her in that dark cellar for two days with nothing but a jug of water and a jar of peanut butter, before he'd come clean and told the police where she was hidden. When they'd found her she was traumatized, covered in bug bites, her fingers clenched around a thick piece of wire she'd dug out of the dirt with her bare hands and used to keep the rats at bay.

"Your reactions are honest," Luke murmured, his gentleness drawing her away from the horrifying memory. "Your fear is real, and with damn good reason. But when it counts, you cowboy up. You do what you need to do. You tough out the pain; you climbed up on that mule. And even though you were terrified, you crawled in here. That's kick-ass in my book, Angelface. And trust me, I know kick-ass when I see it."

He was being kind. Trying to make her feel better about herself.

She managed to smile. "So where does peeing my pants fall on the reaction scale? Because I'm about to do that soon if my heart doesn't quit beating so hard."

"Princess, that's a biological function, not a character trait. And for the record, I'm in awe. You've got the strongest bladder of any woman I've ever met."

"No, I don't," she said on a soft laugh. "When you were getting the mules, I—"

"Did more than pick up potatoes?" he concluded with a grin.

Before she could thank him for being so kind, his head jerked toward the opening of the cave. He didn't have to tell her to be quiet. She knew he'd heard something. And he didn't have to signal for her silence for her to stop their whispered conversation and hold perfectly still.

They were no longer alone. The predators had arrived.

Heart slamming, Val held her breath, then realized

she was getting light-headed and made herself let it out, slow and steady. Beside her, Luke's body tensed into one long, pulsing, tightly wound muscle as he slowly pulled the handgun out of his waistband.

Several tense seconds passed as they lay there. Outside in the forest she could hear twigs breaking beneath the gunmen's feet, the occasional soft curse, and the skitter of loose earth as one of the men slid on the steep terrain.

They were close. Very close. So close, she swore she heard one of them breathing as they passed within a few feet of their hiding place.

Seconds turned to a minute, then several minutes. The strong beat of Luke's heart hammered in the ear she'd pressed against his chest. She could feel the effort he made to keep his breaths even. Sensed the tight coil of strength in his hard, toned muscles that told her that, regardless of the beating he'd taken from his fall off the mule, he was ready to strike if he had to.

She made herself concentrate on steady, even breaths. Willed her heartbeat to settle and her mind to stay focused. Silence counted more than anything and stillness came a very close second. So even though her muscles started cramping from the effort to remain motionless, she didn't let herself move. Only breathe. Only think about surviving this.

And in the midst of it all, while men who wanted to kill her were out there stalking them, she prayed that a spider didn't drop on her face.

Talk about skewed priorities.

Luke finally turned his head toward hers. "I think they've moved on," he whispered against her ear.

"Thank God." She wanted out of here.

"But let's play it safe a little while longer, okay? Make sure they don't get wise and double back."

Oh, God. They were going to lie here and hold their positions. And suddenly she didn't feel so safe . . . but for a totally different reason.

For the past several minutes, Val had managed to avoid thinking about how physically close they were. Now that the immediate threat was over, she was acutely aware that they were pressed together from ankle to head, heartbeat to heartbeat.

It took only but a few of those heartbeats for acute awareness to become hyper-awareness that, somewhere along the way, their breathing had fallen into the same rhythm. And that rhythm—in, out, deep, slow—suddenly riveted her.

In. Out. Deep. Slow.

Like good sex.

A shocking arrow of heat shot straight from the tips of her breasts to her belly.

Whoa. She'd slipped into that thought *far* too easily. It was just the danger, she told herself. And the threat of spiders. And . . . yeah, the intimacy of their positions, so close it was hard to tell which heartbeat was whose. So close their shared body heat had ceased to be a necessity and become the catalyst for this singular kind of quickening of her pulse.

In. Out. Deep. Slow.

She flashed on a visual of them naked, making love, and another rocket of heat burned through her body. This needed to stop. But, since the divorce, her ego had shrunk to the size of a pinhead. Which was probably why she was thinking like one.

It didn't help that his breath fluttered hot against her cheek. That his calloused hand lay at the curve of her hip.

She swallowed hard; suppressed another eddy of sexual heat when his hand moved slightly on her hip. When his breath feathered warm and steady across her brow.

And even though she knew she was playing a risky game, she nestled closer against him. God, it had been so long since she'd felt even a flutter of sexual response to a man. How could she fight the force of it, or deny the delicious rush?

It would be so easy to tip her face to his and kiss him. To morph this moment into something even more reckless and wild, and far, far away from fear.

And fear, she realized with sudden clarity, was most likely the true catalyst for her reactions, the reason she was so close to the edge.

Okay. Deep breath. Regroup.

Luke Colter was a very attractive man. It was easy to want to encourage him to kiss her . . . just to give her something to think about other than Marcus's betrayal and dark holes and gunmen chasing her.

And she might have actually kissed him if she'd

sensed anything sexual on *his* part. But she wasn't picking up any signals—not even a flutter. His hands didn't
roam; his hold was merely protective. He was offering a
shoulder. Safety. Kind words.

She sighed deeply, both disappointed and relieved. It
was a good thing one of them was sane.

9

Luke was going insane.

Break-out-the-anti-psychotic-drugs, dust-off-the-lobotomy-kits, and lace-up-the-straightjackets insane.

All this lush, sexy woman pressed against him was more than he could take. He had the erection to prove it. If she moved her leg up the tiniest bit, she was going to find out the hard way—yes, the *hard* way—just how much trouble he was in.

But when she stiffened suddenly and turned into his arms, he was reminded of how very vulnerable she was. And how foreign and frightening this experience was to her.

"You're doing just fine," he said softly and pressed his lips to the top of her head, giving her the moment she seemed to need to get hold of herself again.

Giving himself a moment to get a freakin' grip.

But then she turned a little closer . . . just a fraction of an inch. His chin brushed against her hair. She sighed, a soft, female sound that was sexy without any effort, beckoning without any guile. And then, Jesus God, her entire body just seemed to give in his arms. Like all the tension, all the fear simply melted away, and she gave herself over to his safekeeping.

He closed his eyes, swallowed hard, and drew on every ploy in his arsenal to distract himself from thoughts he had no business thinking. Thoughts of how easy it would be to shift this delicate balance of trust to a slow dance of seduction.

He might have pulled it off—if she hadn't tipped her head back then, and with a dark, clear-eyed stare, let him know she was both vulnerable and ripe for the picking.

Well, damn it, he was only so strong. And she was so *everything* he'd ever wanted.

His hand trembled when he touched the back of his fingers to her cheek. "You really want to do this?" he whispered, his throat thick with desire as he gave her a chance to stop him.

"We shouldn't," she murmured after a searching look. A long moment passed before she covered his hand with hers. "But, yeah. I want to do this. Crazy, huh?"

He smiled, thanking fate or kismet or whatever cosmic explosion had placed him here, with her, at this exact moment in time. "Crazy good."

Holding her gaze, he shifted his weight until he was propped up on an elbow leaning over her, pressing her onto her back. "You say the word and we red-light things, okay?"

She cupped his head and drew him close, so close her breath feathered against his lips. "No red. Only green."

It was a good thing because he was already gone the

moment she buried her hands in his hair and urged him near. He covered her mouth with his, knowing he probably should be gentle, more reverent. But he'd fantasized about this woman for years—and gentle wasn't even a remote possibility.

His kiss was about pure, hedonistic pleasure.

He lost himself in it. Lost himself in her—the pillow softness of her breasts pressed against his chest. In the slim, supple curve of her hip and thigh molded against him. In the exotic taste of her lips that opened tentatively at first, then wide as he coaxed her to let him in, let him taste, let him take what he'd dreamed about for years.

And damn if reality didn't exceed the dream.

He plunged his tongue inside her mouth, wanting it all. Wanting it now. He sipped and licked and saturated his senses with not only her taste, but her uninhibited responses. She moaned deeply, chased his tongue with hers and sucked it back into her mouth, then held him close with a desperate whimper and a possessive hand in his hair when he would have pulled away to change the angle of their kiss.

His heart went haywire. He levered himself over her, scooped her closer against him, and let his hand roam over her hip, the gentle concave of her belly, then finally filled his palm with the lush weight of her breast. She shuddered and moved against his hand, arching into his palm as he kneaded and shaped her until skin-on-skin contact became the mandate.

He slid his hand up under both shirts, shoved her bra aside, and finally encountered hot, silky flesh. Her nipple pebbled between his thumb and finger, and he was stone hard and straining against his fly when she arched into his hand and made a sexy, needy sound deep in her throat.

He totally lost it then. He wrenched his mouth away from hers, trailed a string of hot, biting kisses down her jaw, then found her bare breast and feasted.

She gasped, moaning throaty and low and long when he sucked her nipple into his mouth. He loved it. Loved it when she writhed against him and whimpered in protest when he pulled back so he could see her.

Perfection. Her breast was full and firm, the nipple dusty brown and delicate, glistening wet and quivering. Beckoning him back. Begging him to dip his head to take her in his mouth again. Because she wanted him to. Because she was wild for him to do exactly what he was doing.

Making her wet. Making her hot. Making her want him the way he'd imagined her wanting him.

She gasped again when he swirled the tip of his tongue over her diamond-hard nipple. And when she cried out and planted her palms against his shoulders and abruptly shoved, he had just enough brain cells still functioning that it registered she was crying out in pain, not pleasure.

He pushed himself up on his elbows, suddenly full of concern. "What? What's wrong?"

Her eyes were pinched shut, her face contorted in pain. "Po . . . potato."

He scowled in confusion. "What? Is that some sort of safe word?"

Her laugh was part pain, part frustration. "No. The potato. It rolled under my back."

He pushed up on an elbow and felt around beneath her shoulders, found the potato and tossed it away. Then he rolled over her again and grinned down at her, ready to pick up where they'd left off.

Only she wasn't smiling.

She was clearly having serious second thoughts about what had just happened, what had been *about* to happen, and what was now most likely not going to happen.

Playtime was over.

He got it. He didn't like it, but he got it. Things had gone from zero to mach 1 and back to zero again in the space of a few pounding heartbeats.

Muffling a groan of disappointment, he got himself back under control. Once he could manage it without groping her, he did the gentlemanly thing and rearranged her clothes until she was covered up like a nun.

She shot him a grateful but embarrassed look.

He smiled and squeezed her hip. "I think you could safely say you were saved by the spud."

Her face flamed red and she covered her eyes with a forearm.

"Hey," he said gently. "Don't. *Please* don't kill this stellar buzz I've got goin' and say that shouldn't have happened."

"I can't believe I let myself get so—" She lifted her hand, let her words trail off.

"Caught up in a moment?" he suggested and pressed

a soft kiss to her brow. "It happens, okay? We're adults. We'll deal with it. And for the record, I don't kiss and tell. But if ever I was tempted, that kiss would be the one to do it.

"And look on the bright side: For a little while there, you forgot all about dark holes and running for your life, didn't you?"

He got the smile he wanted, along with a little eye roll that he'd also expected. That was okay.

And he was more than okay, because he trusted his gut, and his gut was telling him that this was far from over. She might think things had to ended with a mind-bending kiss and a little touchy-feely, but being a betting man, he was going all in on this hand. *This* hand was coming up aces plus one knockout-gorgeous lady, and he'd bet on a hand like that 'til the cows came home.

All in good time, he told himself.

"I'm going to go do a little recon. See if it's safe to move out. You sit tight." He decided to leave her the rifle since she already knew how to shoot it, and it would be much more accurate for her.

"Remember what I taught you?" he asked, placing it in her hand.

She nodded, her face pale.

"Don't point it at anything you don't want to kill."

Another determined nod.

He gave her foot an encouraging squeeze, pulled the Glock out of the back of his waistband, then scrambled out of the cave. "Be right back."

• • •

Several time zones away, Ryang found himself gripping the phone tighter as his man in Peru explained once *again* that the woman continued to elude them.

"What do you mean, you lost her?"

They had retired from the dining room to the living area, Ryang to indulge in a brandy and Jin to read to their daughter. He thought again of how much he adored them both, delighted in indulging them. He'd do anything to insure their future and spare them the poverty and abuse he had endured as the child of a whore, who had been whored out himself to men with twisted sexual appetites.

Keeping his voice low, he cupped the phone closer to his mouth and delivered his edict. "One woman. One man. One purpose. I do not wish to hear excuses. You will find her. You will have her delivered to me. And you will dispense with the man who is helping her with expedience. Report when you have news I want to hear."

He disconnected, then stared at the North Korean flag that hung on the wall above the entry door, a gift from Dear Leader. Who was this man? This man who could kill experienced warriors and continue to elude Ryang's best mercenaries? He must be eliminated.

The woman must be brought to him. Everything in his carefully orchestrated plan depended on her presence for this one last delivery. When she was no longer of use, he would kill her himself for placing him in this untenable position.

"Is all well, husband?"

Jin's melodious voice drew his attention. The crease between her brows troubled him. He smiled for her when her dark eyes met his across the room.

"All is well," he assured her.

All *would* be well. He would see to it. Just as he would see to it that his business ventures would never touch her or their daughter. He would not fail them. He would not fail at anything.

He did, however, need relief from the rage boiling up inside him. The kind of relief a creature as delicate as his wife could never assuage.

"Regretfully, I must meet with an associate," he said, rising abruptly.

"But it is almost time to retire."

He walked to her side, ran a hand over her sleek, stylish hair, then leaned down and tenderly kissed her forehead. "Do not wait up for me. This meeting may run late."

She knew better than to question him. Understood without probing that there were questions best left un-asked or unanswered. Did she know how he had ac-quired his fortune? Did she suspect?

He often wondered. Often regretted. But always he accepted his direction and his destiny.

Her eyes were watchful and concerned as he walked across the room but he did not hesitate. He let himself out of the apartment, placed a call on his mobile phone while in the elevator, then gave directions for his chauf-feur to drive him across the city to the hotel that always kept a room waiting for him.

Wealth made that happen. And wealth, however it

was acquired, made princes of paupers, power brokers of peons.

Ryang had overcome his past and hidden all traces of it from those who could destroy him. Still, he had miles to go before his importance would be fully appreciated in Kim Jong-chul's eyes. It had been unfortunate when Dear Leader, Kim Jong-il, had stepped down and named his youngest son as his successor several months ago. Ryang had been favored by the father. The transition had resulted in a loss of power for him. So he'd redoubled his efforts to prove himself in the young leader's eyes. He now felt he was in a constant struggle to reassert himself in a power position within the government. This Western woman could undo all of his careful attention to detail.

The dazzling lights of Macau's lavish casinos flashed by the windows of the town car as his driver headed unerringly toward the hotel where a diversion from his stress and his rage had better be waiting.

On the off chance that the gunmen decided to double back the same way they came, Luke swung a little wide of what he calculated their path to have been and headed through the trees. He hadn't walked fifty yards when a rifle shot ripped through the silence behind him.

Valentina.

He spun around and headed out in a full-out sprint back toward her.

Three more rapid bursts cracked through the mountain air.

Oblivious to the tree limbs slapping him in the face and the slippery mountainside that repeatedly sent him to his knees, he fought his way back to her. Three more shots followed on the heels of the others.

Then three more.

Then silence.

Ten rounds fired.

Fuck. His heart dropped to his gut. She was out of ammo.

10

An experienced fighter didn't think with his heart during combat. He used his head, called on muscle memory and training and instincts to keep him alive. The emotional warrior died.

Luke knew that if he didn't get his heart out of the equation fast, he *would* die in these mountains. Valentina would be as good as dead, too—if she wasn't already.

He could *not* go there.

He made himself slow down as he neared their hiding spot, then dropped to his belly and crawled silently up the rise that faced the cave.

When he reached the summit, he peeked over the rim.

And damn near swallowed his tongue.

Fifteen yards away, a lone gunman stood in front of the cave, a phone pressed to his ear. Directly in front of him was Valentina.

Alive!

His relief took a backseat to rage when he realized the guy had the business end of a rifle barrel shoved into the small of her back.

Luke made himself breathe deep and take stock. He couldn't hear what the guy was saying and gave up trying to eavesdrop when he spotted the body of another man not ten feet away from them, a rifle on the ground at his side. The shooter was sprawled spread-eagle on his back. Blood still oozed from the rounds Valentina had pumped into his chest at what appeared to be close range.

Kick-ass, ran through his mind as he zeroed back in on the gunman. If Luke had his SIG, he could put a bullet in the back of the guy's head without breaking a sweat. But he'd never fired this Glock; didn't feel comfortable with it. And there was the jerk reflex to consider. Unless he hit the medulla oblongata—in sniper terms, the "apricot" which was the part of the brain at the base of the skull that controlled involuntary movement—it was 99 percent likely that the shooter's trigger finger would spasm and he'd empty the HK's magazine into Val's spinal cord.

He needed to draw the sucker's attention and get that barrel pointed away from Valentina.

He looked around, found a brick-sized piece of deadfall, and hefted it. The wood was hollow, didn't weigh much more than a football, but it would make a lot of noise as it sailed through the lower tree limbs.

He heaved the wood so it whizzed to the left of the gunman's head, crashing into limbs as it flew.

As he'd hoped, the shooter flinched and spun toward the sound. The instant the nose of that rifle barrel shifted away from Valentina, Luke double-gripped the Glock and squeezed off three fast rounds.

The first shot hit its mark and spun the bad guy around. The second went into his open mouth. The third was a little insurance, and totally redundant.

Round number two had been the kill shot. A perfect zero reflex shot that cut the spinal cord from the rest of the body. In combat lingo, a ballistic lobotomy: 9mm in the head, guaranteed to change a man's way of thinking.

The body hadn't even hit the ground when Luke was racing down the ridge toward Valentina. She hadn't fully grasped what had happened when he caught her in his arms and crushed her against him.

"Are you hurt?" he asked urgently.

Her arms clamped around him like a vise, her fingers digging into his shoulders. "No. No . . . I'm f . . . fff . . . ine."

She wasn't fine, but he'd settle for safe. He breathed his first full breath in what felt like hours, though it had been mere minutes since he'd heard those ten heart-jarring rifle shots. He wanted to hold her like this until she stopped shaking, but that could end up getting them both killed. He didn't think there were any more shooters in the immediate vicinity but he didn't want to take any chances.

"How's the knee? Think you can walk?"

"Try to keep me at a walk. I want away from here."

He gave her a quick squeeze. "Hold on for a sec."

Given the scarce cell service and lack of conventional comms in the mountains, Luke wasn't surprised to see that the phone on the ground next to the body was a SAT phone. He reached down, picked it up, and pressed it to his ear. It was as dead as the man who had held it.

Who were these fuckers? And who the hell had sent them?

"Did you catch any part of the conversation?" he asked Val as he reached back into the hidey-hole for his hat and gear, then stuffed the phone inside the backpack. If he could get it back to BOI HQ, the crew could back trace the origin of the call and get a fix on whoever had been on the other end of the line.

She shook her head. "No. They were talking in . . . I don't know. Mandarin, maybe? Japanese? I don't know," she said again, her voice shaky, her eyes glazed and fixed on the man she had killed. "Something . . . Asian."

Which made sense. The man Val had killed looked Korean. There wasn't enough left of the other man's face to tell what he was.

"Don't look at him," Luke said firmly. He knew what she was thinking. Knew what she was going through. Yeah, it was kill or be killed, and the right person had died. But that didn't make taking a life any easier to process.

"Don't look at him," he repeated more sternly when her gaze remained riveted on the dead man.

He quickly stripped both bodies of all the intel that might be of use and could potentially lead them to their boss. He scribbled down the serial numbers of the rifles and handguns, in the event he could track down where they came from or tie the guns to end-user certificates. Then he quickly searched their shirts and pants pockets. One of them was carrying a military medal fixed to a red, green, and gold–striped ribbon. He tossed it in his pack along with their wallets to examine more closely later.

Their clothes were standard cammo pants and T-shirts, something any merc or private contractor would wear, but he cut off the shirt tags anyway in case they led to anything.

Satisfied that he'd gathered everything important, he disabled one rifle and one of the handguns and tossed them deep into the woods. Then he shoved the Glock in his belt, pocketed the extra ammo clips, and grabbed the second rifle.

"Let's get out of here," he said, retrieving his hat and shouldering his backpack.

Gripping her elbow, he steered her east, where he hoped they'd eventually run into a road.

Neither one of them looked back.

Ryang leaned back in the spacious marble tub in the presidential suite of the Mandarin Oriental Hotel and let the hot water shooting from the jets soothe the tension from his body. The girl—he did not know her name, nor did he care to know it—knelt naked on the floor behind him. He watched her reflection in the floor-to-ceiling wall of windows that overlooked the bay twenty-three stories below as her talented fingers massaged the knots from his neck and shoulders, her small, perfect breasts and boyishly slim hips pleasing to the eye.

He would partake of her special talents soon. Now, however, to his absolute annoyance, he still had business that needed tending. He glanced in cold silence at the phone clutched in his hand. One moment he had been speaking with his lieutenant who had headed the team in Peru. The next moment, the line had gone dead.

His man had finally reported in with news that was long overdue. The woman had finally been captured, but at great cost. A total of three of his assets had now been lost. And with the abrupt loss of connection, he must assume he had lost yet another.

Incompetence. He paid lavishly to insure that he did not have to deal with failure. He felt only loathing for these men who had paid for their ineptitude with their lives. Now he must dispatch more resources to clean up the mess.

He glanced at his watch, an elegant timepiece he'd purchased just this morning after a particularly successful night in one of the city's many flourishing casinos. Just as the West had once had no influence in Macau, there had been a time when he had not owned a pair of shoes without holes in the soles. Now Macau was the gaming Mecca of the world, and the eight-hundred-thousand-dollar Blancpain was merely a token of the wealth Ryang had acquired.

Were he not so preoccupied with Valentina Chamberlin's capture, he would have admired the Blancpain's platinum case and jeweled detailing. At the moment, however, his attention was confined to the time.

It was nine p.m. in Macau. That made it early morning in Peru.

"Harder," he ordered in Cantonese as the virgin whore's attention lapsed and the pressure of her massage lessened.

He closed his eyes when she began again to properly apply herself, and let her expertly schooled fingers and the soothing steam rising from the tub clear his mind.

He had not attained his current level of power by allowing mistakes to define his reputation. It still irritated him that he hadn't been able to fully capitalize on the fact that he'd been a favored agent of Kim Jong-il. In some circles, it had even been hinted that he, Ryang, was considered the leader's choice to take over. Of course, that hadn't happened. The control of the country and the million-man army had fallen to a child. A child that Ryang must constantly re-prove his value to.

But Kim Jong-chul was still playing with the reins of power. Ryang would wait. He would continue to prove his loyalty and dedication, and when the time came, he would insert himself into a valued position that would cement his leverage in the upper echelons of the government.

Everything he had worked for was still within his grasp—provided he rectified this situation immediately and insured that Valentina Chamberlin made her scheduled appearance in Sierra Leone next week.

Not only must he avoid losing face, everything he'd built to this point hinged on insuring the woman did not topple his carefully aligned network. She and she alone was the key to his significantly increased sphere of influence. She was the linchpin required to insure his plans were brought to fruition.

The consequences of not finding her would not only result in loss of business, but of his political status. Of his power.

That a woman—a Western woman—might be allowed to derail his machine was unthinkable.

He lifted the phone again, punched in a series of numbers.

"There have been complications with the delivery of the package in Peru," he said in his native Korean when his second in command answered. "There was an unexpected intervention on its behalf. An American, it would seem, has interfered and intercepted."

A man who seemed highly skilled in the art of guerilla warfare. Ryang considered what that meant. Was the man merely a stranger intervening on her behalf? Or could he be an agent assigned to protect her?

"Place a team on the ground at the last known location." His organization was well established internationally. He had resources in place, ready to deploy in every corner of the globe. Peru was no exception. The tracking devices he'd had implanted in all of his assets would assist the new team in locating the dead men and lead him to the woman.

"You must find them very soon. The delivery is scheduled for a week from today. You realize what is at stake." He disconnected, confident Lee understood that failure was not an option.

Satisfied, he turned his attention back to the virgin whore. She was the perfect outlet for the rage that had been simmering since the first report of failure. Perhaps fourteen or fifteen years old, she was older than he preferred, but she had the look of innocence he liked. And since virgins, even at this tender age, were becoming more and more difficult to acquire, she would do.

The fear she tried to conceal when he motioned for her to join him in the water fueled his arousal. She had reason to be afraid. He did not intend to exercise control over his fury any longer.

"Please me," he demanded as she stepped into the steaming tub, then let her know with a measured look that her future was dependent on how well she performed.

He would have no use for her after he'd quenched his lust. If she pleased him, if she went to great pains to satisfy his appetites, he would see to it that she would never have to sell her body again. He would reward her with enough cash that she would be able to make a life for herself on her own terms.

But if she failed him . . . then she would suffer the hard hands of strangers—as he had suffered—for many, many years to come.

"Please me," he repeated, one final attempt to let her know that she held her own destiny in her hands.

11

Cuzco was the gateway to the Sacred Valley and the stunning ancient Incan ruins of Machu Picchu, but Luke had never been impressed by the outer limits of the 11,000-foot-elevation settlement in the Peruvian Andes. They sped through the outskirts of the city, urban sprawl punctuated by the accompanying urban decay that would soon give way to the historical city center that had mesmerized Luke the first time Chewy had brought him here.

A persistent and uncharacteristic June rain beat down on them as they sped along, sharing the open bed of a rusted-out pickup with several bushels of—what else—potatoes.

He tucked Valentina closer to his side in an attempt to shield her against the icy-cold, relentless downpour.

"Almost there," he said against her hair when she shivered violently against him.

It had been four hours since they'd stumbled onto a little-traveled road and the ancient, compact pickup had made an appearance. By the time he'd flagged it down they were already wet to the bone and freezing in the frigid morning air.

Only after he'd been satisfied that the man behind the wheel was exactly what he appeared to be—a farmer on the way to market—had Luke motioned for Val to come out from behind the rock where he'd insisted she hide out. And only after he'd produced a palm full of coins that he'd dug out of his backpack had the mestizo man made room for them in the truck bed.

He'd had to leave the rifle behind. Even in Cuzco, an automatic weapon was going to raise a few eyebrows. Since they hadn't encountered any more bad guys, it had served its purpose anyway. The Glock, however, was still tucked in his waistband under his shirt. The grip poked into his ribs as the farmer managed to hit a pothole big enough to swallow a small pig.

The ride was rough, the potatoes hard, and the rain brutal, but it was a damn sight better than walking. Finally they reached the inner city and the Plaza San Blas, where intricate Incan architecture formed the bedrock from the Spanish conquistadores' period and transported anyone with a little imagination back hundreds of years in time.

Here was where they got out. Luke tapped on the rear window of the truck's cab and motioned for the driver to stop.

"Come on." He helped Valentina down from the pickup bed, then dug into his duffle and handed the farmer the balance of what he'd promised him and what most likely amounted to a week's wages.

Tucking Valentina under his arm, he rushed across the wet, ancient cobbled streets toward the Taypikala Hotel, where he generally stayed when he was in Cuzco for his annual stint with the medical team.

The two-story white building with its sheltering eaves, tiled roof, and large square windows was only four blocks away. But between the street vendors and the street shills constantly grabbing at them, insisting they buy anything from witch's potions to fruit to pottery to guinea pig—a local delicacy cooking over braziers on crude wooden skewers—it was a good ten minutes before they reached the hotel.

Another time, Luke would have taken time to appreciate the local sounds, scents, and flavors of the Mercado de las Brujas, the witch's market. Now all he wanted to do was get Valentina out of sight, get her warmed up and dry, and contact his boss at Black Ops, Inc. to get them the hell out of here. There'd be time later to figure out who was after her.

He didn't have any illusions about the danger she was still in. That hit squad from the train was the first wave. There would be more.

He had to also assume that the local authorities were looking for them. There were three dead bodies on that train. He was responsible for two of them, and there were a lot of witnesses. The policía were going to have questions. Since he didn't have any answers yet, he had no plans of sticking around and being grilled.

Val was shivering almost uncontrollably when they finally walked into the Taypikala's homey lobby with its wide arching doorways. Inca prints hung on walls drenched with warm yellow paint. Despite the fire burning in a huge fireplace, the faint, ever-present scent of mold and mildew permeated the building.

He registered using one of the many fake IDs he carried and made short work of booking a suite for "Adolph and Gretchen Krauss." Then he hustled Valentina up to their second-floor room and locked the door behind them.

"Shower. Now," he demanded, locating the wall thermostat and cranking up the heat.

She stood shivering with her arms around her waist, her sodden hair trailing down her back and her teeth rattling like dice on a craps table.

"Better yet, soak in a hot tub," he suggested, physically leading her into the small bathroom.

"Jesus," he muttered when a violent shiver ripped through her. "You're an ice cube."

He turned on the hot water full blast, adjusted the temp so it wouldn't scald her, then set the stopper in the tub.

"Do you need help?" he asked, watching her with concern. She was at the brittle cold stage. He'd been there. During Hell Week in BUD/S training there'd been times he'd been so cold it felt like his eyelids would shatter if he blinked.

She shook her head, the movement jerky and stiff. "N . . . no. I can do it."

No, he decided after a quick assessment. She couldn't. He started unbuttoning the shirt he'd loaned her.

"Hush," he said when she opened her mouth to protest.

His own fingers were stiff with cold but he worked as fast as he could, then stripped his heavy, wet shirt down her arms and tossed it on the floor.

Next came her turtleneck. He clenched his jaw then tugged it over her head, determined not to buckle when she stood there, naked from the waist up except for a filmy black scrap of a bra. Her nipples, puckered tight with cold, poked like pencil erasers against the transparent bra cups.

Focus, jackass.

With a deep breath, he dropped to one knee and went to work on her jeans . . . then damn near lost it when he finally managed to peel the wet denim down her legs. All that was underneath them besides the ace bandage wrapped around her knee was a tiny black thong.

A man could only take so much before he broke— and he was at the breaking point.

He stood, and abruptly headed for the door. "You take it from here."

He made himself softly close the door, just to prove he had it in him. Then he sagged back against it and counted to ten. When the image of her standing there next to naked refused to roll on out of his mind's eye, he thought, *Fuck it.*

Then he closed his eyes and let himself savor the memory. Every inch of goose-bump-covered, caramel-colored skin. Every sleek, sensual curve. Every delectable detail. Like the tiny, sexy mole high on the inside of her left thigh, where her skin was satin soft; and the little gold stud tucked into her belly button.

Hell, even her navel drove him nuts. He was a sucker for an inny. He wanted to dip the tip of his tongue into that indentation, then lick his way down to the sweet spot between her thighs. A shudder ripped through him when he relived the moment on his knees in front of her. His mouth had been inches away from tasting her.

The sound of sloshing water triggered yet another erotic picture. Valentina naked in the tub, the water lapping over the swell of her breasts, teasing her nipples, swirling between her thighs.

Fire boiled through his blood.

Jesus. What was he, fourteen again?

On the bright side, at least he wasn't cold anymore. Hard as a damn anvil, but not cold.

He dragged a hand over his face, sucked in a controlling breath, then rapped the back of his knuckles against the door before opening it a crack.

"Use this if you have to," he said, placing the Glock on the vanity. "I'll be back in less than thirty minutes. Don't open up to anyone but me, okay?"

Silence, then more sloshing, followed by a soft "Okay."

He quickly shut the door, then shook himself to shed the erotic images of the two of them together. He didn't bother to change into dry clothes. It was still raining and he'd just get soaked again. He dug some cash out of his pack and got the hell out before he did something stupid. Like kick the bathroom door off its hinges, pull her out of that tub, and take her against the wall.

Yeah, that would impress the hell out of her.

Swearing under his breath, he punched the lobby door open with the flat of his hand and stepped out into the rain.

Val had thought she was never going to be warm again. After several minutes submerged to her chin in the hot bath, however, she felt her blood begin to thaw. After several more, she gradually stopped shivering and started feeling human.

She had never been so cold. There had been that time on the beach at La Jolla in January when the photographer had insisted on twenty bikini changes and hundreds of shots before he'd called it a day. But there'd been a tent with a heater, hot coffee, and heavy robes in between each series of shots. She hadn't been on the run since three in the morning then, either. Hadn't hidden for over an hour in a mountainside cave, hadn't killed a man . . .

Another violent shiver consumed her. She did *not* want to think about that. Didn't want to think about how afraid she'd been when she'd heard movement outside in the forest, and knew it wasn't Luke. How she'd instinctively sensed, even before they'd found her, that they would discover her hiding there.

How she had lain there, mouse quiet, hands shaking, and known that she might have to actually shoot that rifle to survive.

She closed her eyes and inhaled the fragrant steam

rising from bubble bath. Yet she still smelled the acrid scent of spent gunpowder. Still felt the kick of the rifle slamming against her shoulder. Saw the deep crimson stain spreading across the man's chest. Remembered thinking that his eyes had died even before his body had fallen.

She'd killed a man.

She sat up abruptly and uncapped the bottle of shampoo set on the rim of the tub. Then she scrubbed her hair vigorously, rinsed, and did it all over again. She managed to keep her hands busy for several minutes before finally making herself get out of the tub.

After lavishing on the entire mini bottle of body lotion she'd found in a basket on the vanity, she wrapped a bath towel around herself sarong style. She was using her fingers to comb her hair when she heard the hotel room door open and close.

She whipped her head around. Listened. Reached for the gun, wondering if she could make herself pull the trigger again if she had to.

"Valentina, it's me."

Her shoulders sagged in relief. She hadn't realized how wildly her heart was jumping until she felt its hard beat beneath her palm. Hadn't realized how vulnerable she felt until she caught a glimpse of herself in the vanity mirror, and saw the reflection of fear on her face.

Pathetic. Disgusted, she turned toward the door when Luke rapped it with his knuckles.

"Princess? You still with me?"

"Yeah. I'm here."

"Open the door, okay? I come bearing gifts."

She clutched the towel tighter around her breasts and cracked open the door. Steam rolled out of the small bathroom; cooler air rushed in.

"Dry clothes." He held out a paper sack. "Hope they fit."

She opened her mouth to thank him, but abruptly stopped. Something on the other side of the door smelled amazing. "Oh, God. Please tell me that's food."

"And not a raw potato in sight. Get dressed, then come out. But toss me a towel first, okay?"

She took a better look at him then and realized he was still soaked to the bone. Feeling guilty, she handed him a towel. Then, forgoing the wet underwear that she'd hung over a towel bar to dry, she pulled on a black sweater that was soft and warm and exactly her size. The jeans were a good fit, too, and the thick black socks felt like heaven.

She walked out of the bathroom tugging her damp hair out from under the cowl neck of the sweater, feeling guilty that she'd been soaking here in the warm hotel room while he'd braved the rain again.

Guilt was shoved out of the way by appreciation when she saw him standing with his bare back to her, pulling on a pair of dry camouflage cargo pants.

He'd slung the white hotel towel around his neck, leaving his broad shoulders bare. Leaving the tan skin of his torso that narrowed to his lean waist bare. Leaving her wondering at the scars that peppered all that exposed skin.

Zipped and buttoned, he tugged a tan T-shirt out of the backpack on the floor. And damn if her mouth didn't go a little dry as she stared at his butt in all its tight, narrow glory. The man was buff. The man was . . . *Oh God.*

She gasped when he turned around and she saw the long, angry scar that ran under his rib cage and wrapped around his waist, where the insulted flesh was thickened and puckered, then disappeared into his pants near his navel. "What happened to you?"

She couldn't keep the horror from her voice. Something that big, something that invasive . . . it could have killed him. *Should* have killed him.

You think I'm not scared?

His words came back to her with the clarity of a diamond. Back when they'd been hiding, he'd told her he got scared, too. She hadn't believed him; had thought he was trying to make her feel better.

Maybe she believed him now.

And when something flashed across his face, something haunted and hunted, she was *certain* she believed him.

Mouth tight, he tugged the T-shirt over his head, then pulled it down over his chest and covered the scar.

"Sometimes the bad guys get in a few licks," he said flatly, then just that fast, Indy Luke was back. A grin on his face, a light attitude once again ruling the hour.

"The clothes fit?" He gestured toward her sweater and jeans.

Okay, so he didn't want to talk about the scar. She

owed him so much, the least she could do was respect his privacy.

"Good guess on the sizes," she said, determined to follow his lead and keep this light.

He flashed a wicked grin. "No guessing involved. When I mentioned that I was a fan, did I leave out the part about a minor obsession?"

His smile was teasing, but she was beginning to think there might be some truth to his words.

"You know, I used to receive love letters from teenage admirers, many of whom took pride in finding out intimate details about me. So tell me . . . were you really one of those love-struck puppies who actually knew my bra size?

He laughed. "My secret's out. But you can relax, Angelface. I already told you I'm not going stalker on you."

She smiled tightly. "And yet, it would make this lovely adventure so complete."

He gave her a sympathetic look. "I'll get you out of this, okay? Just trust me. Now eat."

He'd spread an assortment of food on the low coffee table, from quinoa, a cereal she had come to appreciate while in Peru, to mangos and bananas and hot peppers. He'd apparently hit every street vendor in town. There were anticuchos complete with corn on the cob, boiled potatoes, and chili sauce; tacu-tacu, a seasoned beans-and-rice dish; and ceviche with limes and onions.

"Inca-Kola?" she asked, wrinkling her nose at the cans of soft drink he pulled out of a paper sack and popped open.

"Nectar of the gods," he said with a grin. "Smells and looks like a cross between banana juice and—"

"Llama urine?" she suggested, because anyone who'd ever tried the sickeningly sweet soda pretty much held the same opinion.

"Yum yum." He lifted a glass in salute.

He managed to make her smile again. "I hadn't realized how hungry I was."

"It's the adrenaline," he said as they both attacked the food. "It'll burn right past the hunger. At least for a while. Once it lets down, though, everything else takes over. Fatigue. Nerves. And hunger."

Yeah, she got that part. Especially about the nerves.

"And then there's the pain," he added, glancing at her knee.

He was right about that, too. A dull, persistent ache had set into her knee. Pain, she could handle. The rest of it . . . not so much.

She watched him dig in to the food like he didn't have a care in the world. But she knew he was always tactically aware of their danger.

"How do you keep so cool?"

He grunted and licked a drop of pepper sauce off his finger. "Practice."

She leaned back, suddenly incapable of keeping up the banter. Another question burned for an answer. "How do you . . ." She tried again. "How do you deal with—" She just couldn't say it out loud.

"Look at me," he said softly.

When she met his eyes, his sober expression told her he understood exactly what she wanted to ask.

"You just do," he said firmly. "You remind yourself that if you hadn't killed him, he'd have killed you. You remember that you didn't start this fight. Someone else did, someone bad. Someone who wouldn't blink an eye over the blood he was responsible for spilling.

"That's how you deal with it," he went on as tears pooled in her eyes. "You remember that you're the good guy, and good guys are sometimes forced by bad guys to do bad things."

12

Val swallowed hard. "I still don't understand why anyone would be after me. Why they would go to such lengths to find me."

"We're going to find out," he promised with rock-solid conviction. "We're going to find out who it is, what they want, and then we're going to deal with them."

For a short while, back in the woods, she'd been under the illusion that they *had* dealt with them. The four men who had been chasing her were dead. That was the end of it. They were safe, right?

With a sober look, Luke had set her straight.

"Those men were mercs. Hired guns," he'd told her as they'd hiked away from the bodies, her knee throbbing with every step. "There's a mastermind behind this. Someone big. Someone who has the money and resources to hunt you down."

Despite the hard, vigilant look on his face, she'd kept telling herself that he was wrong. That it was over.

He hadn't said another word. He'd just let her work it out in her mind.

And eventually, on that long, freezing ride in the rain, she had. Luke was right. One gunman had been talking on the phone. Though she hadn't understood what he'd said, she did understand that he was reporting in. Whoever was on the other end of the line wanted her badly enough to chase her across Peru—and apparently he'd wanted her alive, or she'd be lying dead on that mountainside.

It was only after she'd reached that point, that she had accepted the reason Luke had gathered so many items from the bodies. He was going to connect the dots that would lead them to whoever was behind this.

"Hey—you still with me?"

Luke's voice brought her out of her thoughts.

She forced a smile, feeling very contrite suddenly.

"Yeah. Listen . . . I need to say something." But she was at a loss as to how to begin to cover all she had to thank him for. "I need to thank you."

"Hey. I was hungry, too," he said dismissively.

"I wasn't talking about the food. Well, yes, the food, too, but . . . how do I ever thank you for saving my life? Several times. For getting me out of those mountains. For getting me warm. For making me feel like something other than a burden."

He shifted so he was facing her. "You're not a burden."

She smiled and shook her head. "Right. You're being shot at because of me. Don't tell me it's just a typical day in the life of Luke Colter."

The minute she said it, the visual of that horrible scar

came to mind. Oh, God. Maybe this *was* a typical day for him.

He was quiet for a moment, then confirmed her thoughts.

"Actually, that's not too far from the truth."

She met his eyes, recognizing that it was a big admission for him to make. "And what is the truth, Luke?"

He scratched his head, then shrugged. "Screw it," he said, apparently reaching a decision. "You're going to find out most of it later anyway. Earlier, you asked what I did for a living. And you've already figured out I'm not a nine-to-fiver. So here's the down and dirty. I work for a man named Nate Black. Nate was my CO when I was still in the SEALs. He headed up a special task force at the request of and under the direction of President Billings."

President Billings? Whoa. Val steeled herself because she understood that what came next was going to be huge.

"Nate pulled the team together from all branches of the military—Army, Marines, Navy . . . even a couple of company men. CIA," he clarified when her brows furrowed.

"Anyway, we ran covert missions mostly in the Middle East and Africa, all off the grid, all under the directive of the joint chiefs. The unit—Task Force Mercy—was controversial to say the least, and after Billings's second term expired, the new leadership's prevailing consensus was that TFM was a potential political time bomb and needed to be disbanded. And just like that, it no longer existed."

He lifted a shoulder as if it didn't bother him, but she got a strong sense that it bothered him a lot. Just like she understood that he'd glossed over the importance and the dangerous nature of their missions.

"Okay, fine. Shit happens. Power shifts. Life and war go on. So most of the team separated from the service shortly after that, and joined Nate when he set up a private contracting firm headquartered in Buenos Aires."

"Private contracting?" She felt herself go pale. The term raised thoughts of rogue CIA agents and hired assassins. "You mean you're mercenaries?"

His mouth tightened. "Mercenaries hire out to the highest bidder, Princess. Like those bastards back there on the train. Black Ops, Inc. works pretty much the way our old task force worked. Most of our ops are contracted for Uncle and were still doing the same kind of jobs. Only now, the government can disavow any association if an op goes FUBAR. Keeps the PC preachers happy."

PC she got. *Politically correct* was the watchword of the day. FUBAR, however went over her head.

"Fucked up beyond all recognition," he explained, seeing her confused frown. "Only BOI doesn't fuck up. And we're definitely not going to fuck up with you."

She didn't doubt it for one second. Despite his tendency to joke under the most extreme conditions, he was competent, capable, and ruthlessly brutal when he needed to be.

"Wait." She'd skimmed right over something he'd said. Something important. "You said 'we.'"

"I found a pay phone when I went out and put in a call to the guys. You've got most of the BOI team on board now. Nate's working on getting us transpo."

Oh, God. She'd been so caught up in getting warm

and dry and fed, she hadn't remembered a very immediate problem. "How am I going to get out of the country without a passport?"

"You don't need a passport, Princess. You've got the BOIs. Nate's got contacts everywhere. Old military buddies. Diplomats. People whose asses we've pulled out of slings. So don't worry. We're going to get you out of here, and then we will get to the bottom of this for you. I've got to call back in"—he checked his watch—"in a little over an hour. See what kind of bird he's arranged to fly us out of here."

"I can pay," she said without hesitation. If his teammates were half as good as Luke, she'd be willing to pay any price to make this all go away.

He grinned and looked at her like she was a sweet but slightly dim child. "You don't pay, Angelface."

"Oh, yes, I do."

"No, see, you don't get it." He leaned forward, propped his forearms on his wide-spread thighs, and held her gaze. "This might have started out all about you, but those assholes have messed with *me* now. They didn't intend to but the fact is, they did. So now it's personal. And once it gets personal, the entire team gets involved. Okay?"

No, it was not okay, but she could see he was determined.

"Okay." He slapped his hands on his thighs, then stood abruptly. "Excuse me for a minute. That shower's been calling to me."

After digging around in his pack for a razor, he

headed for the bathroom. "Did you leave enough shampoo so that I can smell all girly, like you?"

The idea made her smile. "Knock yourself out."

As the bathroom door closed behind him, she picked up a chunk of mango and nibbled absently. Once upon a time, if someone had told her she would be running for her life from some unknown assailant with unknown motives, she'd have told them to back off of the booze.

Once upon a time, before a night train in the Andes.

Thoughtful, she glanced toward the closed bathroom door. She appreciated that he'd been square with her about who he was and what he did. Sure, it was a little dismaying to realize that she was keeping company with a black ops warrior. Dismaying but also comforting and . . . she had to admit, a little exciting.

He was exciting. And funny. And kind.

And sexy.

And oh my God, the scar. How had a wound that horrific not killed him? From the looks of it, still angry and red, it had happened not that long ago. The idea that a man so vital and heroic could have died . . . it made her heart drop just thinking about it. What if he *had* died? Then he wouldn't have been on that train. She never would have met him.

If she wasn't vigilant, she could let herself become unwisely attached to this man. She was already dangerously attracted to him.

Except for the Indy thing and the hero thing, though, she still wasn't sure why the attraction was so strong. Clichéd as it was, he wasn't her type.

She was constantly surrounded by the most beautiful of the beautiful people. Surrounded by men who dazzled with a smile, a tilt of their head, a blink of a heavily lashed eye. Razzle and dazzle, however, was often all there was to them.

She needed more from a man than surface charm and sex appeal. She needed a gentle man. An intellectual. Someone who shared her hopes and her dreams and . . .

Oh, wait. Marcus had been that man. And Marcus had almost destroyed her.

She glanced toward the bathroom again. Maybe that's why, cute, sexy, funny, brave, and resourceful Luke Colter appealed to her. He was the exact opposite of Marcus. While he was clearly intelligent and he could be gentle, he was a very dangerous man. As a Navy SEAL, he'd done things most men would never do. Seen things most men would never see, experienced things most men couldn't handle.

He'd killed two men on that train without a nanosecond of hesitation. Shot the man who had held her at gunpoint.

He'd saved her life.

He'd run her a bath. How sweet was that?

He'd also stripped her almost naked . . . and walked away, though he hadn't wanted to. As miserable and cold as she'd been, she'd also been acutely aware of that.

He made it easy to remember that a man and a woman could make magic together when everything was right between them. And right now, everything about him felt right.

Her thoughtful gaze was locked on the bathroom door when it swung open.

Luke was clean-shaven and fully dressed — except for his bare feet, which were large and long and for some reason made her smile.

"What?" he asked, his hand stalled mid-air as he towel-dried his hair.

She met his eyes. Said nothing.

It didn't take him more than a second to follow the direction of her thoughts. His eyes darkened danger-ously. A little thrill of anticipation zinged through her body, heating her blood when he balled up the towel, tossed it aside, and crossed the room in several long strides.

"Seriously?" he asked after a close assessment of her face.

"Heart-attack serious," she said, and stood.

They were toe to toe. She could see the pulse beat-ing steady and fast at his throat, feel the testosterone radiating off him in heady waves. He smelled clean and male and aroused. And when she lifted her hands, wrapped her fingers in a light caress around his biceps, he tensed like a coiled spring, the muscle hardening to stone beneath her fingertips.

A shiver went through his big body and she experi-enced an unfamiliar stirring of power, knowing that she could shake him this badly.

His eyes narrowed. "Look . . . if this is about the scar —"

She pressed her fingertips against his lips, not surprised to find them soft yet firm and deliciously enticing. "It's not about the scar."

Every part of him tempted her.

"It's about life," she said, moving into him. "It's about death. It's about making the most of the time in between."

Never had she felt as close to death as she had today. And not since the moment when she'd decided to trust this man had she felt anything as strongly as she felt it now.

"I almost died today," she whispered, holding his gaze. "*You* almost died."

His hands moved to her waist. "Which is why this isn't really a stellar time for you to be making these kinds of decisions, Angelface," he said carefully. "You've been through the wringer. You're running on empty."

She tilted her head, studied his tortured expression, and turned the screws. "So you're turning me down."

"Jesus, no. I mean—yes. But I don't want to." He closed his eyes on a groan. "I mean I *want* to. I *want* to do this. But I don't want to take advantage of you."

She knew what she needed to know now. And she understood exactly what she had to do to bring him around. Not caring that she wasn't playing fair, not even caring that she was manipulating him, she skated her hands down his neck, around his shoulders, feeling his skin heat beneath the trail of her fingertips. Feeling his big frame shudder with the effort to keep himself under control.

A low growl this time. "You are seriously screwing

me up here," he said between clenched teeth. "I'm not in the habit of practicing restraint. Not when it comes to something I want as badly as I want you."

"And I'm not in the habit of coming on to men who throw me out of trains. But I'm making an exception in your case."

He pushed out a helpless laugh, then shook his head as if he were attempting to ward off Lucifer and all of his devils.

"There's a perfectly good bed over there." She let her fingertips drift all the way down his arms again, laced her fingers with his, and felt a kick of excitement eddy through her blood when she realized his hands were unsteady. "Let's take advantage of what's going on here and use it."

She started walking backward toward the bed, tugging him along with her.

"What exactly *is* going on?" he asked, finally giving in and letting her lead him.

"I'm not sure." She wasn't sure of anything but this moment. "Just like I'm not sure it's important that I know. Can't we just be in the moment, Luke? Can't we just make each other feel good for a little while? After what we've been through, would it be so wrong to give that to each other?"

He swallowed hard, and his struggle to do the right thing endeared him to her even more. Made her trust him more. Made her want him more.

"Luke, this is a huge leap of faith for me. I don't do this, okay? Contrary to what the gossip rags say, I've *never* slept around. And I don't *ever* hop into bed with virtual strangers."

His eyes sought more than answers. "Then why me?"

She shook her head. "I honestly don't know. Something about you . . . something about us . . . it changes the rules. Changes so many things. There's only one thing I know for certain. I don't want to question this anymore."

She couldn't believe she was being the aggressor, that she was doing the seducing. But she believed her gut. Believed this was right.

And she believed the conviction that she'd lacked for a very long time. So long, she'd forgotten what a potent drug it could be.

When her legs bumped up against the bed, she released his hands. Eyes locked on his, she reached for the hem of her sweater, then lifted it over her head.

He sucked in a breath as his gaze lowered from her face to her bare breasts. "Jesus. You don't play fair."

She cupped his cheek in her palm, wet her lips and beckoned him with a breathless whisper. "Do things to me, Luke. Do things that will make us both forget everything going on outside this room. Tell me—"

"Enough," he growled. His eyes were dark with desire as he lifted her, tossed her onto the bed, then followed her down. "You had me at potato."

13

Stick a fork in him, he was done.

Done talking. Done trying to do the right thing, be the right man, make the right choices. *Jesus*, he wasn't a saint. *Sinner* came much closer to fitting the bill. And she made him want to be bad.

So he was going to be.

He was going to be damn bad.

It was all about indulgence now. All about sinking into this soft, sexy, blow-his-ever-lovin'-mind woman.

He didn't remember shucking his clothes or dragging off the rest of hers. Had a vivid, visceral memory, however, of her lifting the sweater over her head, of her standing before him, her breasts full and perfect and bare, her small brown nipples tight and erect and asking to be sucked.

No, he was no saint.

Especially when her dark eyes implored him and she begged him to *do things to her*.

Mother of God.

They were both naked now. The bed was fresh

washed linen and softly creaking. Her skin was as hot as fire and so freaking smooth. He couldn't touch her enough. Couldn't taste her enough. Couldn't kiss and lick and suck enough, fast enough, deep enough.

Not enough for her either, apparently, because when he pressed a wet, scraping kiss against her rib cage, just under her right breast, she reared up with a catlike sound, shoved him to his back, and, turning the tables, straddled his hips.

Heart racing, breath ragged, he sensed her need to dominate this round. So he lay spread-eagle beneath her, forcing his hands to stay still—clenched, but still— beside his head and watch her. Just watch her move above him.

She *was* the stuff of fantasies.

He groaned deep in his chest as she ground her pelvis into his, and every muscle, sinew, and tendon in his body clenched into tight steel bands. She smiled in triumph when the heat and the wetness between her thighs pulsed against his cock and it twitched with the need to be inside her.

But she wanted to torture him a little more first. Fine. It couldn't kill him to indulge her, right? Or . . . *oh, God.* Maybe it could.

He sucked in a harsh breath when she planted her palms on either side of his shoulders, then lowered her head and kissed him . . . openmouthed, seeking tongue, all hot and wet and hungry. And when that amazing mouth moved lower to nip and kiss him along his jaw, then lower, to cover and lightly bite his right nipple, he grabbed handfuls of sheet and clung like he was a fingerhold away from falling into a bottomless abyss.

But when she sat back on her heels and took him in her hand, then bent to run her tongue slowly, lovingly, over the ridge of the scar bisecting his body, he totally, *totally* lost it.

He reached down, cupped her head in his hands, and dragged her mouth back to his. He feasted on her lips, then her tongue, feeding his own hunger, then gasped when she broke the kiss and offered him her breast.

He lifted his head off the pillow and latched on. And he wasn't gentle. She cried out when he nipped her, moaned low and long when he opened his mouth wide around her areola, flicked the tip of her nipple with his tongue, then sucked his fill.

Velvet and nectar.

Woman and desire.

He drowned in every facet of her as he skated his hands over the gentle round of her hips, then filled a palm with the weight of one perfect breast, molding her and shaping her with his fingers before turning his head to give attention to the other.

Her breathless sighs and earthy gasps fueled his desire for more as she let him know how much she loved it. Loved his mouth, loved the suction, the wild, wet heat.

Do things to me.

He was just getting started.

Gripping her waist with both hands, he lifted her up,

his mouth never relinquishing its hold on her nipple, and flipped her to her back.

Her eyes were half closed as he knelt between her legs; his hands looked huge and dark and rough against her skin as he stroked from her knees up her thighs to that part of her he had every intention of owning before they left this bed.

Her skin was satin smooth there at the apex, her pubic curls dark and silky. He watched her face as he slipped a finger inside, groaned when she closed her eyes, clenched around him and arched her back, pressing her head into the bedding.

Need shot through him like a Tomahawk missile, lightning fast, fireball hot. Homed in on an irreversible target. And when she opened wider, trusting, vulnerable, inviting, he damn near exploded.

He gripped her hips and dragged her to the edge of the mattress, then he dropped to his knees on the floor.

She made a keening sound as he parted her thighs and, careful of her injured knee, hooked her legs over his shoulders.

"Yes?" he breathed against that sexy mole on her inner thigh.

"Oh . . . God . . . yesss . . ."

He was already seeking that nest of downy curls, his tongue already stroking the core of her sex, his mouth already open and feasting.

She bucked against his tongue, gasped his name as he suckled, spurred on as much by her taste and scent as by the way she writhed against him, fisted her hands in his hair and demanded more. More suction. More pressure. More tongue.

He loved her passion. Almost as much as he loved her taste, and the power of possession. He'd played out this fantasy a hundred times, only in his imagination, he'd been the one doing the begging. He'd been the one pleading for her to let him touch, let him feel, let him see and do and experience the magic of Valentina.

The reality was so painfully sweet he thought he might OD on it. When she convulsed and screamed his name—God he loved that strangled, desperate sound—he eased up, slowed down, let her languish in the riot of sensation, let her glide on the silky rush, and finally catch her breath on the downside of the fall. He reluctantly made himself leave the rich, rare taste of a woman wholly spent, and lay back down on the bed beside her.

Propping himself up on an elbow, he laid his palm over her concave belly and spread his fingers wide. Her flesh quivered beneath his hand, the gold ball in her navel winked between his fingers as she struggled for a steady breath.

Did he still want her? Oh, yeah. Was he rock hard and damn near bursting? *Hell*, yeah. But he couldn't make himself move. Couldn't tear his gaze away from the picture she made lying there. Her breasts were pink and red and wet from his mouth, her thighs were wantonly splayed on the tangled sheets. Moisture from his mouth, from her release, glistened on her silken curls.

"Luke," she whispered and lifted a very limp hand.

"I'm here, Angelface."

"Not close enough." she made a feeble attempt to tug him closer.

"Hold that thought," he whispered, leaned down to kiss her, then briefly left to get some condoms out of his pack, silently thanking Johnny Duane Reed.

"Bang-bang," Reed had said with a grin as he'd tucked a packet of condoms into Luke's hand just as he was about to head out for Peru.

Because it was easier to go along with Reed than cross him and because it was nobody's business that Luke's "vacation" would not be spent on a beach or in a bed with some bombshell of the week, but holding medical clinics for the Quechua, he'd simply stuffed them in his pack.

Yeah, when he got back to B.A., he'd have to thank his teammate.

Right now, though, was all about here. About some unfinished business waiting for him on that bed.

Lord, would you look at her.

He swallowed a huge lump in his throat and stood there, heart skipping like a schoolboy's. Her eyes were closed. Her black hair fanned like a wash of silk over white linen. One hand rested across a delicate breast. The pretty bead of her nipple peeked out from between her splayed fingers.

"Jesus, you're beautiful." The mattress dipped with his weight when he knelt by her hip.

She smiled without opening her eyes. "And you are . . . thorough."

"Oh, Angelface, you haven't seen thorough yet."

As much threat as promise colored his words as he rolled on the condom. As much desire as approval showed in her eyes when she finally opened them and saw the jutting proof that he was just getting started.

She smiled, all mellow and sultry and smug. "You just going to loom over me and make promises, or do you plan to deliver anytime soon?"

He laughed, because damn, she was fun. And damn, she was gorgeous. But when she raised both arms to beckon him, then opened her thighs to welcome him, he sobered like a judge.

"You know," he said, lowering himself and making a place for himself between her legs, "I've wanted to do this since the first time I saw you."

She wrapped her arms around his neck and her legs around his hips. "On the train?"

He reached between them, found her swollen and slick and still pulsing with need for him. "On a billboard near Billings, Montana, about a hundred fifty million years ago."

She gasped and he groaned when he pressed the head of his penis into her opening.

"That's . . . Oh, God." She lifted her hips to meet him when he thrust deeper. "That's a long, long time."

He was drowning in her. Swollen to the max and stretching the walls of her flesh with the most outrageous friction that bred the most astounding sensations he'd ever, *ever*, felt.

"Worth. The. Wait," he ground out, pressing his face

into the curve of her neck and gorging himself on the feel of her.

"Stop talking," she ordered on a thready moan as her arms tightened around his shoulders. "Just . . . move. Please . . . just . . . move."

She hooked her ankles tightly around his hips and hugged him closer, heightening the sense of urgency thrumming through his body as he pumped deeper, harder, faster.

He couldn't talk now if she begged him.

He was fully and wholly immersed in her. The wild, sexy sounds she made as she clung and rocked her hips to meet his. The hot, supple body that vibrated with the need for release.

"Pleasssseee," she hissed against his shoulder, digging her nails into his back.

He lifted his head and clamped his mouth over hers, thrust his tongue inside and mimicked the action of his hips. And still it wasn't enough. He skimmed a hand roughly down the length of her body, tucked it under her ass and lifted, tilting her hips until the contact was so deep, so penetrating, he was afraid he might hurt her.

"You okay?" he panted and prayed to God she was, because this was . . . oh, man . . . this was heaven. The closest thing to a mystical experience he was ever going to get.

"God, yes. Oh . . . please . . . now!"

He heard her through a fog of raw, primal need. Every nerve in his body was focused on the friction and the fusion; every pleasure point felt magnified a million times as he pumped in and out and their bodies melded into one pulsing, hypersensitized organism, both craving the ultimate release.

He was buried deep, deep in desire, yet he still sensed a change in her breathing, from labored to ragged. The change in her heartbeat, from rapid to wild. The change in her body as she stiffened beneath him, cried out against his shoulder, and clung for life as another orgasm ripped through her.

He tried his damnedest to hold on, to hold out, but her release triggered his own. Immeasurable pleasure ripped through him like a wild, sucking riptide as he plunged one last time, and followed her over the edge into oblivion.

Val lay with her eyes closed, vaguely thinking that she should get up. But her bones had turned to liquid. Her blood had thickened like pudding. And the man who had made her feel like a nymphomaniac had a muscled thigh draped over her hips and a warm hand lazily caressing her left breast.

Wow.

Multiple orgasms.

She turned her head and found him watching her.

He smiled tentatively. "Wow," he said, echoing her thoughts.

"Yeah," she agreed and, suddenly feeling a little uneasy, she looked away.

"Several years ago, President Billings made a surprise visit to my base," Luke said softly. "He pinned a silver star on my uniform for an op I'd been a part of in Iraq."

Compelled not only by the tone of his voice, but by his words, she turned her head and looked at him.

"Not too long ago," he went on as he propped himself up on an elbow and smiled into her eyes, "the chief of a remote tribe in the Amazon offered his daughter and a goat in appreciation for helping rid the region of renegade warlords who had been on a raping and killing rampage."

Where was he going with this?

"On my tenth birthday, my dad handed over the reins to a sweet little buckskin mare that I'd been pining over for an entire year."

She gave him a quizzical smile. "And you're telling me this because?"

His warm hand slid to her waist and caressed her. "Because until a few minutes ago, those were the three most stellar moments in my life."

Tears stung her eyes at the sweetness of his words, at the sincerity in his eyes.

He laced his fingers with hers, then he kissed her with a tenderness that touched her far deeper than it should have.

And suddenly she was afraid. More afraid than when the train had been attacked. More frightened than when she'd faced the gunmen from the depths of that dark, damp hidey-hole.

She was terrified of the melting warmth spreading through her chest and the ache in her heart that could only mean one thing: She was falling for this man.

Oh, no. This could *not* happen. She would not open herself to that kind of torment again.

Not even with Luke. Heroic, gentle, sexy, phenomenal Luke.

She quickly blinked back the tears and pasted on a bright smile. Then she set about putting things back in perspective and driving home that what was happening between them was just sex. Just a good time. Nothing more.

"So, you're comparing me to a presidential commendation and a horse—is that what you're saying?"

"And a goat. Don't forget the goat."

"High praise, indeed." She rolled away from him and sat up on the edge of the bed.

She had to get some distance from those eyes. Those all-American-boy eyes and that red, white, and blue heart and those twin dimples that just melted her.

"You're not so bad yourself," she said, determined to sound casual.

When he remained silent, she looked back at him over her shoulder. She expected a flirty smile, but he was watching her with a measured look.

"You okay, Angelface?"

No, she was not okay. She was in danger of being devastated by feelings she couldn't handle, didn't want, and by the veiled hurt in his eyes. She had to put the skids on this before it went any further.

"Actually, I'm not. I'm a little annoyed with myself. What kind of woman lets a man get away with calling her Angelface?"

He laughed and, looking relieved, tugged her onto her back again. "But I'm not just any man, now, am I?"

No, she conceded as he rolled her beneath him, caught her breast in his mouth and, *oh, my God . . .* liquid heat shot from her nipple to her core, and just that fast she was aching for him again. Throbbing for him . . . wet for him as he quickly rolled on another condom, thrust inside her, and took them on another journey to the land that level heads forgot.

14

His mind was officially blown.

Luke's chest was still heaving, his body sated and depleted, his muscles in a state of outrageously blissful atrophy.

He was either the luckiest sonofabitch on earth . . . or the dumbest. Most likely, both.

He glanced toward the closed bathroom door, then back toward the ceiling. Val had been in there for a good fifteen minutes. Didn't take a molecular physicist to figure out that there was a lot of post-heat-of-the-moment regret going on behind that door.

His cheeks puffed out on a thoughtful breath as guilt undercut the memory of just how much heat they'd generated in this bed. *Well, hell. Name me one heterosexual male*, he argued in his own defense, *who could have walked away from "Do things to me."*

Reed, Lang, Jones, Mendoza, Black, and Savage, his BOI teammates.

Okay. That was six men. But they were all married to hot, amazing women who outclassed those lucky SOBs ten ways from Sunday, so they didn't count. So that left: no man. No man in his right mind, at any rate.

Still, he could lie here and attempt to justify his weakness until he got the picture of Valentina naked and orgasmic out of his head—or until a cow really did jump over the moon—but it wasn't going to change a thing.

They'd had sex. Mind-blowing, earth-moving, soul-shattering sex, and he was never going to be the same again.

Like he was never going to be the same since he'd been shot in San Salvador.

Fuck. Why the hell was he going there now?

He ran his fingertips absently over his scar. Felt a latent spark of sexual heat sluice through him as he pictured Val's mouth touching that angry skin. Laving, loving, expressing concern in a way no words ever could.

Look . . . if this is about the scar . . .

She'd insisted it wasn't, but on some level it was. She knew it and so did he.

When the bathroom door finally opened and she stepped out wrapped tightly in a towel, and her gaze lasered in on that eight-inch stretch of flesh before shifting to his face, it pretty much cinched it.

He was eventually going to have to tell her the details. He'd seen that same look in other women's eyes when their heads got messed up by his "warrior scars" and they got to thinking they might be falling in love with him.

He had to make sure she understood that a woman like her didn't ever want to attach herself to a man like him. A man who was no longer certain if he had what it took to walk into the next fire, no questions asked, and lay it all on the line for God, country, and the men by his side.

Case in point, he should be focusing on the bad guys and getting her out of here, not trying to figure out a way to wangle a little more sheet time and still make sure she knew better than to hitch her wagon to his fizzling star.

"Come 'ere," he said, patting the mattress.

"I'm not so sure that's a good idea."

"Trust me, this is officially a testosterone-free zone. I'm gonna need at least a couple of hours to replenish the supply. With any luck, we'll be long gone from here by then. Now come over here."

When she hesitated, he grabbed a corner of the sheet and covered his lower body.

She pressed her lips together, wavered another short second, then slowly walked toward the bed.

"Down," he ordered in a no-nonsense tone and lifted an arm in invitation.

Careful to keep her mummy wrap in place, she eased down on a hip, then fell the rest of the way against him when he tugged her arm and pulled her close.

"Do you manhandle all your women this way?" she groused, but there was a smile in her voice.

"Only the ones who hide in the bathroom and make me feel like the big bad boogeyman."

"You're not the boogeyman," she said, finally relaxing a little and nestling her cheek against his chest. "And I wasn't hiding."

"No?" he challenged.

Silence.

"Just so you know . . . there aren't any women. Or even another woman. Hasn't been for a while," he confessed quietly.

She stiffened and he sensed she was about ready to bolt again.

Jesus, they were a pair. Both of them ready to run if they thought the other one might start thinking the wrong thing and get too attached and yet both of them wobbling on the brink of . . . what?

On a weary breath, he said, "Just chill, okay? I'm not professing love everlasting and I know you aren't, either. I just wanted you to know that I don't do the revolving bed thing, okay?"

"Okay," she said after a long moment. "And thanks for that."

"You're welcome."

He didn't know if that little exchange had accomplished a damn thing . . . didn't even know what he'd been trying to accomplish.

Honesty, he supposed. She'd been honest with him, so he wanted her to know that he wasn't a player, either.

To what end, Colter? The devil was back on his shoulder.

Because I care about her, he admitted to both the devil and himself.

She was vulnerable yet strong, resilient in the face

of danger. She was so much more than an image on a billboard.

He admired her. He liked her. But he wasn't a forever kind of man. Not that one fine roll in the sack conjured notions of forever. Or of making promises. Or of wondering if there was any way in hell they might be able to make things work.

Christ, he felt like a pocketful of change banging around in a washing machine. Completely scattered, in over his head, and somewhere he totally did not need to be.

Disgusted, he glanced at the wall clock. Another twenty minutes before he could go out and make contact with Nate again.

Now what, hotshot? The devil asked lasciviously.

He didn't have any answer to that question. Just like he didn't have an answer when she softly whispered, "How do you see this ending?"

Oh, Christ. How the hell did he answer that? The same way he always answered that kind of question when a woman asked.

You don't want to be saddled with the likes of me, darlin'. I'm not the marrying kind.

"Do you think they're looking for me even now?"

It took a couple of clicks of his brain synapses to realize the ending she was asking about had to do with bad guys, not emotional entanglements.

"Um . . . yeah," he said, not knowing if he was relieved or disappointed. Since relief was what he *should* be feeling, he went with it.

"Like I said, whoever is behind this went to a lot of trouble to hunt you down. They'll keep hunting."

She lifted a hand, exasperated. "It still makes no sense to me."

It was past time that he played devil's advocate. "Other than the fact that your ex had to be the stupidest man on the face of the earth to let you go, what can you tell me about what he's into?"

She wedged herself up on an elbow and met his eyes. "Marcus? Why do you insist on asking about Marcus?"

He worked hard at not getting lost in the deep, dark brown of her eyes. "It's pretty common knowledge, Angelface, that in major crimes, it's almost always the husband or the ex who 'done' it."

She shook her head vehemently. "Marcus is not behind this. He's a U.S. senator, for God's sake."

He grunted. "Right. And we all know the words *shyster*, *illegal*, and *unethical* have never been uttered in the same breath with *politician*."

A deeply pained look flashed across her face before she hid it behind a determined frown. "Marcus would never hurt me," she insisted.

He was more than a little peeved that she was so quick to defend him. "Like the divorce didn't hurt you?"

She looked away.

"The bastard cheated on you, didn't he?" The tabloids had hinted as much.

"That's none of your business."

Yeah, the stupid fuck had cheated on her, all right.

"He's the reason you're down here," he concluded.

"You're hiding out from the fallout, from the tabloids . . . from the embarrassment."

"I don't want to talk about Marcus, okay?"

No, he didn't suppose she did. "I'm sorry if I was out of line."

He drew her into his arms and surprisingly, she didn't resist. She snuggled against him, draping her arm over his waist when he hooked a leg over her hips.

So he kissed her. Nothing sexual. Just kissed her because she looked like she needed to be kissed. And yeah, because he needed it, too.

A few moments passed before her hand slid to his hip, then ever so slowly, her fingers worried their way along the length of his scar. "Were you protecting someone when you got this?"

He had known she would come back to this.

"San Salvador," he said. "Last year about this time. And yes, I was working protection detail."

"For a woman?"

"Yeah. I was protecting a woman. A friend."

He replayed that night in short frames that clicked through his mind's eye like gunshots.

His handgun in pieces on Sophie Baylor's coffee table.

The scent of the gun oil he'd been using to clean it.

The pop pop pop of AK-47s as Vincente Bonilla's Mara Salvatrucha hit squad sprayed the glass patio doors with round after lethal round.

Grabbing his own rifle.

Shoving Sophie ahead of him behind the cover of the kitchen counter.

The sickening realization that he'd been hit.

The blood oozing out of him in a sticky, hot pool.

The darkness that overtook him like black death.

"And is she . . . did she survive?"

Her soft voice snapped him back. "Yeah." He shook his head to clear it. "Yeah, she's fine."

"But you almost died."

He stared across the room. "As my boss always says, I'm too ornery to die."

At what point is enough, enough?

Christ. Join the party, Mom. He already had so many frickin' voices in his head, he was starting to think he was schizophrenic.

"But you almost died," she repeated, pain in her eyes.

He swallowed. "Yeah."

A part of him had died that day. The part that allowed him to walk tall and know without a doubt that he was the same man he'd been before that AK-47 had ripped his guts apart.

He didn't want to think about it anymore, and he sure as hell didn't want to talk about it.

"You get a little rest, okay?" He sat up abruptly, then reached down and grabbed his pants off the floor. "It's about time I made contact with my boss."

He stood, pulling up his pants and zipping in one move.

"Don't open the door to anyone but me," he added, tugging a shirt over his head, then digging into his pack for dry socks.

He sank down on the sofa and tugged them on, then

shoved his feet into his boots. "I'll be back in less than thirty and we'll have a plan of action."

"I'm glad you didn't."

She had rolled to her side, facing him. One hand held the towel together, the other fussed absently with the bedding.

He rose slowly. He should walk to the door. Should not look at that white towel against white sheets, at those long cover-girl legs and that mouth.

"I'm very glad you didn't die," she said, her eyes brimming with emotion.

And he lost yet another battle.

He took one step toward her, then another, feeling an unfamiliar warmth spread through his chest.

Jesus, why did she have to look at him like that? Like it scared her to think about how badly he'd been injured. About how he could have died. About how much she was going to miss him when he was gone.

Well, hell. He wasn't gone yet. To make certain she understood that, he strode straight to the bed, leaned down, cupped her nape in his palm, and pulled her up to him. Then he kissed her like tomorrow might not come and he wanted to experience every nuance, every sigh, every sweet wanton response from the mouth that he wasn't sure he could ever get enough of.

When he finally broke the kiss, her hands were clutching his thigh, and the towel had come undone. The sight of her bare breasts almost brought him to his knees. Her fractured breath and swollen lips damn near had him crawling back in that bed.

"I've got to go," he said hoarsely and, with more will-power than he'd thought he was capable of, he backed away.

His hands were shaking when he dug back in his pack for a black baseball cap and a pair of shades. Without turning around he walked straight to the door, opened it, and closed it hard behind him.

And stood there in the empty hall. Hand still on the knob, he pressed his forehead against the wood. Drew a bracing breath. "Throw the dead bolt this time," he said through the closed door.

A few moments later, he heard the bolt rattle. Several moments after that, he finally mustered the will to move.

He settled the cap backward on his head and shoved on the glasses. Once he was in the lobby, he snagged a couple of city maps out of the rack by the door and, playing the part of a tourist, hightailed it out of the hotel. Away from a woman who could scramble his brain like a short-order cook scrambled eggs.

He was so fucked.

15

Val was fully dressed and as tense as kite string when Luke rapped on the hotel room door almost an hour later.

A very long hour later.

She'd had too much time to think, too much time to panic, too much time to sit there and do nothing.

So she'd done something he wasn't going to like. Something she'd had to do, just like she had to believe it was right.

She walked to the door, unlocked the dead bolt, and let him in.

"Sorry it took me so long." He breezed inside and locked the door behind him. "Had a little trouble making the connection."

"It's okay." She walked back to the small studio sofa and sat down before her knees folded. Second thoughts fruitlessly battled with self-preservation instincts. What was done was done; she had to trust that she'd made the right decision.

Oblivious to her tension, Luke sat beside her,

grabbed a banana off the table, and started to peel it.

"Nate's arranged for a cargo plane to pick us up. Our ride's flying in from Buenos Aires at 1500 hours—about three hours from now. It'll take a couple of hours to off-load their cargo and take on more, and by the time they're done we'll already be on board, stowed away in a shipping container, no one the wiser that we were ever here. We'll be in Buenos Aires by nightfall."

She swallowed hard. "I'm not going with you."

The banana froze halfway to his mouth. Then he looked at her like he hadn't heard her correctly.

She looked down at her hands. "I . . . I can't keep relying on you to take care of me. So I called Marcus and made arrangements to get out of here."

Silence filled the hotel room like a heavy fog. She could feel his gaze boring into the side of her face.

"You did *what?*"

She licked dry lips and forced herself to look at him. His face was hard as stone. "I called Marcus to—"

"I heard you." He glared at her. "I just can't frickin' believe it. You called *Marcus*, your asshole ex?"

"He's got business connections in Lima," she continued, forcing herself to regroup. "A friend with a corporate jet. It should be in the air by now."

A look of utter incredulity darkened his face. "To come here?"

She nodded. "To take me back to the States. They've arranged temporary ID with the U.S. embassy to get me out of the country and through immigration."

For a long moment he just stared at her. Then he

started to say something but stopped himself, stood abruptly, and jammed his fists on his hips.

Luke would never be able to understand the bond she and Marcus had so Val didn't try to explain. Yes, Marcus had betrayed her. Yes, he had almost destroyed her. But the divorce had nearly destroyed him, too. She had no doubt that he still loved her and would do anything for her. Anything but be faithful.

"Jesus," Luke finally said. "I can't believe this. I can't believe you'd trust that bastard over—" He whirled back around to glare at her. "Wait. You left the room? You left the room to call him?"

"I was careful," she said defensively.

He gave a disgusted snarl. "Define *careful*."

She refused to let his anger sway her. "I was just careful, that's all. No one saw me."

"And you used a phone where?"

"I convinced the manager to let me use the office phone. And I apologize, but I . . . I went into your backpack. I needed money for the call and I knew you had some cash."

He dragged a hand roughly though his hair. "Do you not *get* it? Do you not get that you're ass-deep in trouble? Jesus, Val. I can't believe you called him."

Defense turned to anger in a heartbeat. "Okay, look. I don't need your recriminations or your opinions of my intelligence. And I don't need you directing my every move. Yes, I know I'm in trouble. But I'm a big girl. I can make my own decisions. And I can manage just fine on my own."

"Right. Like you would have managed on your own on that train."

She got that he was angry. She also got that he was a little hurt. So she reined in her own temper. "I didn't say that I don't owe you. You saved my life—more than once. I won't forget that. I won't forget . . . anything . . . about what's happened since I met you."

His eyes burned into hers and she knew exactly what he was thinking. But she couldn't let the intimacy of their lovemaking keep her from taking back control of her life.

"But I can take it from here, okay?" she added, beseeching him to understand.

She *needed* to take it from here. Luke had managed to both build and shred her hard-earned self-confidence. He made her feel things she wasn't ready to feel. Made her want things she wasn't capable of having. At least not yet. Maybe not ever.

Making that phone call to Marcus had been one of the hardest things she'd ever done, but staying with Luke would be harder. She was already too attracted to him. He had a way of making her feel like there was a whole lot more than sex going on in that bed.

This trip to Peru had been all about finding herself again, about becoming whole. She was on her way, but her attraction to Luke Colter could send her right back into a dependent relationship.

Even now, she wanted to let him take care of her.

Disgusted with herself, she went to the window, and looked blindly out.

"Valentina. Listen to me." He turned her around to face him. His brown eyes were earnest and entreating as they met hers. "It's a mistake to trust *anyone* at this point. No, hear me out," he said when she tried to pull away.

"For the sake of argument, let's factor Chamberlin out of the equation for now. Say he has nothing to do with these bad guys, okay?

"That still doesn't rule out the possibility that whoever is behind this might be using him to get to you. His house or office could be bugged. His phones could be tapped."

She shook her head. "Marcus is a stickler about security. His lines are secure."

"And you know this how?"

"We had just had a state-of-the-art security firm update everything in the D.C. house before the divorce. Marcus is meticulous to the point of paranoid, especially about his phone lines. It goes with the territory, I guess. I wouldn't have made that call if I hadn't known that Marcus's phone line was secure."

He didn't look convinced. "And this business associate in Lima? This is someone you know and trust?"

This time when she pulled away, he let his hands drop. "No, I don't know him. He's Marcus's acquaintance."

Luke's posture was as stiff as a steel post, his muscles rigid.

"Look, Marcus understands the gravity of the situation," she insisted. "I trust him to ensure my safety. I know you can't understand this, but I know I can count on him to take care of getting me home."

"Because he's such a prince of a guy," he said caustically.

She dug for patience. "Because no matter what happened between us, Marcus still cares about me. I lived with that man for almost ten years. I've seen him at his worst. Seen him at his best. I've cried with him over the plight of the Sierra Leone refugees, witnessed his unflagging determination to make our humanitarian aid missions happen. He's a good man."

And a troubled man, she thought sadly. Luke thought he'd guessed the truth about Marcus's betrayal, but he didn't know the half of it.

She could still see the anguish on Marcus's face the night she'd confronted him. And as painful as it had been for her, she knew that Marcus had been suffering, too. Was still suffering. Which was why she knew that Marcus would do anything to help her.

"You didn't have to call him," Luke said quietly. "You knew I was all over this."

The frustration in his voice broke her heart. "I know. But I've imposed on you enough."

He pushed out another sound of disgust and glanced pointedly toward the bed. "Interesting choice of words."

"You know what I mean. Don't twist what happened between us in this room into something ugly, because it wasn't. It was . . . amazing and beautiful and—"

His jaw hardened. "A mistake? Is that what you were going to say?"

"No, I wasn't."

He looked at her sideways, clearly not believing her. She averted her gaze and, because she owed him the truth, finally admitted, "Maybe."

"So that's what this is really about? You feel you have to run from what we did? From me? Get that idea out of your head right now. No ties, okay? No strings. No regrets."

If she stayed with him much longer, she was afraid that strings were exactly what she was going to want. "I know, and thank you for that. But it doesn't change things. I need to do this on my own. My own way. Please respect my decision."

He was quiet for a very long time. "You're making a mistake."

"Could be," she conceded, "but it's my mistake to make. And you have a life to get back to. We both do."

He glared at the floor, clearly still trying to figure out a way to change her mind.

"Luke," she said softly and touched his arm. "We both know this is for the best."

When he looked up there was pain in his eyes, and reluctant acceptance. "Doesn't mean I'm not concerned about what happens next with you."

"I know."

"These guys aren't going to stop, Val. You need protection until—"

"I'll get it. Marcus is already assembling a security team. They'll be on the ground waiting for me in L.A. when I arrive. I can pay for the best."

"You might be paying for the best, but you won't be getting it."

No, the best was right here in this room with her. "I'll be okay," she assured him.

He finally shrugged in defeat. "Okay. We do it your way. But until I'm satisfied that your Lima connection isn't bogus, and you're on board that jet with the door sealed tight, you're stuck with me. No discussion."

"Appreciate it." She smiled tightly.

He didn't smile at all.

Low-hanging clouds shrouded the mountain peaks forming a semi-circle beyond the concrete tarmac of the Alejandro Velasco Astete International Airport in the center of the city.

The trip from the hotel to the airport had been both infinitely long and achingly short. Other than lecturing Val on the need to stay close and not draw attention until he had her tucked away on the charter jet, Luke had pretty much kept his thoughts to himself.

There was a lot he'd wanted to say, but he saved his breath. She was determined. She was leaving under her own steam. End of story.

A fist tightened in his gut.

As they finally pulled up in front of the terminal, he told himself that leaving her wasn't what was getting to him the most. It was the idea that she trusted Chamberlin that stuck in his craw. He'd known it would end between them. Hell, it never should have begun. He'd had a better chance of winning a lottery than of ending up in Valentina's bed.

They never should have crossed paths in the first place. And yet, they had. And his world was still rockin' in the wake of the experience.

And yeah, he knew that she was right. Splitting up now was for the best. He'd gotten in a little too deep with her, a little too fast. Better that they went their separate ways now. But Chamberlin? *Fuck*.

"Stay put," he told her, got out of the taxi, and with the din of jet engines whining in the background, reconned the area with a long, searching look.

Luke had flown in and out of Cuzco often, so he knew the airport's layout fairly well. He'd had the driver pull up at the far end of the commercial flight terminal where there was a small hangar for the private charters. Past the charter terminal was an area designated for cargo, where he'd catch his own ride a little later.

While he didn't see anything or anyone out of place, he wasn't going to take any chances. Before they'd left, he'd made a few more purchases. Now they were both wearing bright new striped ponchos, dark glasses, and baseball caps—just a couple of tourists headed back to the States, loaded down with bags filled with the local goods they'd bought from street vendors.

Only their bags weren't stuffed with cheap souvenirs. His backpack was concealed in one. Hotel towels filled the other, just to make it look good. And his red, purple, and blue poncho nicely hid the Glock, tucked within easy reach at the small of his back.

The Glock. Yeah. Now things got dicey. While there was a good chance he could make it inside the terminal without anyone detecting the weapon, he'd never make it past boarding security. So since there was no way in hell he was going to let Valentina board any aircraft without inspecting it first, he had to ditch the handgun now.

"Let's get inside," he said, opening the cab's rear passenger door. "The sooner I get you out of the open, the better I'm going to like it."

He took her hand and helped her out, then, as part of their cover and to protect her, tucked her under his shoulder like he had every right. To the casual observer, he was a husband, a lover, a friend with benefits—whatever. But anyone wanting to take a shot had to get past him to get to her.

The scent of jet fuel and exhaust permeated the thin mountain air as he hustled her across the walkway toward the smaller charter terminal. Once they were within a few yards of the doors, he reluctantly tugged the Glock out of his waistband and, under the cover of his poncho, quickly broke it down into two pieces.

"Good-bye, ol' friend," he muttered as he pitched one piece in a trash can and the other in a recycle bin.

"Let's do this," he said and led her the final twenty yards to the terminal.

Because of the tourism trade, the Cuzco airport was always pretty active. Both commercial and charter flights kept the single runway busy. Because of the wall blocking the view of the taxiway and the apron, unless there was a jumbo jet landing or taking off, there was no way to see what planes were jockeying for runway space until they got inside.

Once inside the terminal, he did another visual recon. The charter waiting area was approximately thirty by twenty feet and swarming with travelers who were spread out in back-to-back rows of vinyl and chrome seats, reading newspapers, listening to their iPods, typing on laptops, or watching movies on portable DVD players.

The lone clerk behind a counter that hid everything but her head spoke into a headset, deeply immersed in conversation and looking harried.

To the left of the long counter and the terminal entry doors was a hallway that led to the restrooms. Across from the restrooms was a small door marked MAINTE-NANCE.

Skirting behind the rows of seats, Luke steered Val to an empty corner of the main waiting room near the hallway, keeping the street side exit door in view. Now that they were inside, the three plateglass windows, roughly eight feet square and stacked side by side, offered a good view of the tarmac and the air traffic. A commercial jet on full thrust lifted off down the runway, the roar from the powerful engines rattling the windows.

Closer by, a small Cessna and a pair of Pipers were parked toward the end of the charter flight apron. An older G-3 Gulfstream rolled slowly toward a small maintenance building, then parked outside its open bay doors.

A sleek new G-550 corporate jet had just touched down, turned off the runway onto the apron and, engines idling, nosed straight toward the marshaller who was directing him closer to the terminal.

"That would be your ride," Luke said after consulting the numbers on the bird's tail and seeing that they corresponded with the numbers Chamberlin had relayed to Val in a message he'd left with the hotel clerk.

Luke had gone ballistic over that. "This is Chamberlin's idea of security?" he'd railed after the clerk had delivered the message to their room. "He broadcasts your flight information to any Tom, Dick, or Jose within earshot?"

"Like he had a choice?" she'd pointed out. "How else was he going to get word to me?"

Luke could have thought of a dozen options, none of which would have opened her up to exposure the way that asshole had. But he'd bitten his tongue, grabbed their things, and hustled her out of that room in thirty seconds flat. He wasn't taking any chances that the goons who were after Val weren't on their way to the hotel at that very second. He was no one's sitting duck and he wasn't about to let her be one, either.

During the hour-and-a-half wait for the jet's arrival, they'd ridden in no fewer than five taxis, changing cabs every fifteen minutes in different parts of the city until it was time to show up at the airport.

And he'd just run out of time.

"Well," he heard Val say, "I guess this is good-bye."

16

Luke's heart did a little stutter. Yeah. This was good-bye.

It didn't look like there was anything he could do to stop that from happening, but he would make it damn memorable.

He turned to face her, his back to the terminal, and crowded her into the corner. Even with her hair tucked up under the ball cap, her eyes covered by shades, and smelling like wet wool from her poncho, she looked gorgeous and vulnerable and determined and—aw hell, a little like she might just cry.

Swamped with feelings of tenderness and regret, he touched a finger to her jaw. "So you know . . . I wouldn't have changed one thing about the past twenty-four hours, Angelface. Well," he amended with a grin, "maybe the part about getting shot at on the train. And maybe I'd have picked a different mule. And, come to think of it, I could have done without that damn potato."

Okay. She was smiling now, Just like he wanted. Because if she started crying, he just might do a little blubbering, too.

Jesus, this woman messed with his head.

"Thank you, Luke. Thank you—"

He pressed an index finger to her lips, gently cutting her off. "No," he said, lowering his mouth to hers. "Thank you."

And then he tugged off her shades, looked her deep in the eyes, and kissed her.

How could he not? How could he look into those liquid brown eyes and that valiant little smile and not kiss her one more time? How could he pretend that letting her go was easy, even though he didn't have a clue why it was suddenly so frickin' hard?

He wasn't a romantic. Had never thought of himself as sentimental. But he wanted this one last kiss. One last taste. One last feel of her melting against his lips and telling him without words that she was going to miss the hell out of him, like he was going to miss the hell out of her.

When he finally broke away, her eyes were closed; her fingers were clutched tightly around his biceps.

"Well," he said, his voice hoarse and grainy, "we'll always have Peru."

That actually made her laugh. "Yes," she agreed and, looping her arms around his neck, hugged him hard. "We'll always have Peru."

He held her close for a moment, closed his eyes, and absorbed every feminine inch of her pressed against him . . . and fought a damn-near-overwhelming gut feeling that letting her go was the absolute wrong thing to do.

But she was right, he thought grimly. It was what they both needed.

He reached behind his neck, disengaged her hands, and brought them to his lips. "Don't take any raw potatoes, okay?"

Her smile was a little wobbly this time. "Count on it."

He squeezed her hands one final time, then set her shades back on her nose. "You stay put a sec. The pilot should come into the terminal soon. As soon as I have a little chat with him and I'm sure he's on the up-and-up, I'll walk you onto that plane. But until I'm satisfied that you're in good hands, you're still on my watch."

Luke made another visual sweep of the terminal as he waited for the G-550's hatch to open and the pilot to check in.

The waiting area was still packed with weary travelers. Some were trying to catch a nap, some were reading, some were staring blankly into space; others muddled through the security line. All were tired of waiting for their charter flights and beyond ready to head home. As far as he could tell, there wasn't a ringer in the bunch. No jackets that appeared to be hiding weapons, no sharp-eyed observers, no mercs on a mission to snatch his girl.

His girl?

Strike that. They'd already established that she was not his girl and there were a hundred stellar reasons why, starting with his profession not being conducive to long-term relationships, and ending with the shitload of baggage she was carrying from her divorce.

She was still his charge, though, until she was safely on board that G-550.

The itch suddenly stood the hair on the back of his neck on end, and Rule Number One kicked in with a vengeance.

Instantly on edge, he made another visual sweep of the crowd. Nothing. But then the air pressure in the building changed infinitesimally. The street door opened, admitting traffic noise, jet fumes, and two men whose look and bearing intensified the itch to a scalding burn.

Even if their lack of luggage hadn't tipped him off, one glance told Luke they weren't your typical travelers. The first man was big—around six foot two and a solid two-fifty. He was Caucasian, wore his dark hair in a close buzz cut, and, judging from the width of his shoulders, pumped a lot of iron. The other man was Asian and on the short side, but built like a brick shit house. Both wore scowls, badass attitudes, and oversized black dress suits. They made him think of Belushi and Aykroyd's version of the Blues Brothers, Jake and Elwood, only on steroids.

Enforcers, no doubt about it. And clearly professionals, with their military-sharp bearing, their clear tactical awareness of their surroundings, and their laser-eyed gazes that swept the terminal like radar.

Oh, yeah. They were looking for someone. They were looking for Valentina.

Christ. Who the hell did they work for? More than ever, Luke was convinced that whoever it was had to be a big, big player with a big, big purse and a far-reaching web.

Why the *fuck* was he after Val? It *had* to have some-thing to do with Chamberlin, whether she wanted to believe it or not, because the only way these creeps could have gotten a bead on their location this fast was if someone gave it to them. And the only *someone* who knew she was going to be at this airport at this exact time was her ex.

He'd worry about that later. Right now, he had to get her out of here before they spotted her. The question was, where? A sixth sense warned him that hustling her to the plane might not be the wisest move.

He took a slow step backward so he wouldn't draw their attention and, using a cement support post for impromptu concealment, watched them. They imme-diately positioned themselves just inside the door, flank-ing it on either side, blocking any escape route. Hands clasped in front of them, they stood with their shoul-ders square in those oversized jackets, making it clear to Luke that they were concealing shoulder holsters.

Oh, yeah. Definitely up to no good. And apparently they didn't give two figs about airport security seizing their guns. No one was taking their hardware.

When the big guy, Elwood, flipped open a phone and punched in a number, Luke got a sinking feeling that these weren't the only two snakes to fall out of the tree today.

He whipped his head toward the large windows and saw the hatch of the G-550 open. As the pilot appeared on the top of the airstairs, he reached into his pocket to answer a call.

Snake in the grass number three, Luke surmised as the pilot looked toward the terminal, nodded, and pocketed his phone. A quick glance back at Elwood, who also hung up, confirmed they'd been talking to each other.

Fuck and fuck again.

"We've got trouble." He latched on to Valentina's arm. "I'll explain later but for now, grab your bags and walk with me. Move slow. Last thing we want to do is draw attention."

Her shoulders went stiff with panic but like a good soldier, she did as she was told. Positioning his body between her and the thugs at the terminal door, Luke walked her casually toward the hallway as if they were heading for the restrooms.

He tried the door on the maintenance closet and wasn't surprised to find it locked.

"Showtime," he whispered and backed her up against the door, pinning her there with his body. He lowered his mouth to hers. "Work with me," he whispered as he dug into his pocket for his Leatherman, then wrapped his arms around her and reached for the lock on the door.

She looped her arms around his neck and played the part as he unfolded his pick tool. Anyone looking their way would just see a pair of lovers sharing a parting kiss.

"Got it," he said after a few moments of finessing the lock. "Any eyes on us?"

He gave her a moment to scan the hallway over his shoulder. "No."

Without a second of hesitation, he opened the door, shoved her backward inside, and followed, shutting it quickly behind them.

The small closet was as dark as a cave. He groped around for a light switch and when he didn't find one, reached above him and caught a dangling string. When he gave it a tug, light from a dim bulb flooded the closet.

Valentina whipped off her sunglasses, her eyes huge and round. "What is it? What's happening?"

"Company—and not the kind you want to invite for dinner."

He glanced around the five-by-six-foot closet. A metal shelving unit screwed to the wall held an assortment of hand tools, cleaning supplies, cloths, and a couple rolls of tape—one electrical and one silver duct tape. Several brooms and mops were propped in the corner. A half-dozen hooks held industrial blue coveralls.

"Two men by the door. Both carrying. Searching the terminal for you. One talking to the pilot just as he was stepping out of the plane."

Her face paled. "Oh, God. How—"

He cut her a sharp look. "Jesus, Val. How do you think?"

She slowly shook her head, her face pale. "Marcus wouldn't have done this."

There was more plea than conviction in her statement this time. He would have hurt for her and the disillusion that clouded her eyes if he wasn't so pissed.

"Well, he looks like a pretty solid bet in my book."

She closed her eyes and he could see she was fighting tears. "I never should have made that call. I never should have doubted you, because you haven't let me down yet."

He let out a deep breath. "It's okay. But we're not out of this closet yet."

"What are we going to do?" she asked, as he shrugged out of his backpack and dropped it on the floor.

"*You're* going to stay put. Right here. I'm going to go run a little interference. Keep the door locked. Don't open it unless you hear three sharp raps. Got it?"

She nodded. "Please be careful."

"Careful's my middle name," he assured her and let himself back into the hall.

Luke resettled his baseball cap, shoved his hands in his pockets, and shuffled into the main terminal. Invisibility was his goal, and acting the part of a weary traveler among a group of weary travelers kept him from standing out in a crowd.

The one he'd dubbed "Jake" still held his position by the door. The pilot now waited on the tarmac at the bottom of the airstairs. The taller guy walked methodically through the terminal, clearly searching for Valentina.

Visibly stifling a yawn, Luke rolled his shoulders as though he'd been waiting forever and worked his way around the periphery of the large open area, waiting for the right distance spread before making his move on Jake. When "Elwood" reached the far side of the terminal, Luke ambled over to his partner.

"Your flight late, too?"

As he'd expected, Jake ignored him.

Oblivious to the cold shoulder, Luke kept on talking. "So . . . where you headed?"

"None of your fucking business," Jake muttered.

Luke made a show of looking affronted. "No need to get pissy. Just wanted to pass some time," he went on, just an affable guy too dumb to zip his lip. "I'll just mind my own business and wait for that hot babe to come back."

As he'd planned, the "hot babe" comment perked up the bad boy's ears. "What hot babe?"

Luke sucked in his breath through his teeth, making a scorching sound. "She was sexy as hell, man. Swear to God . . . she looked like that big-time model. Valentina?" He grinned and settled in for a little man-to-man talk. "Long, black hair. Big, gorgeous tits. Man, I'd like to nail some of that, know what I mean?"

Jake was totally on board now. Luke could see in his eyes that he knew he'd hit the jackpot.

"Where'd you see her?"

Luke's grin widened. "I think maybe there's a special waiting area or something for people like her. You know, they don't want to mingle with the riffraff. It's down this hallway. I'll show you where I saw her last."

Without waiting for Jake to order him to stay put or signal Elwood, Luke set out for the hall.

"In there, man," he said with a nod when they reached the maintenance closet.

"It's a fucking closet."

Luke waggled his brows. "Is it? Or is that what they want us to think?"

The seed was planted . . . and it was too much for Jake to resist. He shoved Luke out of the way and gripped the door knob.

In one lightning move, Luke cinched an arm around Jake's neck, applied pressure to his throat, and cut off the blood flow.

The sleeper hold put Jake out in seconds. His body slumped heavily against Luke. He rapped the door three times, then shoved it open, hauled Jake inside, and kicked the door shut behind them.

"Hand me that roll of duct tape." He eased the unconscious man to the floor.

Valentina looked horrified. "Is he dead?"

"Just asleep, if I did it right."

"Did what?"

"Vulcan death grip," he said, taking the tape from her. "My version, anyway."

He did a quick body search and came up with a beauty of a SIG—oh, happy day—and a state-of-the-art sound suppressor, along with an extra ammo clip.

"The bastard's loaded for bear." He handed Valentina all three pieces, then bound Jake's hands together in front of him. After he'd wrapped the tape around his upper body, pinning his arms to his sides, then down around his knees and ankles, was he satisfied he could leave Val alone with him.

"If he so much as moves an eyelid, nail him with this." He pulled a hammer off a shelf and handed it to her.

Then he snagged a pair of workman's coveralls from

a hanger and shrugged into them. They were a little tight across the shoulders and a couple of inches too short, but this wasn't a fashion show. "I'll be right back."

"Wait!" Her hand on his arm stopped him. "Where are you going?"

"To find his friend. We need four for a game of poker," he said with a quick grin.

Dropping the SIG in the roomy front pocket of the coveralls, he grabbed a mop and breezed back out of the closet.

17

Like shooting carp in a barrel, Luke thought as he walked up behind Elwood. Using Elwood's own jacket to conceal the handgun, Luke let him know the SIG was pointed dead center at his spine and ushered him, without protest, to the closet to join his friend.

"All right, then, boys," Luke said amiably when he'd relieved Elwood of a sweet silver Beretta and trussed him up as tight as his buddy, who was now awake and glaring between Luke and Valentina, "first things first. You need to know that I hate tight spaces and it's damned tight in here. Makes my trigger finger all itchy.

"Hers, too," he added with a notch of his chin toward Valentina who, God love her, aimed the Beretta directly at Elwood's heart in a steady, two-handed grip. "So the sooner we can get out of here, the easier it's going to be on all of us, understood?"

Luke very deliberately held the SIG in front of him and with the precision of a man who clearly knew what he was doing, fixed the sound suppressor to the tip of the barrel.

"Nice toy," he said, then turned the gun on Jake.

He was rewarded with a nice little sheen of perspiration on both men's foreheads.

That's right. Sweat, you slimy bastards. You're swimming in a river of shit and I'm just the man to sink you deeper.

"Now, I'm going to ask a few questions," he continued in his good-ol'-boy, I'm-just-the-friendly-type voice, letting the SIG, now aimed at Jake's kneecap, do the enforcing for him. "Let's start with an easy one. Who are you working for?"

Elwood was the first to respond. "Go fuck yourself."

Luke got right in his face. "Hey, asshole. Didn't the professors at bad-guy school teach you that when the guy with the gun asks the questions, you'd better, by God, answer?"

When both men remained silent, Luke jammed the tip of the suppressor directly against Jake's kneecap. "If you ever want to walk again, tell me something to make me happy. Now, one more time: Who are you working for?"

"We don't know," Jake gritted out between tightly clenched teeth. "We don't know who pays us."

Luke slammed the suppressor hard against Jake's kneecap and clamped a hand over his mouth when he howled in pain.

"We don't fucking know!" Elwood insisted when Valentina redirected her aim to his family jewels. "We get a phone call, we're told what to do. Money's wired into a special account—half up front, half when the job's done."

Luke considered him through narrowed eyes. "And what's the extent of this job?"

"Get the woman," Jake supplied, cutting his gaze toward Valentina and having the brains to look guilty.

"And take her where?"

"Just get her on the plane," Elwood said. "After that, we don't know and don't care where she ends up."

Luke had interrogated his share of lug-nuts over the years, and he'd gotten a feel for when they were lying or telling the truth. Unfortunately, he was pretty certain these guys weren't lying. Just like he figured they were merely hired help, not upper echelon. Their allegiance was to a paycheck, not a cause. And without their guns, even that impetus was losing power.

"Tell me about the pilot," Luke demanded, not letting up on the pressure, even though he figured he knew what the answer would be.

Jake shook his head. "Nothing to tell. We were told there'd be a plane. Given a radio frequency to communicate on."

Luke glared between them. There had to be more. Something he could use to reach the mastermind. "Seems to me that once you hand over the girl, you hand over your insurance that you did your job. How do you prove to the top dog that he owes you money?"

Jake looked at Elwood, gave him a nod.

"Snap a photo with our phone," Elwood said.

Luke nodded. "And then you upload the photo and e-mail it to an IP address even NSA can't track down."

Jake and Elwood exchanged another look that told

Luke he'd nailed it. Whoever was pulling the strings had a complex network in place to guarantee anonymity.

"Give me the e-mail address."

"For all the good it'll do you. You'll never be able to trace the origin," Elwood said belligerently, then spat out the address.

Betting man that he was, Luke would lay odds that between B.J. and Tink—Rafe and Johnny's women respectively, who were now employed by BOI—they could nail down the location of the IP address no matter how many servers it bounced off before it finally landed at home base.

"And you know nothing about the pilot?" Luke asked again.

Again, Elwood shook his head. "We were just given contact information and told to meet him here to help facilitate delivery of the . . . package," he finished with a sheepish look at Valentina.

Luke would have loved a chance to question the pilot, too, but time was running out. If he had any hope of getting Valentina out of Peru, he needed to get her out of this terminal and onto the cargo plane Nate had arranged to pick them up.

He checked his watch. Jesus. He'd lost track of time. They had less than five minutes to meet up with their ride.

"How will I know who to look for?" he'd asked Nate when he'd talked with him earlier.

"Oh, you'll know," Nate had assured him with a

smile in his voice. "Just don't make him wait or you're toast."

He handed Valentina the SIG and tore a couple of strips off the roll of duct tape. He didn't like leaving loose ends, liked leaving these two knuckle-draggers to rejoin the general populace even less. But he wasn't a cold-blooded killer and Val had handled about as much trauma as she could take.

"Have a nice life, fellas," he said and slapped tape over their mouths. "And by the way, the name is Luke Colter," he added, looking one, then the other, in the eye.

"You remember that: Luke Colter. You remember that I'm the man who let you live today. But remember this, too: If I ever see your ugly faces again, you won't catch me in such a nice mood."

Luke helped Valentina into a smaller pair of blue coveralls, then knelt to roll up the pant legs while she did the sleeves. Then he tugged the string to douse the light and, locking the door behind them, hustled her out of the closet. Pushing a large rolling trash can that held his backpack and the Brothers' guns, they moved through the charter terminal like they didn't have a care in the world.

He chanced a quick glance toward the G-550. The pilot was waiting on the tarmac at the foot of the airstairs now, an impatient scowl on his face.

"Keep moving," he murmured as they pushed the trash can through the street-side terminal doors. Once they were outside, Luke headed then for the air cargo terminal at a sprint.

"Two minutes," he said as he whipped open the terminal door and, still counting on the janitorial coveralls and the trash can as a diversion, they ducked inside.

The place was another beehive of activity. Outside on the apron, several cargo planes were lined up, and trucks were offloading and reloading the cargo holds.

"Which plane is here for us?" Valentina asked as she bent down to pick up a piece of litter and toss it in the can.

"Wish I knew."

He searched the apron and spotted a couple of older Lear jets, but nothing gave him a clue. A Piper Cheyenne that had seen better days started rolling slowly toward the runway. There was another plane behind it, but he couldn't make it out. Finally, the Piper moved on, revealing a twin-turboprop Beechcraft King Air parked directly behind it. PRIMETIME AIR CARGO was painted across the gleaming white fuselage in glittering red and blue letters.

"Sonofabitch," he muttered around a slow grin.

No sooner had he realized that he'd found their ride than a tall, broad-shouldered man in a silver-gray flight suit came sauntering toward them. He had a diamond stud in his left ear and an unlit cigarette tucked behind the other.

"As I live and breathe." A huge grin split the man's tanned face. "If it's not the one and only Doc Holliday."

"In the flesh, man." Happy as hell to see his old

friend, Luke extended his hand and returned a hearty handshake. "Sonofabitch. Mike Brown." He clapped Brown on the back. "You're a sight for sore eyes, brother. Figured you'd be in prison by now—or dead."

Brown laughed. "Probably should be. Still might end up that way if we don't make tracks. Catchin' up has to wait; Nate'll kill me himself if I don't get your sorry ass and this lovely lady out of here in one piece."

"Valentina, meet Mike 'Primetime' Brown. Best naval aviator to ever fly the unfriendly skies."

"Ma'am," Brown said, his voice dropping to sex-and-seduction mode. "You ready to blow this place, darlin'?"

"Save the sweet talk, Brown," Luke said on a laugh, then grinned at Valentina. "Be warned. The man's got a black belt in womanizing.

"And she's too smart to fall for the crap you dish up," he added, turning back to his friend.

"Pity," Brown said with a wink that had Valentina grinning.

Luke slung an arm over Valentina's shoulders, just because . . . well, just because he could and he wanted Brown to know it.

"You're lucky I don't hold a grudge, Holliday," Brown said amiably as they headed toward the door leading to the tarmac, "or I'd be leaving your sorry ass right here."

"Don't hold it against *me* that *you're* a lousy poker player," Luke reminded him.

"Last time he conned me into sitting down at the table with him," Primetime told Valentina, "he fleeced me for better than three hundred bucks."

"You still harping on that hand? That was ten years ago. And if you could bluff your way out of a paper bag, you might have a chance of hanging on to your money. Speaking of bluffs—you want to tell me how you plan to get us past those security guards?"

Three uniformed men stood between them and the plane, shooting the breeze.

"Security?" Brown's blue eyes twinkled as he whipped out a money clip jammed with large bills. "What security?"

As it turned out, it was more difficult to maneuver the wind currents at eleven thousand feet than it was maneuvering through airport security. Payola spoke louder than security regs this far south of the equator, in Luke's experience. Apparently what was hauled out of the country wasn't nearly as much of an issue as what was hauled in. No one made so much as a peep of protest as Luke and Valentina boarded the plane with Brown.

"The main problems flying into or out of Cuzco are the high altitude and the mountains. Wind coming over the peaks can cause 'mountain waves,' which means heavy-duty turbulence," Brown said as he secured the hatch and headed for the cockpit. "At 10,860 feet it's almost three thousand feet higher than Aspen. But like Aspen, it's at the end of a valley, so you've gotta land in one direction and take off in the other."

"Happy as hell for this little flight briefing, but can we just get out of here?" Luke glanced over his shoulder at Valentina, who was strapping herself into a seat in the cargo bay.

"We're going to have a hefty tailwind for takeoff," Brown went on as he continued his flight check. "Not good. Max tailwind for takeoff on most aircraft is ten knots. We're dealing with a helluva lot more right now. Not to mention that at this altitude, the temperature is very critical. Don't mind telling you, I'd really rather wait until tomorrow morning."

"Not an option," Luke said.

"So Nate said." Grim faced, Brown radioed the tower, asking for clearance for takeoff.

"Thought you gave those things up," Luke said.

Brown reached up and stroked a finger along the cigarette tucked behind his ear. "Did. This one's strictly for emergencies. Never know when an old habit might save your ass."

"And the bling?" Luke asked. Brown was the last man he'd ever figured to wear an earring.

When Brown just grunted, Luke grinned and gave him a little grief. "Well, it looks real pretty."

"Fuck you, Colter. Speaking of pretty, how'd a mud-ugly evolutionary throwback like you score with a woman like her?"

Luke took no offense at the good-natured insults, but what happened between him and Valentina was nobody else's business. "She's a client, smart-ass. Nothing more."

Brown snorted as he flipped switches. "Right. And I'm a virgin. Again."

Luke laughed. "Just do your flyboy thing. Save the wild speculation for the stock market."

"It's your game; we'll play it any way you want to. Better go make sure your *client* is buckled in," he advised after getting the go-ahead for takeoff from the tower. "Then buckle yourself in, too, and hang on for one helluva ride."

18

~~~~~~

Jesus, sweet Jesus, we're going to die!

Val was past caring that she was one note shy of a full-blown hysteria opera.

She'd weathered plenty of bumpy flights and even a life-flashing-before-your-eyes moment when lightning hit her flight over Switzerland a few years ago. But never, as she'd racked up hundreds of thousands of frequent-flyer miles, had she experienced a takeoff like this one.

While the aircraft was clearly loved and well cared for, the Beechcraft hadn't rolled off the assembly line yesterday. The twin-engine turboprop had some years on her. And as the high wind coming over the mountains rattled the plane like ice cubes in a martini shaker, she swore to God she heard rivets pop and seams rip.

The turbulence did its damnedest to throw the small aircraft into the mountains they were attempting to rise above.

The engines whined. The fuselage groaned and creaked. And outside the windows, she was certain she saw the wings flap like a spastic stork as the whipping turbulence conspired with gravity to take them down.

The cargo hold vibrated so hard she had to clench her teeth together to keep them from chipping.

"When will we be out of this turbulence?"

"Soon. Once we get over the mountains," Luke said, looking a little gray as they hit an air pocket and dropped what felt like a mile in a nanosecond.

We're going to die!

"Not today," Luke assured her, and she realize she'd spoken aloud.

She closed her eyes and went to her "happy place," and stayed there long enough that it took several moments to realize the violent shaking had eased into more of a washboard-road sort of ride. And several moments more to realize that Luke was prying her fingers off of his forearm, where she'd locked them like eagle talons.

"Sorry," she said, flexing her fingers to get the circulation back.

"S'okay," he said, gingerly rubbing his arm.

"Really, *really* sorry." God, she was embarrassed.

"And it's really, *really* okay." He shot her a quick grin. "Want to ask Primetime if we can go back and do that again?"

She laughed—he always managed to make her laugh—and checked her watch.

Fourteen hours? Had only fourteen hours passed since this hair-raising thrill ride had begun back on that train? She felt like she'd lived half a lifetime.

She glanced at Luke. What was she going to do about him? And what, she thought, rubbing at a throbbing ache in her temples, could she possibly conclude about Marcus?

Did he have something to do with what was happening to her? Was that how those men had found her?

She refused to believe it. It had to be something else. Maybe whoever was after her had figured out a way to bypass his security, and was monitoring his calls without his knowledge.

Or maybe Luke was right, she thought with a dispirited sigh. Maybe Marcus had betrayed her yet again.

God, she was tired. Tired of running. Tired of being afraid. Tired of trying to figure out whom she could trust.

Luke. She could trust Luke.

When his voice broke the silence with a soft, concerned "You doin' okay, Angelface?" she fought tears.

Nothing in her life was right. Yet this man who had been a stranger only hours ago was the only person in the world she felt she could trust. The one constant she could rely on. Including her own judgment, because she'd bungled things badly when she'd called Marcus.

"I'm fine," she said.

She needed a diversion. "Tell me about our pilot. I gather he's a friend of yours?"

"Yeah, he's a friend," Luke confirmed after giving her a probing look. "Mike was a Navy pilot assigned to Task Force Mercy. Flew us into and out of more scrapes than we should have survived. Best fixed-wing and helo pilot ever attached to our unit. Damn glad to know *that* hasn't changed. I lost track of him a few years ago. Didn't know he'd set up shop down here."

"Why do I get the feeling that 'setting up shop' may mean something different than starting a legitimate business?"

Those twin dimples dented his cheeks. "Let's just say he's one of those guys who always interpreted rules and regulations to mean 'loose guidelines'."

She glanced toward the cockpit door. She'd just bet he did. It hadn't taken more than a glance at the tall, gorgeous pilot for her to recognize a renegade and a rogue. If that flirty white smile weren't enough, his sparkling blue eyes and alpha male swagger cinched it. He was an outlaw, all right. But despite the haranguing he and Luke gave each other, it was also very clear that their relationship was based on both affection and trust.

Cut from the same cloth, those two—though for her money, she'd be more inclined to give Mike "Primetime" Brown a fairly wide berth. The man had *heartbreaker* written all over him.

She glanced sideways at Luke's all-American-hero profile and thought of his Indiana Jones charm, which he managed to pull off even without the fedora that was tucked away in his backpack. Less than an hour ago, her heart had been tied up in a million knots because she'd been certain she'd never see him again. And because she'd known it was for the best that they were parting ways.

It should bother her more that they were still together, but all she felt was a sense of relief. And despite the danger she was in, she just had to look at him to feel her blood heat and her heart rate sprint.

Right, wrong, or somewhere in between, what she felt for him was more than attraction. More than desire. This man continued to drag emotions out of her that scared the hell out of her.

"So, Primetime," she said, determined to distance herself from the emotions clogging her chest. "There's got to be a story behind that nickname."

Luke's smile was filled with nostalgic affection. "The man is a walking chick magnet, as you may have noticed," he added with a grin. "We've always kidded him that he missed his calling. That with a face like that he should be in Hollywood. At the very least, on his own primetime TV show."

"Ah," she said. "Got it. And you're right. He could make some studio a small fortune with his looks."

"He's too much of a high flyer—pardon the pun—to settle for something as predictable as a real job," Luke continued with that same fond smile. "Too much of an adrenaline junkie. I am not surprised that he's down here playing fast and loose with whatever he's playing fast and loose with."

"You don't think his air cargo business is legit?"

Luke scratched his jaw. "What I think is, it's probably best that I don't ask. As long as he gets us to B.A., I don't care what he's into. And I strongly doubt anyone else in this part of the world cares. There are dozens of small, fly-by-night operations—one pilot, one plane—moving around specialty cargo in South America."

"Specialty cargo," she repeated on a yawn. "I guess we definitely fall into that category."

"And you, Angelface, fall into the category of exhausted. I'm going to sit up front for a while and catch up with Brown. Why don't you get a little sleep? You could use it."

She could use a lot of things, she thought as she watched him head for the cockpit. Like that new lease on life she'd come to Peru to find. Like answers to the question of who was after her.

How had she ever had the good fortune to encounter this man at a time when she needed him most, she wondered as she watched Luke drop into the copilot seat.

And how was she ever going to let him walk away when this was over?

If this was ever over . . .

The King Air cruised along at 27,000 feet, eating up the miles between Cuzco and B.A. at round 280 knots. Bleed air from the engine kept the cockpit and cabin at a warm seventy degrees. The interior air pressure was on a par with a commercial jet's, so now that they were clear of the turbulence it promised to be a comfortable, uneventful ride.

Luke checked his watch. According to Brown, B.A. was a five-hour flight. They'd been talking for about an hour, and Luke didn't know a helluva lot more about Brown's post-Navy life than he had when he'd sat down in the copilot seat.

They'd rehashed the good ol' days of Task Force Mercy. Mourned the loss of Bryan Tompkins in an op gone FUBAR in Sierra Leone. They'd touched on Brown's subsequent deployment in the Persian Gulf.

Luke had answered a ton of questions about the old TFM team who now made up Black Ops, Inc. But Brown had managed to dodge Luke's questions about his current life with the skill of a world-class sprinter clearing hurdles.

Okay. The man had secrets. *Don't we all,* Luke thought, catching himself rubbing his side and flashing on the ambush in San Salvador that had almost killed him.

Hell, he'd been on the move for too long now without sleep. And fatigue was the biggest single facilitator of his trips down bad-memory lane.

"And you ended up down here how?" he asked Brown abruptly—both because he wanted to know and to keep himself in the here and now.

Brown worked his jaw and not for the first time, Luke sensed that they had more in common than combat ops.

"Dumb luck," Brown said with a somberness that asked Luke to leave it alone.

Okay. He got it. Respected it. You go through the wars, you got wounds. Physical. Emotional. Whatever. All of his Black Ops team members carried some baggage from their years of covert operations. It went with the territory.

Just like it went with the territory to shake it off and carry on.

He turned his head around and checked on Valentina, relieved to see that she was sound asleep. An uninvited tenderness swamped him as he watched her. Tenderness and an ill-advised sense of possession.

He never should have taken her to bed. Now all he had to do was look at her and his brain scrambled and his heart rate revved and he didn't know what the hell he wanted anymore. Not that it made an ant hill's worth of difference. She knew what she wanted—and that was away from *him*.

"So what's the story with the babe?" Brown's voice broke into his thoughts. "And is she who I think she is? Prince of a guy that you are, you didn't give me a chance to say more than hello."

"Prince of a guy that *you* are," Luke said, eyes front again, "I figured the farther away from you that I keep her, the better. And yes, she's who you think she is. She's also off-limits."

Brown slanted him a knowing smile. "Figured that was the way it was."

Fuck. Was he that transparent?

"Well, you figured wrong," Luke shot back. "She ran into trouble, then she ran into me. I couldn't just leave her on her own, so I'm helping her out of a jam."

"Because she needed you," Brown added, his tone thick with innuendo.

"What she *doesn't* need is a hefty dose of Primetime charm to muddle things even more."

"Just how muddled are things?" Brown said, sobering.

Luke ran through the CliffsNotes version of the

attack on the train, their escape through the mountains to Cuzco, and finally the ambush at the airport.

"Jesus," Brown said. "Something's way off-kilter here."

Luke shifted in his seat. "Tell me about it."

"Got any ideas who's after her?"

"Only one: her ex. Only I can't figure out the motive."

"What's her take on it?"

"Denial with a capital *D*." Luke glanced back at Val again. "Then again, bullets and bad guys aren't part of her everyday routine. As soon as I get her to BOI HQ, where she can take a breath that's not clogged with fear and relax a little, I'm hoping her head will clear and she can give me something to go on.

"I'll tell you one thing," he added, his face grim as he stared into the darkening night, pissed all over again about the terror she'd been through. "When I find the bastard, I'm going to nail his balls to the wall with a railroad spike and a sledgehammer."

19

Val woke to the grinding of the Beechcraft's landing gears. She rubbed the sleep out of her eyes and looked out the window. The glittering lights of Buenos Aires at sunset stretched on for miles as the aircraft smoothly descended toward a ribbon of runway lights.

"Almost home free," Luke said beside her. "This next part's not going to be a picnic for you," he warned her as they touched down.

No, it would not be. The plan involved climbing into a large shipping crate. And total darkness.

"I'll be okay," she said with determination she could do to keep from hyperventilating as the plane rolled to a stop. Luke led her back to the cargo bay, where a refrigerator-sized wooden crate yawned open, waiting for them to step inside.

"Thanks, man." Luke pumped Brown's hand when he came back to join them. "'Til you're better paid, okay?"

"All I want is a rematch. My deck of cards this time."

Luke laughed. "You got it."

"Ma'am." Brown turned to Val with a sympathetic smile that told her Luke had probably filled him in on her situation, including her claustrophobia. "I hope this all works out for you. I hate to rush you, but I need to seal up that crate just in case the nice men from customs decide to come aboard."

She swallowed hard, then turned and faced the music. She felt like she was crawling into a coffin.

"You're doing fine," Luke murmured, lying down beside her. He wrapped his arms around her as Brown tossed in Luke's backpack, then grabbed a huge bag of shipping popcorn and poured it over them until they were covered.

"Half hour max, and we'll get you out of here, okay?" Luke whispered as Brown nailed the container shut, throwing them into total darkness.

It was the longest half hour of her life as she lay there fighting panic, thanking God she had Luke to hold on to, and listening to the sounds of activity around them.

She jumped when the aircraft lurched.

"That's the cargo bay doors opening," Luke told her.

The sound of a vehicle grew closer, followed by the squeal of brakes. Must be the van Luke had said would be waiting for them, backing up to the aircraft.

Brown shouted instructions. "For God's sake be careful with that crate. And if you so much as put a scratch on my bird, you *do* know that I'll have to kill you."

She clung tight to Luke as the crate was lifted, jostled, then transferred to the waiting van. A pair of doors slammed shut near their feet.

Outside, she could hear the murmur of voices, the jumble of aircraft engines prowling on and off the apron, and the scream of commercial jets taking off and landing on distant runways.

"Why aren't we moving?" she whispered against Luke's jaw after several minutes had passed.

"It all takes time," he whispered again. "If they rush this, someone will get suspicious." When she couldn't stop a violent tremor from wracking her body, he said, "These aren't any run-of-the-mill delivery guys. They're *my* guys, Val. You trust me, right?"

She nodded jerkily.

"Then trust them."

This was all about trust. Trust that they wouldn't be trapped in this box. Trust that they wouldn't suffocate. Trust that she really wasn't back in that dirt cellar with the rats and the—

"Hey, hey," Luke drew her tighter against him. "Breathe deep. Come on. Give me a deep breath. That's it. Good girl. Now give me another one."

She concentrated on breathing air in. Letting air out. Focusing on his soothing whisper and the warmth of his body against hers. The scrape of his stubbled jaw against her forehead, the scent of him.

"Think about . . . something that makes you happy," he suggested. "Are you a chocolate kind of girl? Ice cream? How about music—got a favorite song? Tell me. I don't even know what you like."

You, she thought. *I like you, Luke Colter. I like you very, very much.*

"If you were a true fan, you'd know," she whispered back, and felt his smile against her temple.

"Back then it was all about bra size, okay?"

She snuggled closer. "I appreciate the attempt at distraction but I'm okay." Because of him, she was going to get through this.

Finally, the van started moving. A few minutes later, it stopped again.

"Must be at the security gate," Luke said, preempting her question. "Hang on. This is the last hurdle. It won't be long now."

After several long, tense moments, the engine revved and they were rolling again. Not long after, the sensation of speed told her they were zipping down a highway.

They'd made it past security!

Luke started pushing on the lid of the crate, and she joined in with a vengeance until they managed to dislodge a corner of the lid. She gulped in great gasps of fresh air, along with a welcome sense of relief when someone peeled the lid the rest of the way back.

"Whoa. Have a little patience, people." A slow Texas drawl greeted her and a calloused hand reached down to help her to her feet.

"Welcome to Buenos Aires." Strong arms lifted her clear of the container and set her on her feet as foam popcorn scattered everywhere. "Johnny Reed at your service, ma'am."

Mike Brown had nothing on this lean, buff man who smiled at her like she'd just popped out of a birthday cake. His blond hair was a little on the long side; his blue eyes were as sexy and flirty as sin. And as he stood there in tight, faded jeans, a western-cut shirt, and snakeskin boots, Val couldn't help but think, *Good Lord. Doesn't Luke have any ugly friends?*

It became real clear, real fast that the bond between Luke and Johnny Reed was tight and strong, as Reed gave Luke a concerned once-over. Only after he was satisfied that Luke was okay did his killer grin reappear.

"Welcome back, doctorman. Me and the boys were starting to think we'd never see that pretty face of yours again."

Luke brushed popcorn off his chest. "Yeah, I missed you, too. So who's our wheelman?"

Reed hitched his chin toward the front of the van. "That would be the Choirboy."

Choirboy, Val learned as Luke helped her toward the front passenger seat, was Raphael Mendoza.

And holy mother of God. She'd always been a fan of the TV series "Rescue Me," which featured the firefighters from New York City's fictional Truck Company 62. Mendoza, with his caramel-colored skin, deep brown eyes, sensual mouth, and standout physique, could double for Daniel Sunjata, who played the role of firefighter Franco.

Nope, no ugly men, she thought as Mendoza welcomed her to Buenos Aires in a voice lightly laced with a Hispanic accent before he returned his concentration to the highway.

• • •

Val sat staring out the window as the van rolled on and the men talked in the background. She should be participating, but she'd hit the wall. She'd tuned them out. Just as she'd tried to tune out the reality that this was her life, not someone else's.

Night had fallen like a curtain. Traffic was light in this part of the city, and very few people appeared on the streets as they drove deeper and deeper into a squalid neighborhood.

Mendoza turned off on a side street that didn't exactly evoke images of corporate headquarters for a successful paramilitary operation. But after he circled a block twice, cruising past the same building, she wondered if they'd reached their destination.

"Home sweet home," Reed said.

It probably should have surprised her that Black Ops., Inc. HQ was a rundown adobe cantina painted a rusty blood color, but after everything that had happened, nothing much shocked her now. Scared her a little, yes, but shocked her? No.

The dim glow from the streetlights did little to camouflage the building's decay. The thick wooden door was scarred and barred, its peeling blue paint faded in spots to a chalky gray. It looked dark and dangerous—like the men of Black Ops, Inc.

Apparently satisfied that the coast was clear, Mendoza pulled the van into a back alley, then crept along until he came to a tall, banged-up metal garage door. He hit a remote clipped to the visor. When the overhead door silently slid open, he drove through it and down a steep driveway that took them to an underground garage.

Reed jumped out and opened Val's door. "*Mi casa es su casa*," he said, helping her out.

A wall of heat hit her, reminding her they'd descended from mountain cool to nearly sea level.

"So, Reed, how's the wife?" Luke asked with a look that said "back off" as he maneuvered between her and the good-looking cowboy.

Reed just grinned. "Feisty as ever and anxious as hell about you." As he led the way through the dark parking garage, Val spotted two black Suburbans, three black Jeeps, and a pair of motorcycles. "You know how Tink gets when one of her ducks swims out in the deep water."

"Tink—aka Tinkerbelle, aka Crystal Debrowski Reed, is Johnny's wife," Luke explained as Mendoza headed up a set of dimly lit stairs. At the top, he pressed his palm against a scanner mounted on the wall.

"That's new," Luke said, checking out the device.

"Tink and B.J.," Rafe supplied. "They've been updating security."

The panel flashed green, then the heavy metal door opened. Mendoza walked through and held it open for the rest of them.

Inside they walked single file down a narrow, dimly lit hallway. The mournful sound of a Spanish guitar bled through the smoke-stained adobe walls, as did the smell of cigarettes and marijuana.

When they passed by a series of small windows embedded in the thick, rough walls, Val caught glimpses of a smoky cantina. The room was half full of hard-eyed, shadowy men, none of whom she'd want to meet in the light of day, let alone in the dead of night. A pocked-face man with oily gray hair and tired eyes washed glasses behind a long, scarred wooden bar. Spanish tile covered the floor; a ceiling fan spun slowly overhead.

This was their headquarters?

"It's okay," Luke assured her as if reading her mind. "The cantina's a front, and those are one-way mirrors. They can't see you."

Reed planted his palm against the scanner by another door. Another flash of green and the door swung open. When Val followed him inside, she was instantly transported from seedy to state of the art.

Bright fluorescent lights lit a large, rectangular room that housed a bank of computer monitors, half a dozen printers, land lines, a fax, and an assortment of high-tech, big-ticket electronic equipment that blinked, hummed, beeped, and whirred. The floor was utilitarian gray tile, the walls, institution white. There were no windows. Clearly, this was the epicenter of the operation.

"About time you got back here."

Val turned toward the sound of the feminine voice as a petite redhead rushed into the room. She wore camouflage pants tucked into combat boots, a snug tan T-shirt that showcased voluptuous breasts, and gold hoop earrings that a pair of canaries could have used as perches. Her hair was styled in short, spiky wisps around a stunning, pixie face; her eyes were snapping green and her arms were open wide.

"Hey, Tink." Luke hugged her hard.

Reed firmed his mouth and crossed his arms over his chest while Luke made a big production of kissing her smack on the lips. "Missed you, sweetheart. When are you going to leave that overinflated ego of a husband and run away with me?"

Val was fascinated by the byplay as she watched Crystal Debrowski Reed pull back and search Luke's face with concern before she was satisfied that he was okay.

"You do make a tempting offer," she said, hugging him again.

"Far be it from me to break up this little lovefest, but if you value your balls," Reed said with a grin that undercut his threat, "you'll get your damn hands off my wife."

Luke laughed, then let her go. "You are so predictable, Reed."

Crystal chucked Reed on the chin on her way by and marched over to Val. "How you doing, darlin'? Don't take this wrong, but you look like you've been through a war."

In another tone, with a less sympathetic and kind look, Val might have taken offense to the redhead's blunt remark. But there was too much warmth and compassion in her eyes to mistake her intentions as anything but friendly.

Val immediately liked her. Liked even more that another dose of estrogen had been added to the overpowering presence of testosterone that had permeated her life lately.

"I'm Crystal, by the way," she added with a welcoming smile. "And I'd recognize you anywhere. Wow. What a thrill to meet you. Wish it could have been under different circumstances."

She reached for Val's hand. "You look dead on your feet. What sounds good? Coffee? Shower? Food?"

Suddenly, Val was famished. "Food sounds good," she said, smiling her thanks.

"Then food it is." Crystal linked her arm through Val's and led her toward a door at the far side of the room. "Kitchen and mess hall—such as it is—are this way. And you're lucky," she added, tugging open the door. "Rafe and Johnny traded clean-up and kitchen duty tonight. Rafe made chicken enchiladas and there are plenty of leftovers for both of you."

"What is this? Pull-Reed's-chain night?" Reed, looking indignant, ambled lazily behind them. "I could swear you just implied that I can't cook."

"I'd never insult your cooking, darling," Crystal assured him with a grin.

"We would, *darling*," Rafe and Luke said without missing a beat.

"This is what they do," Reed warned Val in a wounded tone. "They gang up on a guy. They're even trying to turn my wife against me."

"Just hoping she'll wise up," Rafe said, opening the refrigerator and coming out with the pan of enchiladas in one hand and a bottle of beer in the other. "Because you're so not worthy."

Val felt Luke's hand on her shoulder and, finally relaxed in the midst of all the good-natured male trash talk, grinned up at him. "Is it always like this around here?"

His smile was long-suffering. "Welcome to my world. Oh, and by the way?" His voice was low as he steered her to a corner away from the activity by the fridge. "Let's just keep that little incident with the mule between us, okay?"

It took a second, then she grinned. "You mean the part where you got bucked off."

His expression was grave. "That cannot get out."

She nodded, pretending to consider. "Because you have your cowboy reputation to uphold."

"Because that information is a loaded gun in Reed's hand. He will *never* let me hear the end of it."

20

"Could I have a minute of your time, please, Senator?" a familiar voice asked.

Marcus Chamberlin silently cursed whoever was responsible for the guest list for tonight's black-tie event. This was supposed to be a charity event for AIDS research, not an opportunity for the press to ferret out sound bites.

But he knew the drill. And he knew exactly how dangerous the veteran reporter from the *Washington Post* could be if he was pissed off.

"Excuse me for a minute, would you, Dex?" He smiled at the freshman senator from Illinois, nodded his apologies to the senator's starstruck wife, who was attending her first big D.C. event, and turned.

"Hello, Cal." He stopped a passing waiter and lifted two glasses of wine, then held one out to the reporter. A string quartet played softly in the background, and he focused on the lilting notes of the Mozart concerto to keep himself centered. "Thought they were going to keep the riffraff out tonight," he said with an amiable grin.

"If I thought you really meant that, I'd be wounded."

Cal Berger was seventy if he was a day. He was a newshound of the worst kind; his dogged determination to leave no stone unturned scared the living hell out of every politician who had skeletons in their closet. Since that encompassed 99.9 percent of the House and Senate, no one wanted Cal as an enemy.

"The social scene isn't exactly your regular beat, Cal," he said, giving the reporter his due. "What brings you out tonight?"

"You. You've been dodging me."

Marcus flashed the smile that had opened checkbooks and stocked his war chest with a surplus of funds that had gotten him elected for his third term. "Now, you know I'd never do that."

"Right." Cal cut to the chase. "What's the word on Valentina?"

Marcus barely managed to keep his smile in place. He was worried sick about Val; he kept hoping to hear word from her that she'd arrived back in the States safe and sound.

"You know that Val is off-limits, Cal. You also know that I have nothing but respect and admiration for her. Since when did you resort to tabloid journalism?"

"Yeah, yeah. I get it. You and Miss Beautiful parted as friends. You wish her all the best. And we all know she more or less dropped off the face of the earth a few months ago."

"She's taking a little time out of the public eye. I respect her need for privacy, so please don't ask me where she is. Because even if I knew, I couldn't tell you."

He hoped to hell she was safely aboard that plane by now, on her way back to the States where he could help protect her. If anything happened to her, he'd never forgive himself. Besides, damn it, he needed her back in time to make the trip to Sierra Leone.

A trickle of sweat ran down his spine. He wished to God he hadn't placed Val or himself in this position. But what was done was done. Now he somehow had to figure out a way to make all parties involved happy without hurting Val.

"Can you tell me if she's going to make the trip next week?"

Ah, this made sense. With the threat of another uprising by the Revolutionary United Front priming the newscasts on both network and cable stations, naturally Cal would want to cover his and Val's involvement in their ongoing joint relief missions.

"What I can tell you is that Val and I are both committed to our cause. The next aid shipment will be delivered next week with or without her presence. Regardless, she will always be there in spirit."

"But I thought she was your ticket past some tricky negotiating with government officials — specifically the minister of commerce, Siaka Bai M'boma, who's reluctant to fall under the scrutiny of the international community."

Ice suddenly flooded Marcus's veins. "Where did you hear that?" he snapped before he could check himself.

"From you. Just now," Cal said with a self-satisfied smile.

"You didn't hear anything from me, Cal," Marcus said calmly, even though he felt himself breaking out in a cold sweat. "And whoever you *did* hear it from doesn't know what they're talking about," he continued. He would not let Berger see how shaken he was. "Yes, Val is our celebrity goodwill ambassador, and yes, she has a certain rapport with M'boma, but those supplies will arrive at their destination even if someone else makes the trip in her place."

"So she's not going."

Marcus didn't fall for the lure this time. "Look, Cal," he said, his voice promising both sincerity and confidentiality. "I appreciate your interest in our cause and in Val's well-being, but I really can't help you. Now if you'll excuse me, there are some very nice people who have generously paid some very big money for my attention tonight."

He turned and walked away. He hadn't made it ten paces when his BlackBerry vibrated in his pocket.

He fished it out, hoping for news from Val. A sick feeling filled his chest when the caller's name appeared on the screen.

He hesitated, his heart hammering, then dropped the BlackBerry back into his pocket.

"Mrs. Fairchild," he said, his smile firmly in place as he greeted the society maven from Cambridge. "So glad you could make it."

He glad-handed and sweated through the rest of the

evening, hoping to hell that with his political future and Val's life hanging in the balance, he hadn't made a tactical error by ignoring that call.

"It's not much, but it's home." Luke felt self-conscious suddenly as he unlocked the door to his apartment. He reached around Valentina and flipped the light switch, then motioned for her to go on inside. After resetting the lock and the security system, he tossed his backpack on the floor inside the door.

His small two-bedroom apartment could be described as spartan at best. He spent very little time here, and since he rarely had company other than the BOIs, he hadn't thought much about neatness or décor.

He thought about it now as Val looked around, seeing it through her eyes, wondering what she thought of the place.

Not much, he figured.

Tan leather sofa and matching chair. Utilitarian black coffee table with a pair of matching end tables. A rust-colored knit afghan was tossed over the arm of the sofa—a gift from his mother a few birthdays ago. A dog-eared paperback lay on the floor by the sofa where it had dropped out of his hand when he'd fallen asleep reading it. Hell, that must have been a month ago.

"Nice painting." Her attention was focused on the large canvas he'd hung on the main wall opposite the big-screen TV.

The oil was the one good piece of art he owned—at least he thought it was good. He'd picked it up at a street fair a few years ago. He wasn't much for abstract art, but this work had drawn him in.

The colors had reached out and grabbed him. But even more, he'd been fascinated by how the artist had slapped on paint in thick slabs with a palette knife and actually created an image. At first glance it appeared to be just a helter-skelter collision of colors, but upon closer look an image materialized of a wild horse, neck arched, mane flying, hoofs thundering.

He liked the wildness of it. The surprise. The sense that the artist totally got that to get to the good stuff in life, sometimes you had to dig deeper.

"Glad you like it," he said. "Among other things, it makes me think of home."

"Right," she said. "Montana."

"Yeah." He leaned down and switched on the lone table lamp by the sofa. "Near Billings."

"Where you lived on a ranch."

"Yeah, where I lived on a ranch," he repeated slowly, wondering where the hint of cynicism in her tone was coming from. He was getting a sense that after all they'd been through, she still didn't believe him.

He knew she was exhausted. Figured she'd absorbed about as much as she could for one day. It was late, and the team dynamic at BOI HQ could be overwhelming. That's why he'd decided to take her someplace quiet and safe, where she could regain some sense of normalcy.

So he'd dumped all the intel he'd gathered with the team, and promised to have Val back in the morning for a complete debriefing.

Tonight was about her. About getting her balanced again.

"Val—what's going on?" he asked softly.

She was quiet for a while, then reluctantly met his eyes. "Do you ever get the feeling that you don't have any control? Of anything?" Her eyes looked a little wild and a lot defeated before she turned away and walked to the window.

"I mean, looking back . . . I never planned on being a model; it just sort of happened to me. *Fame* happened to me. I never planned on becoming a celebrity. Or a senator's wife. Or a divorced woman. Never planned on running for my life, or being dependent on a virtual stranger to keep me alive."

Luke held his silence, gave her the chance to work whatever was eating at her out of her system. She dipped a finger into the closed blinds, then peered out at the city lights ten stories below.

"I've just realized in a very big way," she continued, "that my whole life has been one big delusion. It's never really mattered what I think, what I do, who I believe." She finally turned. "So you say you're a cowboy from Montana? Fine. You're a cowboy from Montana. Whether I believe you or not doesn't matter because whatever's going to happen to me is going to happen. I don't have any say over it anyway."

She crossed her arms tightly under her breasts. "The trip to Peru was all about getting some control back. So the joke's on me, because it seems I never had control in the first place."

He walked across the room to her. "I know you feel like your life is rocketing through space in a tailspin right now, that you have nothing to say about what's happening to you. But it's all going to come back together. We'll figure it out. We'll fix it. This situation isn't permanent."

She closed her eyes for a moment. When she opened them, she looked so sad it broke his heart. "Why do you have to be such a good guy? Why do you have to be so heroic, and sexy and sweet and so . . . Indy?"

Indy? He didn't have a clue what she was talking about.

"I wasn't looking for anything like you in my life, Luke."

So that was the root of her problem. This he could understand.

"I know," he said as they stood there so close, they were almost touching. "I wasn't looking for anyone like you, either."

"It all comes back to the fact that nothing, absolutely nothing, is in my control," she said. "It was all going to happen. *You* were going to happen. And just like everything else, what I feel for you, what I want from you, is out of my control."

She moved in to him, looking beaten, resigned, and as vulnerable as . . . hell, as vulnerable as he was. Worse,

she had developed this notion of who he was—and he
wasn't that man anymore.

"I'm not a hero, Val. Hell, I'm not sure *what* I am
anymore. What happened in El Salvador," he said, forcing the words around the lump in his throat, "the shooting . . . I've brought a lot of guys back over the years,
you know? In the field, on hundreds of ops. I've patched
them up, saved their lives. But as I lay there, knowing I
was bleeding out, knowing I was dying and couldn't do
a damn thing to help myself . . ."

He broke off. Collected himself. "I was so pissed at
myself. For letting those bottom-feeders get the drop on
me . . . for failing the mission to keep Sophie safe . . . for
letting the guys down."

He turned away, scrubbed both hands through his
hair, then wove his fingers together on top of his head.
For a long moment he stood that way, staring off into
space.

"Ten days later when I came to," he said finally, dropping his hands, "the first thing I saw was my mom. Her
face was swollen from crying. She looked so . . . so tired
and scared. So . . . old. And I thought, Jesus, they killed
her, too. We're both dead. And I knew it was my fault.
It was all my fault."

He didn't realize that she'd walked up behind him
until he felt the touch of her hand on his arm. Didn't
realize he had tears in his eyes until he felt the burn of
them.

Shit. He blinked them back. Cleared his throat. Got
himself together.

"Anyway, I haven't been able to stop thinking about it. About how I was there, then how I almost wasn't. Can't stop thinking about my mom. Of how much pain I'd put her through."

When she slid her arms around him and pressed her cheek against his back, he let out a breath that felt like it had been backed up in his lungs for hours.

"I'm not the man that I was before," he said turning in her arms and resting his cheek on the top of her head. "I question things now. Why am I doing this? When's the next bullet going to finish the job? When is enough, enough? And you can't do that. In this line of work you just can't do that. Sooner or later, it'll get you killed. It'll get someone else killed."

"And yet you're still with the team," she said quietly. "Why? Why haven't you gotten out?"

The little lady had just asked the million-dollar question. He wrapped his arms tighter around her. "Because of them."

"Reed and Mendoza," she concluded accurately.

"Yeah. And Jones and Green and the rest of the team that you haven't met. They're my brothers," he said quietly. The whole world, it seemed, had suddenly fallen quiet. "We've been through the fire together. Bled for each other."

"And you nearly died for them."

"Sometimes I think I really did die," he said, fighting a despair he'd been beating back for months now. "Sometimes . . . hell, sometimes I feel like I'm a ghost of the man I once was. So . . . get the hero notion out of your head, okay? I'm not that man. Not anymore."

She tipped her head back and looked up at him, her eyes shining with something that made his heart clench. "You *are* that man. You are that man and so much more."

She slipped her arms around his neck and kissed him with so much tenderness, he felt it clear to his soul.

When she pulled back, her eyes were glittering as she caressed his cheek with her fingertips. "You're my Indiana Jones. My white knight. You're the man who told me that it's how you react to the fear that says who you are, and then you showed me exactly what you were talking about. Don't you see that? Can't you feel what strength you have inside of you? You *are* my hero. And you are definitely *not* a ghost."

Not a ghost.

Her words hit him like a freight train. And for the first time since this wild ride had started, he realized that with her at least, it was different. With her, there was no hesitation, no doubt. With her, he was who he was trained to be. His reactions were automatic. His mission clear. Protect. Defend. At all costs.

Because there was no way in hell was going to let anything happen to her.

No way in hell was he ever going to lose her.

He touched his hand to her face. Looked deep into her beautiful, soulful eyes and knew he would die to protect her.

Without another word, he picked her up, lifted her

in his arms and, eyes locked on hers, carried her to his bed.

He laid her down and turned on the bedside lamp. Then he undressed her slowly, lingering over each inch of satin skin, caressing her with his eyes, adoring her with his hands, cherishing her with his mouth, telling her without words what a wonder she was to him. What a gift.

When they were both naked, he knelt above her and moved between her open thighs. She was crying softly when he entered her, as overcome as he was with emotions too complex and too deep to put into words.

He made love to her with a tenderness he hadn't known he was capable of expressing. With a reverence that he hoped showed her that this wasn't about sex. This was about communion. This was about seekers who hadn't even known they'd been searching. About lost souls who had defied fate and found themselves in each other.

Yeah, it was crazy. It was incomprehensible that this could happen. But his entire life had changed since he'd met her.

He totally got it now. It was this kind of connection, this against-all-odds union that had turned womanizing, self-indulgent Johnny Reed into a devoted husband. This was what Gabe and Sam and Rafe had discovered with the women who had become their wives. What Nate and Juliana had found to sustain a bond that defied all logic. This was what Wyatt and Sophie, separated for over a decade, had held on to that had inevitably drawn them back together.

Was it love? He didn't know. But as he buried himself deep, poured himself inside her, he couldn't imagine anything else in this world that could even come close.

21

Everything had seemed clear in the intimacy of the night, in the heat and intensity of the most profound emotional and sexual experience of Luke's life.

Then morning, the bitch, showed up and muddied the waters again.

As soon as he woke up and the cobwebs had cleared, Luke realized he was alone in his king-sized bed. The aroma of coffee told him Val was up and that she'd been busy. The scent of his soap permeating the air told him she'd showered.

And even before he rose, dragged on his boxers, and followed his nose to the kitchen, he'd suspected that just because the walls between them had crumbled last night, that hadn't kept her from building them back up this morning. The closed-off look on her face confirmed it.

He leaned a shoulder against the doorframe and crossed his arms over his chest, watching her. "'Morning," he said, his voice gruff with sleep.

She nodded but wouldn't meet his eyes. "I hope you

don't mind." She lifted a hand toward the coffee pot. "I needed a caffeine fix."

And he didn't need a crystal ball to read what was going on in that busy mind of hers. If this was a marathon, she'd have already put miles between them.

"You okay?" He pushed away from the door, then picked up the mug she'd filled and shoved toward him across the island that divided the kitchen and living area.

"Yeah, I'm fine." She met his eyes briefly, then busied herself refilling her own mug. She was dressed again in the sweater and jeans he'd bought her in Cuzco.

"You could have worn a pair of my sweats," he said. "They'd have been big, but at least—"

"It's okay," she said with a quick, tight smile. "I'll make do until I get a chance to buy something else."

He watched her above the steam rising from his mug. Yeah, she'd built that wall up good again. Brought in an entire crew with backhoes, cement trucks, and big-ass trowels to rebuild. There was no way in hell he was breaching it this morning.

The part of him that still believed he was half ghost was too chickenshit to even try.

He suddenly felt very tired. And very resigned.

Maybe she was the smart one here. Maybe until this was over and both of them could think past who was out to get her, it was better to just leave it alone. To back off to where they didn't have to think about what the hell was happening between them.

Time to do his part. "Let me grab a shower, then we'll head back to HQ, okay?"

She nodded. "Yeah. That would be best."

Oh, yeah. Like him she'd chickened out, decided to deal with it by not dealing with it at all.

This was why he didn't do relationships. Everyone brought too much baggage to the party.

"Sorry I don't have the kitchen stocked, but there should be a loaf of bread in the freezer. Peanut butter's in that cabinet. Last I knew, the toaster worked."

"You want me to make you some?"

"Sure, if you don't mind." He headed for the bathroom.

Sure, let's pretend that last night didn't rock our worlds into the next galaxy. After all, falling couldn't-draw-a-deep-breath in love happened to him every frickin' day.

An hour later, they arrived at BOI HQ. Compliments of Crystal, who had rustled up a change of clothes, Val was now wearing a clean black T-shirt and tan cargo pants.

"Not exactly material for a *Vogue* cover shoot, but they're clean," Crystal had said with a grin.

"They're perfect," Val had said, thanking her. She'd used the locker room to change before joining the team in their situation room.

She now glanced around the large rectangular table. Besides Mendoza, Reed, and Crystal, two more team members, Gabe Jones and Rafe's wife, B.J., had been there to greet them when she and Luke had arrived a few minutes ago.

While Crystal was a petite redhead, outgoing, friendly, and a blatant flirt who was clearly enamored with her hunky hubby, B.J. Chase-Mendoza was Crystal's exact antithesis. She was a tall, willowy blond with a tangle of long corkscrew curls that she'd done her damnedest to wrestle into a ponytail at the nape of her neck. Her severely cut black pantsuit and crisp white shirt were all business and seemed to be designed to minimize her figure, just as her lack of makeup and utilitarian hairstyle appeared to be deliberate attempts to play down her striking good looks. None of her tactics had worked. B.J. was a beautiful woman. And until Val had seen her interaction with Rafe, the Choirboy, she would have assumed she was as cold as Alaska's Malaspina Glacier, where Val had once done a very nippy photo shoot.

When B.J. looked at Rafe, her face transformed to a look so soft and vulnerable and intimate that Val had had to look away, feeling like she was intruding on a very private moment.

Gabe Jones . . . well. There was no mistaking who he was nor what he did. He was a warrior. He was also a big, brooding man who literally filled up the room with his presence. That he was yet another excruciatingly handsome operative didn't surprise her anymore.

Every minute that she was in their company, observing their easy camaraderie, and the precision with which they functioned as a team, it became that much clearer that these weren't ordinary men and women. They were highly trained, highly skilled, and profoundly dedicated to their cause. It didn't take the American flag hanging on the wall above the bank of computers to tell her that they were also patriots.

One other thing had become clear. Last night in the kitchen over Rafe's enchiladas, Crystal's rundown on the other players making up Black Ops, Inc. had made Val realize that every man among them had paid some price for what they did.

Looking at Luke, who sat across the long table from her, his jaw hard, his eyes averted, she saw that he was as determined as she was to avoid dealing with whatever was happening between them. That he was struggling with it just like she was.

Wrong time. Wrong place. Wrong life.

She fought the urge to tell him how life-altering last night had been. To confide that she was scared senseless of the feelings she had for him, that she'd made so many bad decisions in her life about men that she couldn't afford to make another.

The door to the situation room door opened, drawing her attention to a tall, lean man with eyes as sharp as razors.

The sound of a metal chair scraping on the tile floor filled the room as Reed shot to his feet, stood at attention, and saluted crisply.

The man stopped, scowled, and heaved a heavy sigh. "All right, you clown. At ease. It hasn't been *that* long since I've been here."

"Just showing my respect, sir," Reed said with a smart-ass grin. "It's not often we're fortunate enough to be in the company of such greatness."

"You are such a drama queen, darling," Tink said, her affection tinged with forbearance.

"What he is, is a kiss-ass." Mendoza fired a paper clip across the table at Reed, who laughed and dodged the missile. "And payday was yesterday, so you're wasting a performance."

"Val," Luke said, breaking into the mix, "this is Nate Black. Nate—Valentina Chamberlin."

The moment he'd walked in the door, Val had suspected that this was the head of Black Ops, Inc. The man had a commanding quality that exuded control, leadership, and respect. According to Crystal, Black spent most of his time in Bahía Blanca, where he oversaw the business from a remote location and supported his wife in the medical clinic she ran there. From the curious looks on the faces of the people around the table, they were surprised to see him, too.

"It's a pleasure," Black said, extending his hand. "Crystal has been keeping me apprised of your situation. How are you holding up?"

"I'm fine," Val said, returning a handshake that was as strong and steady as the man delivering it. "And very appreciative of your team."

His dark eyes were as kind as they were sharp as he smiled. Then he planted his hands on the back of a chair. "Someone give me a sit rep," he said, taking command of the meeting with a no-nonsense style that his team clearly respected and responded to.

Crystal took the lead. "Still digging for clues as to who's after Valentina and why. Luke brought us tons of goodies." She spilled the contents of a large manila envelope in the center of the table.

Val felt a chill when the wallets Luke had taken from the bodies of the men they'd left in the mountains fell out. The tags he'd cut from their shirts and the red, green, and gold ribbon holding the medal he'd taken from one of the bodies were also in the mix, along with the SAT phone.

Gabe leaned forward and reached for the medal. "Military. North Korean?" he speculated, glancing at Crystal.

She nodded. "Combat decoration. We ran it against a database B.J. managed to 'borrow' from her friends at DIA."

Val glanced at B.J. Crystal had told her that before B.J. joined the BOI team, she had been a field operative with the Department of Intelligence Agency. She and Rafe had met as adversaries when they'd been at cross-purposes on an operation in Caracas.

"Tough as nails, that one," Crystal had said with admiration in her voice.

Val could see that. B.J. was *kick-ass*, as was Crystal.

"Only four of these medals have been awarded to North Korean military personnel in the past decade." B.J. lifted a remote control and pointed it toward the far wall. A viewing screen dropped down from the ceiling, then four headshots appeared side by side.

"Number three. That's our guy," Luke said flatly and

without hesitation, IDing the man from the mountains after a quick glance.

Nate scowled at the screen while B.J. made a few clicks, dropping the other three photos and enlarging the one of the man Luke had identified. "So what's a decorated soldier in the North Korean army doing in Peru chasing an American model?"

"*Former* N.K. soldier." B.J. clicked to another screen that showed an official-looking document written in what Val assumed was Korean. "According to this, our guy separated three years ago."

"To do what? Become a hired gun?" Eyes on the photo, Gabe leaned back in his chair and laced his hands together behind his head.

"Walks like a merc, talks like a merc, must be a merc," Reed said, rising to grab the coffee carafe and refill his cup.

"Dig up everything you can on this guy, Tink," Nate said unnecessarily. She was already tapping away at the keyboard on her laptop.

"As expected, we got no hits on the IDs from the wallets," Rafe added. "Which means they were fakes, which is information in and of itself. These guys didn't want to be ID'd dead or alive. The labels from the clothes are pretty standard issue. Could have bought them online, army surplus, or Mercs-R-Us. So the clothes are a dead end."

"What about the serial numbers I lifted from the weapons?" Luke asked.

Tink glanced up from her laptop. "Dead end there,

too. I tried tracking the numbers for their point of origin or to tie them to end-user certificates, but came up blank. CYA well in play."

"Cover your ass," B.J. explained when Val's puzzlement must have shown.

"Tink dumped the SAT phone data last night," Reed told the room at large. "With luck we'll be able to back-trace the origin of the call, maybe get a fix on who was on the other end of the line. Should have some results soon."

"I also convinced the two goons at the airport to give up an e-mail address they had been instructed to use to confirm they'd fulfilled the terms of their contract," Luke said.

"We're running that, too." B.J. glanced at Nate. "But I'm not looking for much on that end."

"Big effing bingo." Crystal sat forward in her chair, her excitement drawing everyone's attention. "I got a hit. And wow. This is interesting. Hold on. I'll send it to the screen."

Every pair of eyes in the room focused on the viewing screen, waiting for Crystal to do her magic. Her fingers scrambled across the keys as she manipulated the image of the merc and reduced it to fill only half the screen.

When another photograph popped up beside it, Val felt the blood drain from her face.

She heard Crystal's voice through a fog. "Meet our North Korean medal recipient's last known 'associate.'"

"I've seen him before," Val said breathlessly as she studied the photograph.

"Where?" Luke clasped his hands tightly together on the table.

She shook her head, continuing to squint at the image. "I . . . I'm not sure. I just know I've seen him."

She *knew* she had seen that face. But try as she might, she couldn't place where or when.

"Ryang Wong Jeong." There was a lethal edge in Luke's voice Val had never heard before.

"You *know* him?" Her heart drummed like crazy, her frustration growing as the missing piece of information she needed to connect his face to her memory continued to elude her.

"We know him well." All attention shifted to Nate. "Anyone fluent in illicit international arms dealing knows about Ryang. He's a big player in the North Korean political arena. Was highly favored by Kim Jong-il, but lost a little of his stock when the youngest son, Kim Jong-chul, took over the reins. Ryang's been redoubling his dirty dealings ever since to impress the new head honcho."

"Prince of a guy and a total whack job," Reed added irreverently. "Jacket on him says his mother was a prostitute who used to pimp him out to her clients who had, shall we say, more exotic tastes. Fought his way out of the slums, joined the army. Started his climb. And now look at him. A self-made rat bastard."

B.J. leaned back in her chair. "He was a busy boy paving his way to a power position in Dear Leader's cabinet. Worked into the big time."

"We figure he's had a hand in close to a quarter of the international black market arms shipment deals made in the past three years," Gabe added.

"All in the name of North Korean patriotism," Crystal said caustically. "Rumor has it, Ryang had actually been considered as a successor to Kim Jong-il because of his ruthless dedication to the cause."

"And because the oldest son, Kim Jong-nam, is a total fuck-up," Nate added. "Ryang was counting on the younger son's lack of experience to keep him out of the position. I'm thinking Ryang was beyond pissed when the kid was tagged for the spot anyway."

It became very quiet in the room, and all of the team members suddenly seemed to be avoiding eye contact with Val. Sensing a dramatic shift in mood, she felt very ill at ease.

"I don't understand. Why would this Ryang be after me?"

Nate looked pointedly at Luke, who heaved a troubled breath, then finally met her eyes. "Marcus heads up the House Committee on Armed Services, right?"

She blinked, shook her head. "Yes, but he participates in a lot of committees."

"But as *head* of that particular committee, he has access to highly classified information that, if it landed in the wrong hands, could—"

"Wait." An edgy panic had her hands sweating as she realized what he—what all of them—must be thinking. "You think Marcus is somehow linked to Ryang?"

She stood abruptly, and glared at Luke. "And that somehow he's gotten me mixed up in some . . . I don't know. Some *arms* deal?"

No one would look at her. They were all looking at

Luke, waiting for his cue. Yet, their silence was answer enough. That's exactly what they thought.

"No. You are *so* off base. Marcus would never do that. In the first place, he would never do anything illegal. In the second, he would never put me at risk. The idea is just ridic—"

She stopped midsentence when her synapses suddenly snapped her elusive memories of Ryang Wong Jeong's image together.

A sick feeling roiled in her stomach. Heart racing, breath shallow, she jerked her attention back to the photograph. "Oh, God." She dropped heavily into her chair.

"What is it?" Luke voice was edged with tension.

Wanting to deny what she now knew, but unable to fight the truth, she clasped her hands tightly in front of her. "I . . . I just realized where I'd seen Ryang before."

She forced herself to meet Luke's eyes. "Several years ago, we were at home. I'd been in the kitchen. Marcus was in his office. I went to tell him that dinner was ready, but his door was closed and I knew he couldn't hear me. I knocked once . . . then swung the door open. He . . . he whirled around, furious that I had interrupted. He snapped at me to get out and close the door behind me."

"What had you interrupted?" Crystal asked in an encouraging tone.

"A video conference call." She looked down at her hands again before meeting Luke's gaze. "I caught a glimpse of Marcus's computer monitor over his shoulder. That man . . . I saw his face on the monitor. Ryang was the man Marcus was talking to."

22

The situation room fell deathly quiet. Val looked like she wanted to curl up and die because she'd just realized that her ex-husband had consorted with a North Korean official—an act that was as good as collaborating with the enemy.

Though Luke wanted to save her from this, there wasn't a damn thing he could do to soften the blow. A long moment passed. "Give us a minute, would you, guys?"

Without a word, everyone stood and walked out of the room, leaving the two of them alone. And even though Crystal squeezed Val's shoulder in support on her way by, Luke got the very distinct impression that Val had never felt more alone in her life. Or more adrift.

Tears filled her eyes. "I know this looks bad. But there's got to be some explanation. Marcus couldn't be involved in any international criminal activity with that man."

It was the last straw.

"Jesus, Val, Get a clue!" He was pissed at Chamberlin. Pissed *for* her, and yes, *at* her because she was still attempting to defend her piece-of-shit ex. "No one in the U.S. government communicates with a North Korean official without a directive from POTUS. And if the president *does* approve such a dialogue, you can damn well bet it makes international news. It's not done in secret. Chamberlin is neck deep in something that reeks of espionage and treason. And whether you want to accept it or not, he's somehow involved you in it, too."

She looked so heartsick, he made himself back off. "Look . . . maybe he's been forced into it. Maybe he's being threatened."

"Threatened?"

He shrugged a shoulder. "Hell, I don't know. Ryang might have threatened his life. Or yours. Or maybe Chamberlin's being blackmailed."

Her face paled, and suddenly she looked away.

And he knew in that instant that she was hiding something from him.

Fuck.

He leaned forward in his chair, clasped his hands together on top of the table. "Did Marcus have secrets, Val? Secrets that if they got out could kill his career?" *And maybe ruin a marriage*, he thought as he saw her struggle and her pain.

But he couldn't back off now. She needed to come clean, and she needed to do it now. So he spelled it out for her. "Consorting with North Koreans is a treasonable offense. Illegal black market gun shipments are violations of not just U.S. but international laws. Still, it happens all the time. Corrupt government officials will act on their own for personal gain. And if they aren't corruptible, then men like Ryang find one who's vulnerable and capitalize on it."

She still wouldn't look at him. "And you think Marcus was corruptible?"

"I think," he said, "that it's time we talked about the reason for your divorce."

Half an hour later, Luke left Val alone to pull herself back together and deal with some very ugly, sordid truths. He found the team in the kitchen, where Reed and Crystal were rustling up lunch.

Nate leaned back against the counter and crossed his arms over his chest when Luke walked in the room. "And?"

Luke cupped a hand behind his nape, where a headache throbbed like a bitch. Then he gave them the nutshell version of the cheating husband story with a nice juicy twist.

"So," Reed said when Luke finished, "the senator is a total prick. He not only cheated on Valentina, he used her to keep his secret and his closet door closed."

Luke dropped into a chair, feeling like he'd just kicked a kitten. Repeatedly. "Amazing what old money can buy. Chamberlin managed to keep the lid on his homosexuality for years. If Val hadn't caught him in a compromising situation, they might still be married."

"Look, I've got no problem with what goes on between consenting adults, but I've got a major beef with a cheater. The bastard should be strung up for that alone," Crystal sputtered, making it clear that she'd already developed an allegiance with Val. "Add on what's starting to look like fraternization with the enemy, and the counts are stacking up against him."

"How could a man keep something like that from his wife?" Rafe was clearly confounded. "She really didn't suspect anything?"

"Yes and no," Luke said. "They both had busy careers that didn't allow for a lot of together time. The last few years were particularly grueling. Chamberlin always had a lot of excuses for why they couldn't have sex, and yes, she was concerned and confused. She even blamed herself, worried that he'd lost interest."

"Lost interest in a woman like that?" Reed looked flabbergasted. "Does she never look in a mirror?"

"Anyway, it wasn't until she came home unexpectedly that the proverbial cat jumped out of the bag," Luke went on. "Chamberlin was 'entertaining' in their bedroom. Guess it had been going on since before they were married."

"I still don't get it." B.J. snagged a carrot stick from a veggie tray Crystal set on the table. "So he's into men. So what? It's not the fifties, for God's sake. Why does he think he has to hide it?"

"Family? Political pressure? Who knows? Apparently he's been in denial his entire life. He thought marrying Val would 'cure' him—and yeah, he actually used those words in a teary confession when he begged Val not to leave him or reveal his secret."

"Like I said," Crystal spoke up again, "I've got no beef with his sexuality and if anyone here does, then you're not the people I think you are, but this guy sounds like a spineless piece of shit. He used Valentina to enhance what he calculated would be his best image."

Luke couldn't have put it better. Yet Val had still defended him.

"He's a good person. He hates himself for what he did to me. He's been in agony for years, confused, ashamed, and riddled with guilt."

"And how do you feel about him?"

"I'm past the anger. I just feel regret. In his own way, he loves me. And a part of me will always love him. I don't expect you to understand, but Marcus was the first man in my life who treated me like something other than a commodity. He helped me through my mother's death. We believed in the same things. Championed the same causes. Or so I thought . . ."

Until she'd found out the bastard had been using her.

Luke glanced at Nate. "I think it's time to have a little chat with Chamberlin. Joe's in D.C. with Steph, right?"

Joe Green was a charter member of Task Force Mercy and the BOI team. These days he spent a lot of his downtime in D.C., and it was no secret why. Ever since Joe had been tagged for a temporary protection duty assignment for Stephanie Tompkins, the sister of the TFM team member they'd lost in Sierra Leone years ago, Joe and Steph had found as many excuses as possible to spend time together.

Nate confirmed Luke's assumption. "I'll give Joe a call. See if he can visit Senator Chamberlin, have a little come-to-Jesus meeting, and get this sorted out."

B.J. looked troubled. "If Chamberlin is as guilty as he looks, he's facing treason charges. I can't see him talking."

"Then we'll have to make certain that Joe explains to him that he's run out of options," Nate said.

Luke checked his watch. It was an hour earlier in D.C. "Something tells me the senator is going to miss lunch."

"Or lose it, when Joe's finished with him," Gabe said with a grim look as Nate left the room to make the call.

"A word, please, Senator Chamberlin."

Christ, Marcus thought as he rushed down the steps of the Senate Office Building. *Would these reporters just leave me alone?*

"Sorry," he said without turning around. "I'm already late for a meeting."

"You're going to want to take time to talk to me."

The cold calculation in the man's voice made him stop and turn around—to face a very big man. NFL-defensive-line big. He looked hard and mean and not one thing about him told Marcus that this guy was someone he wanted to talk to.

"Do I know you?"

"Not yet. Let's go back to your office and have a

chat. Or would you rather have this conversation about Ryang Wong Jeong in public?"

Marcus's vision went foggy for a moment. Then fear, heavy and debilitating, roiled through his gut. "Who are you?" he demanded, fighting to keep his voice steady.

"Your office, Senator?" There was more warning than invitation in his tone.

"You've got five minutes," Marcus said, and headed back up the steps.

He snapped at his staffer as they passed his desk. "Call Senator Helfer and let him know I've been delayed."

He closed his office door behind them and turned to face the stranger with as much authority as he could muster. "All right. I can give you five minutes."

"You're going to give me," the man said, moving in hard and fast, "whatever I want." Big hands grabbed his lapels and shoved him up against the wall. Hard.

Jesus. Jesus.

Marcus fought back a cry of pain as he was slammed up against the wall again.

"Did . . . did Ryang send you?" He was shit-his-pants scared. He'd been dodging Ryang's calls, hoping to buy time, to find Val and fix this problem.

"What about Ryang?"

"Look, I know he's upset. But I'm working on finding her. Tell him . . . tell him—"

"Ryang didn't send me," the man snarled, his face mere inches from Marcus's. He was so close Marcus could feel the rage seeping from his skin, so close he could see the cords and veins in his thick neck bulging. "I'm a friend of a friend of Valentina's."

"Valentina? You . . . you have Val?"

"Let's just say Ryang doesn't have her—no thanks to you."

Relief cut through the terror. "She's okay?" he choked out. "God, please tell me she's not hurt."

"She's fine. Look, I'll make this easy for you. We don't like what's happening to her. And we don't like the connections we've been making with you and Ryang. So why don't you enlighten me on what your arrangement is with him, and why he sent a squad of goons to Peru after Valentina?"

"I begged him not to do that. Not to hurt her."

"Save the remorse, you slimy bastard. You're in this neck deep."

"No, you have to believe me. I've been trying to keep her from getting hurt." Tears stung his eyes. *What a mess. What a fucking disastrous mess.*

"And look how well that's worked for ya. I'm not a patient man, Senator. I want answers and I want them now."

The man threw him down in his desk chair and leaned over him, wrapping his fingers around Marcus's throat and squeezing so tight he couldn't breathe.

"Are you ready to talk to me?"

Marcus felt his eyes bulging, his oxygen supply going south. He nodded jerkily, then gasped for breath and clutched his throat when the pressure let up.

"So talk," the man demanded again. "And don't leave anything out."

23

"Well, you know what they say." Crystal lifted the pitcher of sangria and refilled Val's and B.J.'s glasses. Sunshine sparkled through the leafy trees shading their table at an outdoor café on a vibrant Buenos Aires street. "If it has tires, testosterone, or experience with Tomahawk missiles, it's going to give you trouble."

"I'll drink to that," B.J. said in solidarity.

Val couldn't believe she was laughing. She'd laughed a lot during the past four hours, since Crystal had taken on the role of social director and personal shopper.

"You need clothes, right?" Crystal had pointed out after dragging her out of the situation room where Luke had forced her to take off her rose-colored glasses.

"We're on hold until we hear back from Joe and our computer programs finish running, so let's shop," Crystal had reasoned with a grin. "Maybe get manis and pedis, too. It's been a damn long time since I've had a girly day."

"Knock yourselves out," B.J. had said when Crystal had invited her to join them. "I'm behind on my reports."

"Oh, no." Crystal wasn't having any of it. "You need to get out of here for a while, too."

When B.J. had still balked, Crystal had added, "Don't make me get Nate involved."

Apparently Nate had been after B.J. to take some downtime, and the mention of their Boss's name was enough to break her.

"Fine," B.J. had grumbled, "but only for a couple of hours. And don't expect me to buy anything."

"God forbid you find some sassy lingerie or, *gasp*," Crystal had teased with round eyes, "a hot dress to seduce your husband."

B.J. had just snorted, snagged her purse, and headed toward the door. "Let's get this over with. But I'm not shopping. And I'm not letting some stranger play with my feet."

They were an unlikely trio, Val thought as the sun warmed her shoulders. The effect of her second glass of sangria eased the tension that had been her constant companion for days.

Crystal, with her irreverent and quick wit, was a woman Val could truly like and trust. She also liked the stoic and serious B.J. who, at Crystal's dogged insistence, was now the owner of a pair of killer black stilettos and the siren's dress and lingerie to go with it—and yes, a new manicure and pedicure. They were bright, capable, and funny women. And they were both packing serious weapons in the hobo bags hooked over the backs of their chairs.

"But *you* make it work," Val pointed out in response

to Crystal's tires, testosterone, and trouble remark. After B.J. and Crystal had told Val how they had met and fallen in love with their men, Val didn't have a doubt that their marriages were bedrock solid.

"Only because my gun is bigger than Rafe's," B.J. said.

"Don't ever let him hear you say that," Crystal said around a laugh.

"So." Crystal turned to Val after their waiter delivered a sampler platter of deserts Crystal had insisted they all try. "What's the story with you and Luke?"

"No story," Val said quickly. Too quickly, based on the knowing glances Crystal and B.J. exchanged.

Crystal shot her a grin. "Sweetie, the looks between you two could torch a forest."

Val played with the napkin on her lap. "Look. Luke . . . is amazing. I don't even want to imagine what would have happened to me if he hadn't been on that train."

"But?" Crystal held a forkful of something chocolate and decadent over her plate.

"But I just met him. And even if running for my life weren't muddying my decision-making process, I have a history of making bad choices about men. I can't afford to make another one."

"He's a good guy," B.J. said.

"I know that," Val agreed. "A great guy."

"We almost lost him," Crystal said quietly. "Last year. In San Salvador."

Val nodded. "I know that, too. What?" she asked, when the two women exchanged another quick look.

"He talked to you about it?" B.J. leaned forward, her brows creased with interest. "About getting shot?"

The surprise in both women's eyes confused her. "Yeah. He did." And then she got it. "You mean he doesn't talk about it with any of you?"

Crystal shook her head. "He's been spooky silent on the subject. We've been worried about him. It's good to know he's finally letting it out."

Unspoken was the fact that Crystal thought it was significant that Luke had opened up to Val.

"We've been through some pretty intense stuff together." If she could convince them it wasn't significant, maybe she could convince herself. "I guess . . . I guess extreme circumstances net extreme reactions. It was probably just time he got it out."

But what they'd shared last night—in words, in emotions, in the most physically intense and intimate lovemaking she'd ever experienced—had been profound. And earth-shattering, for both of them.

And completely futile. Because the connection they'd made had broken down barriers neither one of them had been prepared to breach. And because both of them were gun-shy of commitment.

She should be relieved that he'd let her pull away from him this morning—yet she felt bereft and disappointed that he'd simply walked away. More proof of how screwed up she was.

She suddenly realized that her silence had garnered more curious stares.

"For God's sake, will you two stop with the looks? I

don't deny that I care about Luke. But I can't get involved with anyone right now, okay? My life is a mess—he doesn't want to get involved, either."

Crystal looked at her kindly, then covered Val's hand with her own. "I hate to break this to you, honey, but you two are already involved."

Val looked at B.J. and Crystal. B.J. had been a field agent for DIA. Crystal had trained to be a cop, but a slight hearing loss from a childhood illness had kept her from passing the physical. Nothing stopped either one of them from doing what they wanted to do.

They were the kind of women Luke needed in his life. Val wasn't and never would be. Deep down, she suspected Luke got it, too, which would explain why he was willing to let her shut down and pull away. Any woman who teamed up with him would have to be strong. Much stronger than she was.

Yeah? And whose fault is that?

Suddenly she was tired of shying away from her own shadow. Looking at these strong, capable women made her look back on her own life differently. Because of the trauma of the kidnapping, she'd been coddled and pampered ever since. It had made her dependent, malleable, and naïve.

It was time she fixed that. For most of her life she'd let people use her and think of her as little more than window dressing, but that didn't mean she wasn't capable of becoming more. So she'd made bad choices, choices that had led to her believing that she didn't deserve anything better.

Why not take a shot at becoming more than what people expected? More than she'd expected of herself? She'd risen to the occasion in Peru hadn't she? She'd been scared, but she'd kept it together. So why not see if she had what it took to become worthy of a man like Luke? Why not fight for what might be the best thing to ever happen to her? Why not take a giant step toward being the strong woman Luke thought she was?

A rush of decisiveness washed over her, and she knew exactly where to start.

B.J. choked on her sangria when she told them what she wanted to do. "Say what?"

"I want you to teach me how to handle a gun."

When both women gave her dubious looks, she explained. "I killed a man in the mountains. If I hadn't, I'd be dead now instead of him. I *shot* him because I was scared to death and because I didn't have any choice.

"I want the option of saying, 'Don't make me shoot you,' and knowing that they'll understand I'm more than capable of doing it. I need to know how to defend myself to do that."

"Val," Crystal said gently, "if someone pulls a gun on you, it's way past time to talk."

"Fine," she said. "Then teach me how to handle a gun because I'm fucking tired of being scared."

Val's reprieve from reality came to a jarring end when the entire team met up in the situation room again a couple of hours later.

"Sit down, Val." Nate Black pulled out a chair for

her. His eyes were kind but she could tell by his somber expression that what he had to tell her wasn't going to be good. "You're a part of this, so I want you to sit in on the briefing."

"Joe came through?" B.J. asked.

"In spades," Nate said with a grim look.

Crystal and B.J. each took a seat on either side of Val. She appreciated their show of support. Squaring her shoulders, she braced to take the bad news.

"While Senator Chamberlin was initially reluctant to talk, when Joe convinced him that your life was on the line, he became much more forthcoming.

"There's no easy way to say this," Nate went on, "so I'm just going to lay it out. Several years ago, shortly after Chamberlin was appointed head of the arms committee, he made a trip to South Korea for an international summit on the growing illicit arms problem and its impact on terrorism. While he was in Seoul, Ryang Wong Jeong made arrangements with a South Korean asset to set up a sting involving the senator." He stopped and glanced at Luke.

His jaw hard, Luke looked Val in the eye. "The man lured Chamberlin into a highly compromising situation involving an underage male prostitution ring. Then he had the episode videotaped."

Her vision blurred. *Underage male prostitution ring. Videotape.*

Oh, God.

"Shortly after that, Ryang started leaning on Chamberlin," Black went on, "using the threat of going public with the tape. At first, all he asked for were in-nocuous bits of information, but over time his requests escalated. As Ryang's status with Kim Jong-il grew, so did his appetite for more power. He dragged Cham-berlin in even deeper with his demands for inside in-formation.

"Ryang's network was growing and he needed someplace to set up shop instead of scattering his in-ventory all over the globe." Nate ticked off his next point on his fingers. "Someplace where the govern-ment was weak, corruptible, and the country was in chaos. Someplace where al-Qaeda and their splinter groups could funnel in a shitload of money to keep things stirred up and take some of the heat and focus off them."

He looked straight at Val. "He found an easy answer, in Sierra Leone."

It took a moment for the information to jell. And when it finally did, when the implications became clear, she didn't know if she could stand to hear the rest of this.

"The aid deliveries you've been making to Sierra Leone? They're a front to help Ryang smuggle in huge shipments of illegal arms." Empathy filled his eyes.

Her hands trembled. "Marcus . . . Marcus told you all of this?"

He nodded.

"I don't understand." A wild desperation kept denial burning. "I . . . I was part of every delivery. I was there when they opened the boxes. I helped pass out food . . .

medical supplies . . . tools . . . schoolbooks. I didn't see any guns."

"No one did, because they were all busy looking at you." Gabe Jones added his voice to the mix. "You were the perfect beard for the operation. Your celebrity? Your looks? Think about it. The paparazzi swarmed all over you on those trips. You couldn't take a step without tripping over a reporter with a camera. Like Angelina Jolie's visits to Darfur, *you* were the story in Sierra Leone. You were the diversion."

Gabe was right. By design, each trip has been a media frenzy.

"Oh, God. And I just blindly agreed with it. My celebrity was supposed to bring attention to the cause." Her heart sank as she accepted that she'd played a part in hurting the very people she was trying to help.

"Then add Chamberlin into the mix," Rafe said, "A popular U.S. senator endorsing the missions, greasing palms, and ensuring that the inspections were fudged, and it's foolproof. No one was looking for smuggled guns. Who was going to question a senator from the country leading the fight against global terrorism?"

"So, that's why they needed me," she said hollowly. "A pretty diversion." She'd been so proud. For once, her face was doing something for the greater good instead of for commercial gain.

"It doesn't end there." Nate's voice warned her that the worst was yet to come. "You were more than a diversion. You were Ryang's signal to his end buyers that he'd come through on his promise."

"I don't understand."

Nate glanced at Luke. "You want to take this?"

"The buyer wants proof that he's not going to take heat on his end," Luke explained. "Ryang gives him you. The buyer sees your face all over the TV, sees you on the ground in Freetown—that's Ryang's signal that not only have the goods arrived, the coast is clear."

"That's why Ryang was after you in Peru," Nate said, filling in the blanks. "You've got another aid mission coming up, right?"

She nodded, fighting light-headedness. "Next week. I was heading back to the States when the train was attacked. I wanted to be back in time to make the trip."

"Only Ryang didn't know that," Luke said. "You'd dropped out of sight. Marcus hadn't been able to deliver you. Since this next arms shipment—apparently the biggest one yet—is tied to you being there, Ryang had to find you. His buyer was going to back out if you didn't show. He not only stood to lose money, but risked total disruption of his operation."

"And, worse, he would lose face with Kim Jong-il," Gabe added. "The equivalent of signing his own death warrant."

"So," she said slowly, working through the disbelief and horror, "it would be best if I don't go. Is that what you're saying? Then Ryang loses, right?"

The room rang with a deathly stillness. She glanced at Luke, wondering why everyone wasn't agreeing with her. He looked ready to spit nails.

"We need you to accompany that shipment, Val,"

Nate said. "We've been on Ryang's trail for years. He's sneaky and elusive, and except for one op when we got lucky and confiscated a small shipment of arms in Panama last year, he always manages to slip past our net. This is the closest we've ever gotten to nailing him.

"Now, thanks to Chamberlin, we know Ryang's MO. We know where the shipment is going to make port, and we know the delivery method. The only thing we don't know is who the buyers are. With your help we can not only divert the shipment, we can nail his end users and cut off Ryang's major pipeline."

"And if it happens that the rumors are true, that remnants of the RUF are regrouping for another attempted coup, we can also settle an old score," Gabe said quietly.

The girls had told Val today how one of their own, Bryan Tompkins, had died in an ambush in Sierra Leone.

They all had a personal interest in returning to Sierra Leone. They'd lost a brother in arms there, and they'd never stopped wishing they could go back and find the murderous RUF who had killed Bryan.

So she understood why Gabe saw this trip to Sierra Leone as an opportunity to settle up.

"I don't want Val in the mix," Luke challenged his boss, bringing her back to the conversation.

"That makes two of us, but we've been over this. Without Val," Nate said, "we're dead in the water. Sure, we can cut off the shipment. But we lose our best and possibly only chance to nail the buyers on the receiving end."

"There's got to be another way." Luke stood so abruptly, his chair clattered to the floor. He planted his palms on the table and glared at Nate. "It's too dangerous. We can't take the chance of her getting caught in the crossfire if things go south."

The two men glared at each other, Luke with fire in his eyes, Nate with a cold, calm authority that warned Luke to stand down.

They could argue all they wanted.

Val understood what had to be done.

24

"I'm going," Val said.

Luke whipped his head around and glared at her. "No, you are not," he snapped before facing off with his boss again. "She is *not* going."

Heart pounding, Val held her ground. "Inadvertently or not, I played a part in making this mess. I need to play a part in fixing it."

Luke's hard eyes lasered back to hers. "You don't know what you're signing on for."

"And that's news?" she fired back. "Apparently I've been in the dark for years. He used me, Luke. *Everyone's* used me. Marcus, Ryang, and God knows who else. And innocent people, the people I thought I was helping, could be hurt because of it."

She was so angry, she was shaking. "No more. If I'm going to be used, then let it be to *stop* these bastards."

Filled with a determination fueled by both purpose and humiliation, she turned to Nate. "I'm all yours. They want Valentina showing a little leg? A lot of cleavage? They've got her."

Nate gave her a measuring look, then an approving nod. Beside her, Luke simmered with anger, but said nothing as Nate continued.

"The delivery, complete with the dog-and-pony show the press will stage all on their own, is set for four days from now. We've got very little planning time, major flight time, and zero time to run this up the flagpole and wade through miles of bureaucratic red tape to get the blessing from the powers that be. So, we're on our own on this one."

Crystal leaned over and whispered in Val's ear. "What Nate's saying is that we don't have time to turn this info over to U.S. authorities. They won't be able to okay an op on foreign soil without an executive order, and since this is Sierra Leone, that's not going to happen with UN watchdogs monitoring every move. So it's better we act now and answer questions later. With luck, we'll establish a permanent roadblock in Ryang's arms pipeline."

"Tink."

Crystal returned her full attention to Nate.

"Get hold of Ann Tompkins at DOJ. See if she's heard any scuttlebutt about Chamberlin, just in case there's something else she can add to the mix. We're also going to want someone on the Hill to know what we're up to, in case the mission goes FUBAR. Ann's our best option."

Ann Tompkins was Bryan Tompkins's mother. B.J. and Crystal had told Val how Ann and Robert Tompkins had opened up their home to the guys after losing Bryan. How they all thought of the Tompkinses as extended family—even how Ann had played a part in Crystal's rescue from an Indonesian crime lord after he'd abducted her and held her prisoner in Jakarta.

"In the meantime, what about Chamberlin?" Gabe asked, bringing Val back to the immediate dilemma.

"Joe's got him contained. He's not going anywhere and he's not talking to anyone until this is over.

"He doesn't want you hurt, Val," Nate said. "He's made that clear. He'll cooperate with whatever we ask him to do."

As consolations went, it was a small one.

And as anger went, she realized, turning her attention back to a darkly brooding Luke, his was as big as a house.

"Yes," Marcus told Ryang in a placating tone, "Valentina will participate in the delivery as planned."

His palm was so slick with nervous sweat that he almost dropped the phone. "She's making preparations for the trip as we speak," he assured Ryang again. "I don't know what else I can tell you. She'll be there. We'll both be there as originally planned."

He closed his eyes, and listened as Ryang castigated him one more time for avoiding his calls.

"I've apologized," he said. "What else do you want me to say? I regret not getting back to you but the truth of the matter is, I panicked. And frankly, that's on you."

Ryang's silence told him how angry he'd just made him. "Again, I apologize, but when Val called me she was scared to death. I still don't understand why you had to send those men after her. They shot at her! And you . . . you attempted to have her abducted again at the Cuzco airport."

Again, he reined in his anger. The last thing he wanted to do was make Ryang suspicious of his boldness.

"Forgive me," he amended penitently. "I understand that you found it necessary to take matters in your own hands, to make certain she accompanied the shipment. I realize what's at stake for you."

Marcus had never doubted that the North Korean was a cold-blooded killer. Just like he had no delusions about how this was going to end for him. His career was dead. His life was over.

Frankly, he was past caring. All that mattered now was Val. She was a good person. She'd kept his secrets in the face of the humiliation he'd caused her. He was so ashamed of himself for falling into Ryang's trap, for knuckling under to Ryang's demands. For selling out a country he had sworn to uphold and protect. And he was so, so sorry for dragging Val into the muck with him and exposing her to such danger.

"No," he said, tuning back into Ryang's ranting. "I already told you. Apparently the man was simply a fellow traveler who came to her rescue. He found her a place to hide out. He put her in touch with the American embassy, who issued her a duplicate passport so she could get back to the States," he lied, pushing past Ryang's accusations that Marcus had hired a team of mercenaries to protect her.

"I must beg your forgiveness, but I have to go," he said abruptly, before Ryang could engage him in further conversation. "I'm expected at a meeting. Yes, an arms committee meeting, and if I don't show up they're going to come looking for me. Please rest assured the timetable will be met. The delivery plans remain unchanged."

Ryang issued one more threat detailing what would happen to both him and Val if he didn't come through, then hung up. Marcus's hands were damp with clammy sweat as he hung up his own phone. He drew a shaky breath, then looked up at the man who had identified himself as Joe Green. Marcus had no idea who he worked for. He knew only that the man scared him almost as much as Ryang did.

"Did he buy it?" The look on Green's face made it clear that Marcus had better have the right answer.

Marcus nodded. "I think so. Hell. I don't know. You heard the conversation." In fact, Green had practically dictated the dialogue word for word. "Ryang's a loose cannon. Intimidation and threats are his life."

And his own life was as good as over, he thought again. In a way, it was almost a relief. The subterfuge, the guilt . . . the shame. All of it had been eating him alive.

"I do care about Val," he said.

"I don't give a rat's ass what you care about, Senator. All I care about is making this deal go down and putting an end to Ryang's arms operation."

"And keeping Val safe," Marcus insisted. "You said you and the men you work with were going to keep her safe."

"Little late to be worried about her now, isn't it? After the way you screwed her over?"

He deserved that. He deserved a lot more, and fully understood that he would pay the price for his sins against her and against his country.

He propped his elbows on his desk and lowered his head to his hands. He hoped Val knew what she was doing. That this group of men could be counted on.

Joe could hardly bear to be in the same breathing space as Chamberlin. The man was a gutless coward. A traitor involved in a scam that transported illegal arms shipments to Sierra Leone.

Sierra Leone. It had been too many years since they'd lost Bry in that shithole. It had been an illegal arms mission back then, too, that had led to Bry's death. It had eaten at Joe for years . . . just like the way that mission had gone FUBAR had eaten at him.

As a rule, he tried not to think about it at all. He and the BOI team had their plates full in the here and now. But what had happened on that long-ago mission . . . hell. It never should have happened.

He thought about it more than ever lately. Because of Steph, he supposed. Because they had this thing going . . . because he cared about her. And because when she hurt, he hurt.

She still mourned her brother's death. He hated seeing the pain on her face when she looked at Bryan's picture. Hated knowing that her parents, Ann and Robert, who had offered their home, their hearts, their love to the TFM team in the years since Bry's death, had died a little, too, the day they'd buried their son.

Most of all he hated knowing that Bry shouldn't have died that night. There wasn't supposed to have been an RUF patrol within ten miles of their position. And yet they'd been caught with their pants down in an ambush.

For years, he'd been pissed with the talking heads running command central and calling the shots from hundreds of miles away, relying on drone and satellite surveillance to micromanage their operations, when what the team had needed were eyes on the ground. The consensus was someone had simply screwed up. They'd received bad intel.

But Joe had always wondered if it hadn't been a screwup at all. If maybe they'd been set up.

He glanced at Chamberlin and anger knotted his gut. How many politicians had sold out their country, their troops, their souls, for money or to simply save face?

He turned away, walked restlessly around the office—then stopped short in front of a framed group photograph on the far wall.

There were around twenty people in the picture, but his gaze snagged on one specific face.

What the fuck?

He felt the room sway before he pulled himself together again.

"Tell me about this photograph."

• • •

Green was standing with his hands on his hips, scowling at one of several framed eight-by-ten photographs hanging on the wall opposite his desk.

"It's a group shot of the stateside and Sierra Leone teams who organized the first aid shipments six years ago," Marcus said as Green leaned in close, his expression hardening as he studied the photograph.

When Green turned around to face him, there was a look in his eyes that could only be described as bloodlust. "I want a complete list of names and the personnel file information for everyone ever involved with the aid missions. Both stateside and in Sierra Leone."

Anger radiated off Green in violent waves. Something, or someone, in that picture had set him off.

"That's a lot of names," Marcus said carefully. "Takes hundreds of people to make something this big work."

Green whirled around and slammed the picture on the desk. The glass cracked as the frame shattered, sending shards of glass flying everywhere.

Jesus!

"I don't give a fuck how many names there are." He peeled the group photo out of the decimated frame, rolled it into a scroll, and shoved it in a deep pocket on the leg of his cargo pants. "Just get me the damn information. And don't leave one person out."

Marcus lifted a trembling hand and reached for the phone to buzz his aide.

Green grabbed the phone from his hand and dropped it back into the cradle. "No. *You* do it. Copy the files on everyone having to do with the initial S.L. project onto a flash drive. Do it now."

Green stood with shoulders squared, breathing deep as if he was using every ounce of concentration to keep himself from reaching across the desk and strangling Marcus with his bare hands, while Marcus pulled up the files on his PC, copied them onto a flash drive, and with a shaking hand, handed it to Green.

"Now what happens?" Marcus asked, braving the dark, brooding anger in the younger man's eyes.

"Now you keep your mouth shut until I personally notify you otherwise. And a word to the wise, Senator. If you run, I will find you. And if you do anything but the right thing, you're a dead man."

He tucked the drive in his hip pocket and left the office.

Marcus slumped back in his chair, staring at the door Green had shut behind him.

And the walls came tumbling down.

He stared at the empty spot on the wall where the photo had hung. Then he shifted his attention to the shot of him shaking hands with the president. The framed photo covered his wall safe. Inside the safe was a Colt revolver.

He rose on shaking legs and crossed the room, broken glass crunching under his feet. He carefully removed the photograph, then set it on the floor.

His hand was trembling as he spun the dial and meticulously worked through the combination. The lock gave with a gentle click and the door swung open.

The gun sat inside the safe like a bomb, just waiting to explode. It was big and black and felt cold and heavy in his hand.

He walked back to his desk. Tested the pistol's weight in his palm. Experimented with the feel of the trigger beneath his finger.

For long, heart-pounding moments, he envisioned himself lifting the weapon, pressing the barrel into his mouth, and firing.

Then he laid his head on his desk and cried like a baby, because he knew he didn't have the guts to do it.

25

"We should talk about this," Val said.

Apparently, however, they weren't going to.

All she got was silence as Luke reset his apartment's security system, then stalked past her toward the kitchen.

They'd come straight here after the strategy session about Sierra Leone. Her mind was still reeling at the sheer volume of operational details that needed to be worked out. They needed a flight crew from B.A. to D.C. Ground support in Freetown, Sierra Leone, for possible extraction if things got dicey. A backup extraction plan. An emergency medical treatment plan in the event there were causalities. The list went on and on.

By the end of the day, she had a firm grasp on just how dangerous this mission was—and why Luke was so opposed to her participation. These people were professionals; she was not. They lived and died by their wits, their skills, their experience; she did not. She understood that even though they needed her, she was also their single biggest liability, because in addition to carrying out the mission, they needed to worry about her safety.

To say that Luke was still angry was like saying bombs went *boom*. She was certain he was going to blow at some point but for now, he had yet to even speak to her.

"Luke, we need to talk," she repeated, following him into the kitchen where he stood with his back to her, jerking open kitchen cupboard doors.

"I've said what I had to say. You didn't want to hear it." He banged a pan onto a burner on the gas stove, then set a can of soup and a can opener on the counter beside it. "Dinner. Knock yourself out."

Taking great pains to avoid both eye and body contact, he moved past her. "You can take the bedroom tonight. I'll sleep in my office." He walked out of the kitchen, down the hall, and slammed the door to his office behind him.

The old Val would have left him alone, rather than incite a confrontation. But that Val was gone. She'd died in the mountains of Peru, perished in the ruins of Marcus's betrayals.

That woman had experienced two epiphanies today. The first, while she'd sat in the Argentina sunshine with two women who inspired her. The second, in the situation room when she'd realized that most of her life had been a lie and that she had let it happen.

Phoenix rising from the ashes?

Not by a long shot. She had a way to go before she'd feel absolved of her sins of submission. A lot to prove to herself, and to the people who mattered to her.

And Luke Colter mattered.

She headed for his office. Not bothering to knock, she swung the door open and stepped inside.

His office consisted of beige walls, a single window, a small desk with a PC, an overflowing bookshelf, and a brown sofa against one wall. The room felt utilitarian, spartan and lonely.

He looked lonely, sprawled on his back on the sofa, one arm over his eyes, one knee cocked, one foot on the floor.

How often had he lain alone in the dark here or in his bed and relived the horror of San Salvador, she wondered, her heart aching for him. How often had he questioned who he was, what he was?

Sometimes I think I really did die . . . sometimes I feel like I'm little more than a ghost of the man I once was . . .

Now, more than ever, he needed to be reminded of how very vital he was. And if it would snap him out of this funk, she was ready to pick a fight if that's what it took to make him see the light.

"I didn't figure you for a pouter," she said.

He grunted. "Yeah, well, I didn't figure you for a martyr," he spit back.

"Fine." She crossed her arms tightly under her breasts. "We can do this all night. I'll label you. You can label me. We can be as judgmental as hell. It'll be fun. Your turn."

For the longest time he didn't move. Finally, he lifted his arm and looked at her. "I'm sorry," he said quietly and sat up. He let his head fall back against the cushions and closed his eyes. "I don't want anything happening to you."

"Like it happened to you?"

His eyes snapped open. "This has nothing to do with me."

"Doesn't it?" she asked, already certain of the answer.

His jaw clenched as he leaned forward, clasped his hands together, and dangled them between his knees. "Okay. Let's make this about San Salvador. Let's talk about life and death and the fact that this isn't an action adventure movie you're getting yourself into, Val. This is real. Like San Salvador. This is as real as it gets. People get hurt. People get killed. You are not prepared for what's going to happen when that plane sets down in Sierra Leone."

He swallowed, then looked at his tightly clenched hands. "And I'm not fucking prepared to lose you."

Her heart swelled. So did her tears as she walked over and knelt in front of him.

"I have to do this," she whispered, placing her hands on his knees. "The same way that you have to do this."

"I know," he said, sounding miserable. "Doesn't mean I like it. Doesn't mean I have to support it."

He looked at her then. His eyes were tortured, his expression grave.

And her heart broke when she realized how truly afraid he was for her.

She couldn't remember anyone ever looking at her that way. In all her life, she couldn't remember feeling a connection so strong. Last night he'd almost destroyed her with the intense intimacy of his lovemaking.

She'd never felt so connected, so possessed, so completely vulnerable to any man, and yet so empowered by one. But she understood that her emotions were under siege by everything that had happened to her. She knew that she couldn't fully trust these intense feelings. So she still couldn't risk telling him the things he made her feel.

But she could show him, she thought, aching for his anguish. She knew exactly how to show him.

"Make love to me," she whispered. Because when he was holding her, when he was inside of her, there was no fear. Only trust. Only pleasure and passion and the perfect illusion that everything was right in her world.

"I don't think that's such a good idea. Go to bed, Val." He slumped back against the cushions. "Just . . . go to bed."

He was still angry. Because he was afraid for her.

He cares. He cares so much.

A tear trailed down her cheek as she moved in closer, then slid her palms slowly up his thighs. His muscles tensed beneath her touch.

His eyes shot open, then flamed with desire when he realized her intent. He shook his head slowly, but the denial didn't reach his eyes.

"Don't," he whispered when she brushed her fingers along the seam of his zipper, then caressed him, feeling the unmistakable swell of his response beneath her hand.

"Don't," he managed gruffly, but didn't stop her as she undid the snap at his waist.

"Don't." His eyes pleaded but the single word held little conviction as she slowly lowered his zipper.

"Jesus, Val." He groaned her name when she freed him, when she took the long, hard length of him in her hands, then traced the tip of her tongue over the engorged head of his penis.

His hands were in her hair now, an aborted attempt to push her away before he surrendered with a low growl, begging her, "Don't stop . . ."

He was hers now. No fight, no regret, only pleasure as he helped her shove down his pants.

Thrilled with her victory, she drew him deep into her mouth and showed him that she adored him, couldn't get enough of him, couldn't bear to think about life without him.

He sucked in a harsh breath and stiffened when she cupped his testicles and gently squeezed. He was hot and full and heavy in her hand.

The next thing she knew, he'd gripped her under her arms and dragged her up his body. He lifted her arms around his neck and caught her mouth in a deep, carnal kiss. She hung on for her life as he tore open the snap on her new jeans, wrenched down the zipper, and shoved them and her panties roughly down her hips.

She managed to kick her jeans free, and then she was straddling his lap as he guided himself to her opening and thrust inside.

She gasped against his mouth, shocked and thrilled and stretched to the limit as he gripped her hips and held her while he pumped hard and deep with an aggression bred from passion and turmoil.

The pleasure was so intense, so exquisitely wild and

carnal, she wanted to scream and claw and bite him like an animal. As the salty taste of blood registered on her tongue, she realized how out of control things had gotten.

And as he flipped her onto her stomach, then dragged her to her knees and moved in behind her, she realized how much she trusted this man.

He braced a knee on the sofa between hers, parted the wet, pulsing lips of her vulva with his fingers, and plunged inside her again.

With a primal moan she arched back against his pumping hips, loving the feel of him inside her this way as his big hands guided her hips and set a rhythm that raised the sensation to a fever pitch. She cried out again when he reached around her and finessed her clitoris, enhancing the friction as he filled her again and again until finally, he tensed with a low, guttural moan.

His entire body stiffened; his grip on her hips tightened, and he slammed into her on one final, deep thrust as his orgasm overtook him. She buried her face in the sofa cushion and screamed as her own release ripped through her, long, intense, and electric.

She was still gasping for breath when his big body curled over hers. He pressed his cheek between her shoulder blades and wound his arms tightly around her ribs as he, too fought for breath, clinging like he never wanted to let her go.

He brushed her damp hair away from her eyes. "What you do to me," he murmured against her nape, then slowly withdrew from her body.

She felt his weight sink down on the sofa behind her, then he ran a fingertip over her hip and trailed it lazily down her thigh. "And me without a camera."

She pushed out a weak laugh. This wasn't exactly a Kodak moment for either of them. He was wearing only a T-shirt; his pants were jammed around his ankles where they were stuck on his boots. Her bare butt pointed skyward; her T-shirt was bunched up around her shoulders. Both of them were drenched in sweat, smelling of sex, and wrung out within an inch of their lives.

No, not a Kodak moment—but a very, very good moment.

She collapsed then shifted around and snuggled up against him, where they stayed for long blissful moments.

The euphoria lasted until they staggered into bed.

As exhausted as they were, neither could sleep. Because nothing had changed, nothing *could* change until Sierra Leone was behind them.

So they lay in the dark silence, and waited for morning to come.

"Men like Ryang are successful because the flow of weapons is so difficult to police," B.J. said as she and Crystal walked Val to the shooting range the next afternoon after lunch. "Small arms and many light weapons have legitimate military, law enforcement, and even sporting and recreational uses."

"So governments can't flat-out ban them," Val surmised as B.J. unlocked a cabinet that held a huge selection of handguns.

"Which makes it difficult to enforce restrictions."
B.J. pulled out a sleek black pistol, double-checked to
make certain the chamber was empty, and slid it into
her belt holster. "And because they're so plentiful and
easy to conceal, small arms are a smuggler's dream and
a law enforcement nightmare. Hundreds of thousands
of small arms in leaky government arsenals are vulnerable to theft, loss, and diversion. Once Ryang and his
ilk make a buy, the weapons are smuggled across bor-
ders in every conceivable way—hidden under sacks of
vegetables in the back of pickup trucks, packed into
household appliances that are then loaded onto cargo
ships, even air-dropped out of old Soviet military transport planes."

"Or in humanitarian aid supplies," Val said, grimly.

"Yeah," Crystal agreed with a sympathetic look.

"I feel like such a fool. How could I have been so
oblivious?"

"Look. You weren't the first to be used. You won't be
the last," B.J. said in her typical straightforward style.
"Government officials who are trained to spot this stuff
get the wool pulled over their eyes all the time. Last
year, Ryang was in collusion with a Colombian arms
dealer operating out of Panama. They duped the Ni-
caraguan government into selling them three thousand AK-47s and 2.5 million rounds of ammunition.
The bastards convinced them they were procuring the
weapons on behalf of the Panamanian National Police,
using a forged end-user certificate.

"Anyway," she went on as she loaded a clip with

ammo, "they cut the deal and loaded the weapons into a Panamanian-registered ship and headed out from Nicaragua. Two days later the shipment arrived in Colombia, where members of FARC—a terrorist paramilitary group—were waiting to claim their prize."

"Only they got a surprise. We were there to intercept it," Crystal added. "Score one for the good guys."

"And we'll turn this into another score," Val said with determination.

"Try this one," B.J. said, keeping on task. "You look like a Glock 19 girl to me. Should be a nice fit."

Crystal passed around headsets to protect their ears and shooting glasses to protect their eyes. "Come on, girlfriend." She headed for the door to the shooting range. "Let's go turn you into Jane Wayne."

The day was warm and overcast, the light breeze heavy with the promise of rain.

"Four cardinal rules," B.J. said gravely. "Treat all guns as if they're loaded; never point the gun at anything you don't want to destroy or kill; finger off the trigger; and be one-hundred-percent certain where your bullet will end up. Memorize them, live them."

A couple of hours and a hundred rounds of ammo later, Val had the fundamentals down. She knew how to load and reload. How to rack the slide and chamber a round. How to adopt a solid stance and a firm, two-handed grip, align the sights, and squeeze, not pull, the trigger.

"Breathe," B.J. reminded her more than once. "Take a breath, let half of it out, and then caress the trigger."

"Think about the way Luke touches you," Crystal added with a grin.

Val rolled her eyes. But the advice helped. Once she softened her trigger pull, her accuracy improved.

She was still only hitting the paper target fifty percent of the time, but she'd finally conquered a limp-wrist problem that had resulted in the empty brass spitting out and hitting her in the forehead.

"I think that I'm seeing a depth perception issue," B.J. said as they'd discussed her tendency to shoot high and to the right. "With practice, you'll learn to compensate."

"We've got another day before we leave, so we'll give it another go tomorrow." Crystal grabbed a broom and started sweeping up their spent casings.

Since her arms were trembling from muscle fatigue and she had a raging blister on the web between her thumb and forefinger, Val didn't argue. "Sounds good." She felt a long way from marginally able, and one more day wasn't going to make a big difference.

Her concern must have shown.

"It'll come," B.J. assured her. "In the meantime— you do realize that you're never going to come within a football field of the line of fire on this op, don't you?"

Yes. She knew that. They'd had a team briefing first thing this morning. Along with tying up some loose ends—among them the news that they'd linked both the gunman's call on the SAT phone in the mountains and the IP address from the e-mail addy Luke got at the airport to Ryang—Nate had reiterated that

Val's only part in the operation was window dressing.

That fact was pounded home again a few minutes later when she, B.J., and Crystal filed into the situation room after their session on the shooting range. "One last quick briefing," Nate said, "then we'll call it a day."

One look at Luke's face, however, and Val knew that this day was far from over.

26

"Santos, Carlyle, and Waldrop." Nate tossed the folders on the three operatives across the table to Luke. "Work for you?"

Feeling the eyes of the rest of the team on him, Luke glanced at the folders, then drummed his fingers on the table. He still wanted to be pissed, but he actually felt some relief.

Several months ago, when they'd needed additional manpower for job in Nicaragua, he'd personally vetted these three men, whom they'd then contracted for that op and several others after that.

Enrique Santos, a retired Marine, was in his early thirties. The short, stocky Latino was born in the Bronx and wore his head shaved, sported a soul patch, a Semper Fi tattoo on his left pec, a tribute to his mother on his right, and easily bench-pressed an impressive 275 pounds. When he didn't have his nose buried in Tolstoy or Kafka, he was on the shooting range honing his expert marksman skills.

Brett Carlyle was an Iowa boy. With his auburn hair and lanky six-foot frame, he looked all of sixteen instead of thirty. He'd been a pentathlete in the Army, had training as a medic, knew how to handle an arsenal of different weaponry, and God help the fool who saw Boy Scout instead of warrior when they looked at him.

Josh Waldrop was the senior citizen of the group at thirty-seven. Waldrop clocked in at a honed one-eighty on a five-foot-eleven frame. He was a former SF staff sergeant, a martial arts expert, favored his custom Bowie knife for close-quarters combat and never went anywhere without a pocketful of Red Hots candies.

All three were combat veterans of Iraq and Afghanistan. And to a man, they were solid, steady, competent, and trustworthy.

Luke would feel comfortable with them watching his back any day. And since Val's celebrity came with a built-in expectation of bodyguards, the extra muscle wouldn't rouse any suspicions.

"Her protection exclusively." He met Nate eyes. "They don't pull double duty working any other aspect of the op."

"Done," Nate agreed.

Luke still wasn't happy. "I want them on her like white on rice. Every second, every minute, every hour."

"White on rice," Nate agreed without hesitation.

His boss made it hard to stay pissed.

"One more thing," Nate added. "Brown's signed on for the ride."

"Primetime?" Rafe grinned. "Excellent. He's missed us, huh?"

"Us? Maybe," Nate said. "The action, absolutely.

He'll be on the ground when we get to Freetown. By the time we arrive, he'll have extraction transpo arranged if we need it. So let's hope we don't.

"That's it. Unless anyone has anything else to discuss, we're done for the day."

Luke gathered up the jackets on Santos and company and held them out to Nate. "Thanks," he said with a grateful nod.

"Jesus, I'm glad you two finally kissed and made up." Reed made a big production of looking relieved. "I was beginning to think we were going to have to break out the dueling pistols."

"Stow it, Reed," Nate said as he walked out the door.

Never knowing when to quit, Reed snapped to with a sharp salute. "Stowing it, sir."

Crystal pumped a closed fist into his breadbasket.

He folded with a grunt of pain. "What'd you do that for?"

"Because you made it so easy. And because one of these days, he's going to get tired of your lip and give you the boot."

"Naw." Reed slung an arm over his wife's shoulders and pulled her close. "He *lurves* me. We're going to go pick out a china pattern tomorrow."

"Wear gloves when you go to the range tomorrow," Luke said as he applied ointment to Val's hand.

They were back at his apartment, after stopping at the market and shopping for dinner. Then they'd cooked it together, washed dishes together, lingered over a couple of glasses of wine, done the whole domestic-bliss scene.

He had to keep reminding himself that it wasn't real—even though he was beginning to want it to be.

Which was pure lunacy.

"Do you want to talk about it?"

He cut his gaze to her face. The gravity of her expression told him she was referring to the trip they would be making in less than forty-eight hours.

"No," he said, putting his medical kit back together. "I don't want to talk about it."

He got crazy just thinking about what could happen to her and he didn't want to ruin the mood.

"I want to finish this glass of wine," he said, leaning in and kissing her, long and slow and deep. "Then I want to take you to bed." He trailed his mouth along her jawline, nipping, sipping, teasing with the tip of his tongue. "Work for you?"

For a moment, he thought she was going to pressure him into talking. Thankfully though, she only tilted her head back and allowed him easier access. "Works very well."

Later he lay in the dark, mellow, sated and spent, listening to her breathe, loving the feel of her naked and warm against him.

Wondering how he could arrange the rest of his life around her, this bed, and the occasional meal.

Finally admitting that he wanted this. Wanted her to be a part of his life.

But it wouldn't be fair to her to ask.

The job took such a fucking toll on everyone. Gabe had lost a leg on an op, and for a while he'd lost his direction as well. Sam Lang had lost a sister, and until Abbie had come along, none of them had thought he'd ever drag himself out of the abyss of self-recrimination. Johnny Reed—hell, Reed had been lost before he'd ever teamed up with the crew. It had taken Crystal to make him whole again. Even Wyatt had lost the better part of himself somewhere along the way—so much so that he was still on an extended leave after his honeymoon with Sophie. No one knew when or if he was coming back.

The danger, the close calls, the death and destruction . . . it took too much. And with every life Luke took—even the lives that needed taking—a little part of him had died, too.

So, yeah. The BOIs had been through the fire, yet all of them had managed to recover then hang on to the things in their lives that held them together. Their integrity. Their moral compass. Each other. And for most of them, that included hanging on to a good woman.

Luke was one of the last single men standing. He'd been fine with that. Never wanted the responsibility that came with partnership. Even if he had, he'd never figured a woman would want to sign on for the ride.

Val sighed in her sleep and snuggled closer against him. And stirred his yearning for more.

B.J., Tink, Jenna, Abbie, and Sophie had all taken the leap. Even Nate and Juliana, who had danced around each other for years, had finally committed to each other. They were making it work.

But him and Val? He pressed his fingertips to his temples and rubbed at the dull ache there. Hell, look at her. Look at her life. As soon as they got through this op she had a career to get back to. The limelight. Adoration. Fame.

No way in hell would she want to put up with the stress that came with his line of work.

He didn't even know if he had what it took anymore to do the job. And yet, what else was there?

How could he possibly saddle her with *that* man?

Easy answer. He couldn't.

Easy decision. He wouldn't.

End of the fucking discussion.

After a ten-hour flight from B.A. to Dulles, in D.C., Val was settled on board the Operation SR Foundation's Boeing 737 and waiting on the tarmac to take off for Sierra Leone. She'd established the foundation six years ago, using her own money and donations from both hers and Marcus's high-profile friends. Their first purchase had been this older-model Boeing, that had been reconfigured to a cargo bus, with extra fuel tanks in the belly to support the transatlantic flights from D.C. to Freetown. The cargo compartment filled half of the passenger space, and a cargo door added to the back end of the plane allowed for even more storage.

Both cargo holds were already loaded with the humanitarian aid supplies when Marcus stepped on board the aircraft.

She'd been dreading this confrontation.

One look at the haggard and drawn shell of the vital man she had married, and it was as though years had passed, instead of months. He was broken. Beaten. Ashamed.

Even through her anger, her heart clenched with compassion and pity as he walked down the narrow aisle toward her.

"I am so, so sorry, Val," he whispered.

She met his eyes through a film of tears, then quickly looked away.

There was nothing to say. Nothing she could say.

"Back of the plane, Chamberlin," a big man—Joe Green, she assumed—said from behind him, and Marcus moved on down the aisle.

"You okay?" Luke sat down in the seat beside her.

She gripped his hand when he covered hers and didn't even attempt to lie to him. She wasn't okay. Nothing felt like it would ever be okay again.

The last time the team had landed in Sierra Leone, it had been the dead of night and they'd HALO'd in— high-altitude, low-opening parachute drop. They'd been hundreds of miles away from the capital city of Freetown, where the upper echelon of the RUF regime had set up shop while their enforcers, armed with military uniforms, guns, and machetes, viciously maimed, raped, and killed hundreds of thousands of defenseless villagers throughout the country.

This time it was bold daylight, early afternoon. No flares were necessary to lead them to their landing zone;

the control tower guided the pilot down to Lungi International Airport.

They touched down and the interior lights blinked on. Luke watched the faces of the men who were as close to him as brothers, and knew every one of them was thinking of Bryan Tompkins. Though the RUF ambush had been over ten years ago, none of them had ever forgotten.

Beside him, Val was somber. Her hair hung loose and free and shone like silk. An hour ago, they'd cleared out what had once been the first-class section of the modified 737, pulled the privacy curtain, and she'd changed clothes.

When she'd stepped out from behind that curtain, Luke had flashed on an unforgettable photograph of Princess Diana dressed in a simple white shirt tucked into tan pants, a flak vest, and a clear protective face shield as she walked through an Angolan minefield to bring attention to her own personal cause. He'd been so impressed by her. Her love and caring and approachability was what had shown through that day.

He saw that same courage, commitment, and integrity in Val as she settled back down beside him wearing tailored white slacks and pale pink silk blouse. Hell yeah, the pants hugged that fabulous ass like a second skin and hell yeah, the blouse showed off her world-class breasts. She was like a Monet under a perfectly placed exhibit spotlight—a draw for the press, which in turned drew attention to her cause. She carried it off like an American princess, and he'd never been so proud of anyone in his life.

By design, all eyes would be riveted on her stunning beauty. She was back in international-celebrity mode but it was very clear to him that beneath her meticulously applied makeup and her game face, she was as tense as piano wire.

That made two of them. Though they'd planned for every possible contingency, their run-through had been only on paper. The team didn't have the luxury of practice runs for this op. They were prepared for all the known threats, but it was the unknowns that were driving him crazy. That, and the fact that once he and the BOIs left the aircraft, what happened to Val was out of his hands. Even knowing that she had a basic grasp of how to fire the Glock 19 tucked inside her black leather clutch, and that a GPS transmitter was sewn into her bra, he was damned edgy.

Once she was out of his sight, her safety fell on Santos, Carlyle, and Waldrop's shoulders. Broad shoulders, he reminded himself. Capable shoulders. He had to let them do their job so he could do his.

All three men were dressed the part of professional, hired muscle in dark suits, white shirts, and ties. Only a practiced eye would realize they were carrying concealed; all three wore shoulder and ankle holsters. Luke was also betting that Waldrop's Bowie was strapped on him somewhere. And because of their security-guard status, no one would question their earpieces and throat mics or suspect that in addition to communicating with each other, they could send and receive commo to the BOI team.

"Lock and load, boys and girls," Nate said from the seat ahead of him.

Because transporting even legitimate firearms was tricky business, the BOIs had packaged their equipment as medical aid and stowed it in the cargo bay with the humanitarian aid supplies. Tink, being the smallest team member, had already shimmied in and out of the cargo bay through a hatch designed for electrical maintenance. She'd dug out only the arms and ammo they could carry concealed on this first leg of the mission.

Luke unbuckled his seat belt and glanced out the portal as the jet taxied toward the waiting throng.

Besides a good fifty media mongers lined up with their cameras and booms along a security rail set up by airport security, several dignitaries decked out in ceremonial garb stood in a receiving line for a meet-and-greet photo op.

The circus had definitely come to town.

"Remember," Luke said, absently nodding his thanks as Crystal handed out khaki coveralls to each team member. "You stay within two feet of Santos, Carlyle, and Waldrop at all times."

"I know," Val said, touching up her lip gloss.

"You are never to leave their side."

"I know," she repeated as she tucked away the tube. "I know what to do. I know what's expected." She shot him a smile. "I'll take care of me. You take care of you, okay?"

God. She was so gorgeous, so determined, and so out of her element.

If she was scared, she didn't show it. But even though they'd taken every precaution to ensure she wouldn't be anywhere near the action when the fat hit the fire, he was damn scared *for* her.

"You take your photo ops, you stay on task, we make the last delivery, and you're gone. Santos and the guys will drive you back to the plane. The pilot has orders to wait for you, then immediately go wheels up."

She hadn't much liked it when she'd found out she was leaving Sierra Leone without him. He hadn't much cared. He wanted her out of here yesterday.

"Be careful," she whispered, the look in her eyes telling him how afraid she was for him. "Please, please, be careful."

"You forget, Angelface, careful's my middle name."

He was determined to leave it at that—until she touched her fingers to his face and whispered a tearful good-bye, and it hit home that this might be the last time he'd ever see her.

He dragged her into his arms and kissed her like there was no tomorrow, because, damn it, there was a real chance there wouldn't be.

"Stay safe," she whispered against his lips.

Both of them jumped when the rumble of the opening cargo bay door reverberated through the floor of the plane.

Showtime.

In a few minutes, the team would don workman's coveralls and ball caps, tuck their weapons inside their uniforms, and step into their roles as delivery boys and girls and truck drivers. While Val did her celebrity ambassador thing and Chamberlin did his U.S. senator shtick, the BOIs would fade into the background as part of the crew overseeing offloading the humanitarian supplies—along with their own weaponry.

If the information Chamberlin had fed Joe was accurate, a quartet of trucks would be rolling onto the tarmac any moment to receive the goods from the 737.

"According to Chamberlin," Joe had told them earlier, "Ryang's arms shipment arrived via a coaster—a small, shallow-hulled ship," he explained when Crystal held up a hand. "It rendezvoused off the coast with Ryang's freighter earlier today. From the coaster, Ryang's guns and ammo, packaged in containers labeled MEDICAL, SCHOOL, and CANNED GOODS, were then loaded onto the four trucks."

The BOIs had gotten their own personal weaponry past Dulles security by taking a page from Ryang's playbook.

B.J. had done the research on the trucks. "The transport vehicles are open-bed trucks decommissioned from the Sierra Leone military fleet several years ago. The drivers are local day laborers. They have no clue what they're carrying."

Nate glanced at Rafe. "You handle the drivers. Pay them off. Convince them we'll get the trucks back later tonight—whatever it takes to ensure they keep their mouths shut and just go away. Then make certain our personal gear gets on the first truck so we can access it ASAP."

From that point on, they would follow the protocol established on the very first aid mission six years ago—a protocol that had repeatedly enabled Ryang's buyers to pick up their "merchandise" without generating any attention.

"Quick huddle." Nate tacked a map up on the bulkhead wall. "One last run-through. Three stops—the church, the school, and the hospital." He X'd each location with a marker. "Each stop equals a photo op. Val and Chamberlin pass out a token number of boxes, make nice with the good people, the press get their shots. Then Val and the senator head back to the airport, and we take it from there."

While Luke hated that Val would be out of his sight, he'd be damn glad at that point to get her out of the mix.

"By design," Nate went on, "the rest of the aid—which conveniently includes Ryang's illegal weapons—stays on the trucks and we deliver it to a warehouse north of the city, ostensibly to be stored for distribution at a later date." He marked the location of the warehouse on the map.

"What has always happened next was that the trucks pull out and the warehouse is locked up. Nobody's home. A little later, Ryang's buyers roll in, collect their weapons, roll back out, and no one's the wiser. Foolproof plan."

"It was until today," Gabe said grimly.

Because the BOIs, playing the role of mercenaries would be waiting for Ryang's men.

If all went as planned, the team would not only prevent the exchange from happening, but also smoke out the big buyer and contain him—alive, preferably, but dead worked if he wanted to play rough.

"Any questions?" Nate asked the group as he tucked a pistol into an underarm holster, then zipped up his coveralls to hide it.

"Only one." Reed looked annoyed as hell when Crystal handed him his coveralls. "What's with this khaki crap? I specifically requested blue to match my eyes. All right, people, 'fess up. Who dropped the ball on this one?"

Eyes rolled because they were all used to Reed's attempts to cut the tension before a dicey op.

"It was you, Tink?" He made a *tsk*ing sound and grinned wickedly when Crystal gave him a long-suffering look. "Well, then, I guess we all know who's goin' get punished when I get her home, don't we?"

"Do you suppose maybe you could focus on the mission?" Nate grumbled as he stepped into his coveralls.

"Focusing, Si—"

Crystal clamped a hand over her husband's mouth. "Shut. Up. Just shut up."

27

The primary airport for both domestic and international travel was located in the coastal town of Lungi, which was separated from Freetown by the Sierra Leone River. For Luke's part, there might as well have been a river separating him from Val as he stood on the tarmac, the sun blazing down like a ton of hot coals. He watched her through his dark glasses. She was posed in the 737's open hatch, and, despite the oppressive heat, looked cool and collected as she waved and smiled for the press piranhas crowding the metal rails airport security had positioned at the foot of the airstairs.

He checked the GPS—a cutting-edge unit Nate had access to before it had even gone into production because he had test-driven it for a friend who was eager to get it on the market. He was receiving a signal from her bra transmitter loud and clear.

He tucked the palm-sized unit back in the chest pocket of his coveralls and glanced up at her again. Chamberlin stood in the shadows behind her. As much as he hated the bastard, Luke had to give him credit. He was holding up his end of the charade and had cooperated on all counts.

"Valentina! Over here!"

"Perfect! That's it. Big smile. Fantastic! You've never looked better, babe!"

"One more shot. Look this way! Yes! Hold it right there, okay?"

"Christ," Gabe grumbled. He stood beside Luke at the bottom of the airstairs. "Like goddamn sharks in a feeding frenzy."

Luke's thoughts exactly. He didn't like that Val was so exposed. But he *did* like the way Santos and Carlyle were stacked in front of her while Waldrop held a position behind her.

He had to let them do their job. He had his own part to play.

"Just got a call from Brown," Nate said, ducking under the wing of the plane. "Says he located a nice big bird. He's standing by if we need him."

"Good to know," Reed said and fell in step behind Nate as he headed for the trucks.

Luke lingered for a final look at Val. He slid his dark glasses to the top of his head and watched her, her smile radiant as she waved to the crowd that included, in addition to the press and several lower-level dignitaries, the man Luke recognized as the Sierra Leone minister of commerce, Siaka Bai M'boma.

Beside him, Joe glared at M'boma, his jaw clenched, his fingers balled into tight fists. Because it was unchar-

acteristic for Joe to show any emotion, Luke felt a curl
of alarm. "Problem?"

He'd started to think Joe hadn't heard him, when the
big man gave a slight shake of his head. "No. Everything's peachy."

Yet the simmering rage in Joe's eyes was hotter than
the heat boiling up from the tarmac.

"Let's just get this done," he said and followed Nate
to the trucks.

"What's with Joe?"

Luke glanced over his shoulder at Gabe. "Don't
know. He's pissed about something."

Ever since he'd boarded the plane in D.C., Joe had
seemed distracted. More brooding even than usual.

Luke glanced back to the plane. Val was just beginning to walk down the airstairs.

"She'll be fine." Gabe clasped a hand on Luke's
shoulder.

She *had* to be fine—because Luke had finally come
to the irreversible conclusion that he was not finished
with this woman.

Logical or illogical, good or bad, he'd decided there
was no way in hell he was going to let Valentina Chamberlin walk out of his life.

When this was over, they were going to have a little
talk. Strike that. They were going to have a big-ass
talk.

But first he had to get her out of this dangerous country safe and sound.

● ● ●

"You are watching the news feed?" Ryang pressed the phone to his ear as he sat in front of the flat-screen TV in his Macau apartment.

The international press had been providing news coverage for the past five minutes of Valentina and Senator Chamberlin as they waved from the hatch of a 737, then waded through a reception line of Sierra Leone dignitaries on the tarmac at the Lungi airport.

"I am watching," Augustine Sesay confirmed. "As always, I appreciate both your competence and the confirmation that my delivery has arrived, and that the path is clear to pick up the shipment. As agreed, I will wire payment for the balance of the cargo within the hour and our deal will be completed."

"Forgive me, General." Ryang flicked off the TV. "If you would indulge me for a moment, I wish to offer a proposition that you may find appealing."

Ryang waited through a short silence before Augustine Sesay spoke again. Augustine had taken up the torch after his grandfather, Issa Sesay, head of the defeated RUF political party, had been convicted of war crimes and sentenced to life in prison close to ten years ago.

For six years now, Augustine had been stockpiling weapons, secretly reassembling an RUF military force, and making grandiose plans to stage another military coup against the now democratic nation of Sierra Leone.

That his efforts would be fruitless was without question. The young hothead would wage his war, quench his thirst for blood, and would eventually be crushed by a superior national military.

But Sesay's fate did not concern Ryang. He'd made his money from men such as Sesay. Tyrants in training, religious zealots, drug cartels. He cared nothing for their success or failure. Ryang's only interest in Sesay now lay in what the self-appointed general could do for him.

"Speak," Sesay said finally.

"I wish to forgive the balance of the payment you owe me for the shipment," Ryang said, dangling his bait, confident that Sesay would pounce like a tiger on raw meat.

"In exchange for?" Both distrust and curiosity colored the general's tone. No gift came without cost in their business. And no business deal was ever struck without careful manipulation.

"In exchange for facilitating the untimely deaths of the American woman and the senator."

Ryang had given this much thought. Admittedly, his anger with the woman and the senator over the trouble they had caused him had been the impetus for his decision. Upon further examination, however, there was much merit to having them both eliminated.

"They have been useful pawns for the cause," Sesay continued. "Why would you choose to dispense with two such valuable tools?"

Ryang chose his next words carefully so that Sesay could grasp the import of his proposal. "Chamberlin has become a problem. It's become clear to me that he's in the process of developing a conscience. I am concerned that he may no longer be controllable. If he were to divulge our activities . . . well, it could drastically affect our business dealings and bring me unwanted attention on an international front."

"And the woman?" the general asked after another thought-filled pause.

"The woman also knows too much," Ryang said, working to control his rage toward this pampered Western princess who had cost him the lives of four reliable assets and forced him to have two others eliminated for their bungled job in Cuzco. "She is aware of the leverage I hold over Chamberlin. If she is not killed, I have no doubt that she will make my involvement with the senator public. Again, this would place all of my business transactions under increased scrutiny. I would be forced to suspend shipments. Consequently, your arms supply will dry up."

Sesay didn't need to know that Ryang had already decided to cut ties with him. He was already in negotiations with a new buyer with even deeper pockets.

"This is a very risky endeavor," Sesay said after measuring the weight of Ryang's proposal.

"Which is why I'm forgiving the balance of your payment. It is not a paltry sum," he reminded the general. "No doubt you have numerous uses for that much capital."

Like feeding your troops, Ryang thought acidly, although Sesay would doubtless find more self-serving outlets for the unexpected windfall.

"This would be a delicate operation," Sesay said slowly.

At that point, Ryang knew he had struck a bargain. "I'm certain you will figure something out. I have only two conditions. You must act now, while they are on the ground in Sierra Leone. And you must kill them both immediately.

"I need your answer now. If you would rather fulfill the terms of our agreement with cash, so be it. I'll arrange an alternate solution to my problem."

"No. No, that won't be necessary," Sesay said quickly. "Consider it done."

Ryang breathed deeply, well satisfied with the way this conversation had gone. "Very good. I'll expect to be watching new and tragic news footage when the deed is done."

He disconnected, then absently set down the phone while he contemplated Valentina Chamberlin's fate. His only regret was that he couldn't personally watch the life drain out of her body.

"He broke into a smile when Cho ran into the room. "Hello, my little flower. For me?" he asked with surprised delight when she handed him a paper covered in vibrant watercolors that she'd splashed on the page with a child's joyous abandon.

Cho's smile was the light that guided his life. "It is very beautiful. As beautiful as its creator," he said, lifting her onto his lap and glancing adoringly at his wife, who stood in the doorway with an indulgent smile on her face.

The trip from Lungi to Freetown was generally made by water. Since taking a ferry across the waterway wasn't an option for this size of convoy, they had to drive to Freetown via Port Loko.

Five hours later dust and heat and the smell of despair seeped in through the open window as the four-truck convoy lumbered through the noisy, crowded city with Rafe and Luke in the lead. B.J. drove the second vehicle; Reed rode shotgun. Gabe and Crystal were next—Nate specifically broke up the married couples to avoid inherent emotional combat decisions—and Green sat behind the wheel of the last truck with Nate on lookout beside him.

With the bulk of their gear still packed away, each truck had to make do with the light fortification of a MP5-K mini sub-gun, stashed low and out of sight. The MP5-K was a compact thirteen inches overall and weighed in at under five pounds, handy as hell and fairly easy to conceal if they got stopped by the local police.

In addition, they were all armed with their personal handguns. Reed, like Luke and Rafe, preferred a SIG; Crystal and B.J. both carried Glock 19s. Joe preferred the Glock 17. All three weapons shot 9mm rounds, but the 17 had a bigger magazine. Gabe, as always, swore by his 1911-A. Only Nate was old school and preferred a revolver to their automatic weapons. His seven-shot S&W Model 686 Plus .357 magnum was the culmination of old technology meeting new. In Nate's expert hands, the revolver rivaled the speed of an automatic.

Val, Chamberlin, and team Santos with Waldrop at the wheel were ahead of them in a black armored limo, compliments of the Sierra Leone government. A pair of black Suburbans, loaded with rifle-toting government security guards, flanked the limo and transported M'boma, the mayor of Freetown, and a handful of lesser dignitaries.

Luke kept eyes on Val's vehicle. The armored limo was as impenetrable as a tank. He'd insisted on it. Two-inch-thick polycarbonate bullet-resistant windows, and Kevlar in the door panels, floorboards, roof, and engine compartment. The tires would run flat no matter how many holes were shot in them.

It wasn't as if they expected trouble on the drive between Lungi and Freetown. Even so, it was with no small measure of relief that they made it across the city without incident. Even without the complication of sitting on a shitload of weapons and an impending arms transfer, Freetown was a dangerous place. So when their truck got stalled in traffic and both Suburbans and Val's limo drove out of his line of sight, Luke fought to keep it together.

"Step on it," he said sharply.

"Easy, bud," Rafe said reacting calmly to Luke's tension. "You might have noticed that there's a semi blocking my way. Now relax, would ya? We'll catch up. In the meantime, Waldrop and company have things well in hand. Let 'em do their job."

Luke knew that Rafe was right, but he'd feel a damn sight better if he had eyes on even though he was tracking Val's progress with the GPS. He could raise them on the SAT phone, but that wasn't the point. The point was, he wanted to see where she was every mile of the trip. *Deep breath.* He needed to trust the three men they'd hired to keep her safe.

He shifted in the seat and made himself tough it out. And was damn relieved a few minutes later when they finally caught up with the limo again.

"So this is Kissy," Rafe said as they rolled into a crime-ridden slum on the east edge of the city. "Not exactly a Top Ten vacation destination, I'm guessing."

"Why Kissy?" Luke had asked Val when he'd found out the ghetto, which had once been the Waterloo refugee camp at the height of the bloody RUF-run government, was their primary stop. "You couldn't have picked a more dangerous part of the city."

"Which is exactly why they need the help," she'd said. "We have always gone to Kissy. The program is built around the mission there."

Luke looked around the littered streets as they rolled slowly by graffiti-splashed buildings with broken-out windows and ripped awnings. Despondent eyes stared back at him from street corners and sagging stoops. He was no stranger to third-world poverty. Still, he was sickened by what he saw. If anyone needed help, it was these people.

Ahead of them the limo stopped. Rafe pulled in behind it. The heavy scent of diesel fumes and the squeak of the transport truck's brakes accompanied the cheers of a small crowd that had gathered in front of a dilapidated Methodist church. A hand-painted WELCOME, VALENTINA! banner was draped above the double entry doors. A choir of barefoot children with bright smiles and mismatched clothes sang a welcome tribute as others swarmed around Val, squealing with laughter when she stepped out of the car.

He watched from the truck, his heart going all squishy when she leaned down and picked up a grubby little boy with big brown eyes and a fairy-tale smile, set him on her hip, and carried him up the front steps of the church. Children and adults alike followed her inside like she was the Pied Piper.

Luke climbed down out of the truck and made himself concentrate on his job. All seven BOI team members followed suit and started loading supplies into waiting hands.

He just kept telling himself that Val was safe. She was secure. There was no reason to anticipate she would be a target of any kind.

It was clear that the local populace loved her, not only because of her philanthropic gestures but because of who she was. A celebrity of international fame. A shining beacon who spread her light twice a year into a world that was for the most part ugly and dark.

Still, he was relieved when Santos and company herded her and Chamberlin out of the church and back into the limo an hour later. One stop down, two to go, and Luke was that much closer to sending her home.

28

This was it, Val realized two hours later as she stood on the front steps of the Good Shepherd hospital, saying her final good-byes to the mayor and Mr. M'boma. Her show was over, but it was the beginning of the real danger for Luke and the team. And like it or not, this was where they parted ways.

M'boma and the mayor were due at meetings on the other side of town. She and Marcus would be driven back to the airport with Santos, Carlyle, and Waldrop providing protection. Luke and the BOIs would drive to the storage facility and set their trap. Even the reporters had peeled off one by one, no doubt leaving to write their sound bites and get their footage ready to air on the evening news.

She caught her lip between her teeth and looked over the head of Mrs. Koroma, who had been the head nurse at the small rural hospital since the missions began. Luke was standing by the front fender of the truck he'd been driving, waiting for the rest of the team to gather. He looked rugged and lean, competent and heroic, and suddenly she couldn't bear the thought of leaving him.

She wasn't supposed to acknowledge him in any way . . . but she just couldn't let him leave without telling him good-bye one last time.

"Excuse me, Mrs. Koroma," she said, pulling out of the woman's embrace. "The drivers have been so helpful. I want to thank them personally."

"Of course."

Ignoring Marcus's warning look, she made her way through the reporters and lingering curiosity seekers lining the steps outside the hospital entrance.

"Thank you," she said, surprising Luke when she appeared beside him. "You and your crew have been wonderful help."

"Our pleasure," he said, and gripped the hand she extended in a formal shake.

"Please be careful," she whispered for his ears only. "I don't want to lose you."

Before she could give in to the tears stinging the back of her eyes, she spun around and walked to the limo, nodding a quick thank you to Waldrop, who immediately opened the door for her.

Only after she was alone in the backseat did she let herself look back at Luke. The tinted window was covered with road dust, but she could still see him as he climbed up into the driver's seat of the transport truck parked fifteen feet away.

Her heart leapt when he looked directly at her window. She knew he couldn't see her through the tinted glass. Just like he knew she *could* see him.

She watched his lips move as he mouthed something to her . . . and her heartbeat shifted to a flat-out sprint.

She inched closer to the window, frustrated because she couldn't lower the thick, bulletproof glass.

And watched as he said it again.

No question this time. His lips formed the words—*I love you*—before he settled his dark glasses over his eyes.

Her heart tripped, flooded by sensations that were frightening and thrilling and yet oddly calming.

I love you, too, she whispered, not even aware of the single tear that trailed down her cheek. God help her, she did love him.

His truck grumbled to life, then eased forward. Close behind him, the rest of the BOI team followed suit.

She was so intent on getting one last glimpse of him, it hardly registered when the three bodyguards and Marcus climbed into the limo. Waldrop sat behind the wheel. Santos and Carlyle slid into the seat directly opposite and facing her. Marcus sat quietly beside her.

"You ready to roll, ma'am?"

She met Josh Waldrop's earnest blue eyes in the rearview mirror.

"I guess I have to be."

"The guys have the situation well in hand," Brett Carlyle assured her.

In spite of the gravity of the situation, she couldn't help but smile at the boyish-looking bodyguard.

"Thank you, Brett," she said, and was rewarded with

a full blush that pretty much blew his image as a macho warrior.

"Jesus, Carlyle. I thought you finally grew out of that."

Instead of being embarrassed by Santos's ribbing, Brett just shrugged. "It's hereditary. And a curse."

"Just like you're my curse," Santos grumbled good-naturedly.

"What say we leave the lady in peace for a while," Waldrop suggested with a glance over his shoulder. "And heads up, boys. We've got a four-hour drive back to the airport. We don't want to drop the ball this late in the game."

The limo rolled out into traffic. Val closed her eyes and let her head rest against the plush leather seat. It had been hours since she'd slept and the fatigue had finally caught up to her. She must have immediately fallen asleep, because when she opened her eyes and checked her watch, almost an hour had passed.

She looked out the window. They were driving through a stretch of fairly open road before heading into the throbbing pulse of the center of the city. She dragged a hand through her hair, combing it back out of her eyes, and felt Marcus watching her.

So far she'd managed to avoid any one-on-one conversation with him. She didn't know what to say. And wasn't even certain what she felt anymore.

"You're in love with him, aren't you?"

She froze momentarily, then slowly turned her head his way.

"The one they call Doc," he said, looking weary and drawn. "You have feelings for him."

She glanced up to see both Santos and Carlyle were totally engrossed in their own conversation and oblivious to her and Marcus.

"I don't think I want to talk with you about this," she whispered.

"I understand. It's all right. I just . . . I just want you to know that I hope you find happiness, Val."

She swallowed hard. Nodded. She didn't want to hate him. Yet how could she ever forgive him for everything he'd done?

"I know I can never make up for what I did to you . . . for any of this," he said, lifting a hand in a gesture that encompassed not only their sham of a marriage but his subterfuge and treasonous acts. "I'm going to turn myself in as soon as we get back to D.C. It's too little, too late; I know that. But it's time to do the right thing."

Tears burned her eyes for the man she had once believed in. And when he slid his hand across the seat toward her, she hesitated only briefly before covering it with hers and holding tight.

A split second later, Waldrop swore under his breath. "Get 'em down. Now! We've got company."

Santos grabbed Val by the arm and jerked her to the floor. Carlyle flew forward and wrenched Marcus down beside her.

A Jeep roared past, then cut sharply in front of them. Two more vehicles flanked them on either side. A quick look behind her confirmed that a fourth Jeep had joined the others.

They were surrounded. And they were under attack. A barrage of automatic weapons fire battered the bullet-resistant limo.

A hand landed hard on the back of her head and pushed her face into the floor—but not before she saw that at least half a dozen men manned each vehicle, all with automatic rifles, all firing in nonstop bursts from the backs of the open Jeeps.

She felt the car shift, then drop several inches.

Oh, God. They'd shot out the tires.

"Hang on! We're getting the hell out of here." Waldrop hammered down on the gas pedal.

Between the blown tires and the weight of the armor, the limo was no match for the lighter, more maneuverable Jeeps. She could feel the vehicle losing speed.

She lifted her head again to see what was happening, just as a huge cloud of white vapor exploded from under the limo's hood.

"What's happening?"

"Bastards have armor-piercing rounds," Carlyle said. "Just blew through the engine block."

The Jeep on the driver's side swerved in and rammed them hard. The limo fishtailed, throwing Val against the side door. No sooner had she gathered herself when they were hit from the other side.

"Brace!" Waldrop yelled, then jerked the wheel hard right and slammed into the Jeep crowding them on the passenger side.

The next instant they were airborne, then they landed with a bone-rattling crack as the limo tipped to a forty-five-degree angle, teetered several yards on the wheel rims, and finally fell on its side.

Val landed hard against the door; the world became a reckless tumbling of arms and legs and pain. Steel screeched against concrete as the car skidded along the pocked pavement; sparks flew past her face on the other side of the glass. Smoke streamed from the engine block.

Sheer instinct had her scrambling for something to hold on to. She grasped at the seat in front of her, but lost her precarious hold when the limo flipped completely over on its top. Upside down, she rammed into bodies, seatbacks, the ceiling, then bounced off the floor when the limo rolled one more time and stopped.

Her head slammed against something hard; stars burst behind her eyes. Then pain stabbed through her head and sucked her into suffocating blackness.

Luke was running out of patience. Once the BOIs split from the limo, they were out of radio contact. Point-to-point commo was low power by design, because too much power made it possible for the bad guys to home in on your signal. That's where the GPS was supposed to come in.

Only it wasn't working.

Now they were in the back of the fucking beyond, miles away from any town, working inside an isolated warehouse in the middle of an exposed field.

He swore under his breath. He'd been out of contact with Val for over an hour and it was driving him crazy.

An odd tingle slithered down his spine.

Don't ignore the itch.

Something wasn't right. He could feel it.

"Could use a hand here, bro." Sweat soaked Rafe's shirt as he trudged past Luke carrying a ninety-pound case of ammo on his shoulder.

Since the buyers were expecting the warehouse to be abandoned, the guys had driven the trucks inside the sweltering heat of the twenty-five-by-seventy-foot metal warehouse that drew the sun's warmth like a bitch in heat drew strays. No electricity, which meant no lights so the big roller door on the south end of the warehouse was open wide, letting in enough late-afternoon daylight for them to see what they were doing.

They were setting up for the upcoming meet-and-greet with Ryang's buyers, who were going to be surprised—and not in a "happy birthday party" sort of way—when they swung by to pick up their guns and found that Black Ops, Inc. had come a-callin'.

Luke pushed away from the truck's bumper and stomped up to Nate, who was directing the placement of their weapons.

"You tell your buddy, Farmer," he said, getting in Nate's face, "that this state-of-the-art GPS he wants to manufacture doesn't work for shit."

"Noted," Nate said without glancing up from his checklist. "Give it to Tink and see if she can get it working. Unless you want to stand around and finger bang it to death for another hour, because, wow, you're really getting results with *that* method."

Nate glanced up at him then, and the look on his boss's face relayed that it was an order, not a suggestion.

Without a word, Luke headed to the far side of the warehouse, whipped off his shades, and searched the shadowy interior until he spotted Crystal.

"Tink," he bellowed and walked across the dirt floor toward her. "Make this sucker sing and dance."

"Hey." Reed bulled his way in between them. "Who died and made you emperor?"

Luke set his jaw and glared at the tall Texan. Reed rarely got pissed, but he was good and mad right now. They were all hot, sweaty, and edging toward cranky. They'd been loading and unloading heavy crates all day, and they still hadn't completely set up shop to welcome Ryang's buyers, who could arrive at any moment.

"Now let's try that again. Ask my wife nice," Reed ground out, butting his chest against Luke's, "and maybe I'll let you sleep in the same bed as your teeth tonight."

"It's okay, Johnny," Crystal said. "He's worried about Val."

"No," Luke said, feeling like an ass. "He's right. I'm sorry, Tink. Yeah, I'm worried, but that's no excuse to bark at you."

"Better," Reed said and backed off. "She's in good hands, bro," he added, letting Luke know there were no hard feelings.

Tink took the GPS unit. "Tell me what's happening."

"Nothing good." The signal from Val's tracker had

told him they were right on course, right on time. Then it stopped. Just blacked out.

"It's frozen."

"Let me see what I can do." She squeezed his arm. "It might not even be the unit. GPS needs to see the sky to get fixes on the satellites. Something could be blocking the signal. Maybe the armored limo's the problem. When they get to the airport and she's out of the car, we'll probably pick her up again."

"Why don't you just freakin' call Waldrop and get it over with?" Reed suggested.

He should do exactly that—it would piss off the security detail, but at this point he didn't care. He cupped the back of his neck, rubbed at the slight tingle again.

Don't ignore the itch.

Fuck it. He whipped out his SAT phone, dialed— and got a "subscriber not in service" message.

"Try again later," Crystal said with a sympathetic smile. "But Johnny's right, Luke. Any potential threat to Val ended when she parted ways with us. On the off chance something does come up, those guys know what they're doing. No one's getting past them to her.

"Now go." She gave his arm an affectionate pat. "Don't make my baby hurt his back doing all the heavy lifting."

"Yeah," Reed said, looking all put-upon and poorly. "Don't make baby hurt his back."

Luke rolled his eyes and headed back to the trucks.

They'd arrived at the storage site over an hour ago. The warehouse was built of metal with a corrugated roof and no window. No other buildings within fifty yards. A lone tree struggled for survival twenty yards down the road.

At least the site and the building were isolated, so no one could approach the place without being spotted—which was why the buyers had arranged it as the drop spot. As soon as they'd arrived, Nate had sent B.J. out as lookout. Armed with binocs, she was positioned on a low rise that overlooked the entire valley. No one was going to sneak past her.

Luke was on his way past Nate with another load of ammo when Nate held up his hand for silence.

He touched a finger to his earpiece and spoke into his throat mic. "Talk to me, B.J." He listened for several seconds. "Roger that, scramble back on down here."

Everyone stopped what they were doing and waited for Nate to fill them in.

"B.J.'s got eyes on. Two trucks on the roll from the south heading our way. Driver, shotgun, and four more men in each truck bed. AKs all around. One sub-gun.

"We've got approximately ten minutes to showtime, boys and girls. And remember: Today we're big bad mercs. Gear up like Rambo, get into position, and let's throw these nice kids a party."

29

Augustine Sesay was a proud man. A man of vision. His grandfather had been such a man. He had been a devoted follower of Foday Sankoh, the great leader of the Revolutionary United Front. Now his grandfather rotted in prison because an international tribunal had convicted him of war crimes.

The regard Augustine held for the tribunal could fit on the tip of a bullet. But the conviction that drove him to avenge not only the injustice meted out to his grandfather, but the killing of his father by enemy forces during the siege of Freetown, could not be contained within the boundaries of the country he intended to take back.

Tomorrow was both the eleventh anniversary of his father's death, and the tenth anniversary of his grandfather's imprisonment.

Augustine had marked his time. He had studied the Sankoh doctrine. He had quietly built his forces, but kept them dispersed all over the country until the time was right to gather them into an undefeatable force and reclaim what was rightfully his.

He believed it was his legacy to resurrect the RUF movement. To regain control of the Kono District and reap the profits from the diamond mines that had once been under RUF control.

The mines belonged to his people.

And his people belonged to him.

All of this rolled through Augustine's mind as he sat in a tattered canvas chair beneath the shade of an awning, his temporary base of operations in the territory north of Freetown. He was not enamored of this nomadic life. Was not disposed to living in tents, or sleeping in abandoned mine shafts, but he had done so willingly for the past ten years. He had sacrificed for the cause.

But the time for sacrifice was over. And his last bit of business with Ryang Wong Jeong would make what was about to happen possible.

Augustine's gaze swept the encampment with satisfaction. A small complement of men accompanied him. Including the ten he'd sent for his weapons, there were forty men. None questioned the strict obedience he required.

Their faces were gaunt, their bodies were weary, yet they practiced their drills without complaint. Of course, they feared him. Fear was a true leader's discipline of choice.

But today, they also understood that soon they would feast on the fatted calf. Again, compliments of Ryang Wong Jeong.

Augustine rose from his seat. He despised the North

Korean, with his superior attitude and endless conditions. He had played Ryang's game for six years now, meeting his demands and prices for his grossly expensive weapons.

Yet today, Ryang had handed him a windfall. Of course he had agreed to Ryang's terms—as he had always been forced to agree to Ryang's terms, or find himself without a weapons supplier.

What the North Korean did not know was that Augustine had no more need for his services. With this final shipment of weapons, which his detachment of soldiers was now en route to secure, his armory was complete.

And since he had no more need for Ryang Wong Jeong, he had no compunctions about altering the terms of their final agreement.

He smiled to himself as he walked to the entrance of the abandoned mine shaft. He was pleased with the diligence shown by the six-man guard unit who stood watch over the two new arrivals being held inside.

He glanced toward the thicket where the three others were strung up by their wrists, beaten and unconscious. These three were warriors. They had fought to protect the others and he respected their loyalty. But they would still die for their poor choices eventually.

He had decided that he would save them for later. Within the week, he would gather his entire army together and begin their finest hour. These three would provide many hours of entertainment when he turned them over to his men to exact slow, bloody deaths that would fuel their bloodlust and prime their thirst for war.

But the other two?

"*. . . you must kill them both immediately.*"

Kill the golden geese who could be worth a small fortune in ransom? *No, my North Korean friend.* He would not kill Marcus Chamberlin and his whore of an ex-wife. Not until after he had extracted several million dollars for the guarantee of their safe return.

Someone would be willing to pay. Someone would be willing to pay dearly. He need only bide his time until he located the perfect mark.

The warehouse was dark and silent when the trucks pulled up outside.

The team was in position and ready. Between their own combat gear and some of the toys they'd uncovered in Ryang's shipment, the cache was a mercenary's wet dream.

Despite his new lightweight body armor, sweat rolled between Luke's shoulder blades and trickled into his eyes as he waited in the hell-hot shadows of the closed warehouse. He pushed his concern for Val out of his mind and concentrated on his assignment as he stood out of sight behind one of the transport trucks, his SIG holstered on his belt, the MP5-K in a sling over his shoulder, and a big-ass machete strapped to his thigh. The entire team was tricked out with boom-booms, blades, and attitude.

Thin slices of sunlight knifed in between cracks in the galvanized roof and the sheets of tin nailed to the wall studs. The light inside was dim, but he could see the rest of the team where they manned their stations inside the warehouse.

Rafe, channeling his inner Rambo, stood to the left of the closed warehouse door, a blue do-rag knotted on his head, full bandoliers crisscrossing his chest, and toting a Thompson submachine gun. Reed, not to be outdone, could have been his twin. He manned his post on the opposite side of the door.

Tink and B.J. were positioned on their bellies in the rafters with sniper rifles tricked out with night-vision scopes.

Joe and Gabe were out of sight like Luke, behind the cover of the transport trucks.

They were ready.

The door slid open on the rusted overhead rail, and Luke's pulse kicked up a beat as sunlight crashed into the warehouse.

He ducked farther into the shadows. And waited.

A truck door slammed.

An engine revved.

The lead truck rolled into the warehouse, the second vehicle right on its tail.

In the few seconds it took for their guests of honor's pupils to adjust from sunlight to shadows, the team was on the ten men like fleas on a junkyard dog.

"Don't even think about it." Nate flicked on a battery-powered spotlight that illuminated the warehouse, so the new arrivals could see exactly what kind of buzzsaw they'd just run into.

Joe shouldered his M-4 and took a bead on the guy with the sub-gun. "Give me a reason."

The gunner froze, then carefully laid the gun across the roof of the truck. He laced his hands on his head and dropped to his knees.

"Toss 'em." Rafe stepped forward with the Tommy.

Ten AK-47s clattered to the ground.

"So glad we understand each other," Nate said from a stack of rifle crates they'd lined up against the wall. He lounged like a king on a throne of automatic weapons, an M-16 propped back on his shoulder, his S&W revolver holstered low on his hip like a wild-west gunslinger.

Round one was over, and just as they'd hoped not a single shot had been fired.

"I feel like such a bully," Reed said, deadpan, his head cocked to one side, his tommy cradled loosely in his arms as he stood guard over their motley assortment of prisoners.

"God, they're just boys." Crystal shook her head, her face drawn with anger.

B.J. leaned back against a truck fender, folded her arms beneath her breasts, and watched them chow down on the MREs Nate had passed out. "They're also starving."

The way they were diving into the meals said it had been a long time since these boys had food in their gaunt bellies. The old "catch more flies with honey" trap had worked in spades. All it had taken was the promise of food, and the youngest boy—he couldn't have been more than twelve—had started talking. Not long after, the rest of them chimed in, answering Nate's questions.

The team now knew who they were dealing with. And the news wasn't good.

It was Augustine Sesay, the grandson of the disbanded RUF's most brutal leader, who had purchased the shipment from Ryang. And these boys had just confirmed that the rumors dancing around the international intelligence community were true: Sesay was reassembling an RUF army. This shipment was to be the catalyst to stage another coup.

But, there was some good news. Sesay's troops were still mostly scattered all over the country, awaiting his call to arms. And Sesay himself was bivouacked near an abandoned diamond mine not more than two hours away. Thirty men remained behind with him.

Crystal handed a bottle of water to a boy who was shirtless, barefoot, and stared back at her from an ebony face pocked with scars.

"Give 'em each another one," Nate said, and Rafe dug into the carton of MREs.

"I don't fuckin' believe this." Joe glared from Nate to the prisoners. "I don't give a shit how young they are; they're Augustine Sesay's soldiers. That makes them killers."

"Easy, Joe." Luke shot his friend a concerned look. "We got what we needed from them."

Joe rounded on him, rage in his eyes. "You think that if the tables were turned, they'd be giving us their food? They're fucking RUF wanna-bes! Their leader is the grandson of a murdering psycho. And now we're playing wet nurse?"

He stopped short. Dragged a hand over his head. And tried to settle himself.

The warehouse was deathly quiet.

"Take five, Joe." Nate's tone held equal measures of understanding and warning. "Go get some air."

Joe shook his head and got control of himself. "Right." Then he spun on his heel and, M-16 still in hand, trudged out into the fading sunlight.

For a long moment, no one spoke. They all knew he was thinking about Bryan, and they all sympathized. Just like they understood that the barrier defining the good guys from the bad guys sometimes eroded without warning. Joe was in conflict with everything he stood for.

Hell, Luke had had his own share of dark moments. This just happened to be Joe's. Despite the odd way Green had been acting since they'd hooked up in D.C., Luke was confident that Mean Joe Green would work it out. Find true north on his moral compass again.

But he hoped to hell he found it fast, because they'd been out of contact with Val for over two hours now. The GPS *still* wasn't working and he'd tried several more fruitless times to raise them on the SAT phone. And the itch just kept getting stronger. He wanted to get this show on the road, get back to frickin' civilization, and make sure she was safely winging her way back to the States.

He heaved a breath of relief when Nate approached the boy who seemed to be in charge, and extended the SAT phone Crystal had found in the glove box of the lead truck. "Call your general. He's going to want to hear what I have to say."

Augustine held the SAT phone to his ear, his fury growing by degrees as a man who would not identify himself dared to dictate terms by which his own weapons would be released to him.

A Westerner. An American. He could hear the arrogance and sense of entitlement in his voice.

"You're a businessman," the mercenary said. "This is a simple business proposition. I've found something that's yours—let's just say I'm holding it for you in safekeeping. All I require to turn it over to you is a finder's fee. Half a million American dollars seems like a fair price, do you agree?"

He did not agree. "Where are my guns?"

"Safe with me, as I have already assured you. You let me know when you can get me the money, and we'll arrange a transfer. How long it takes to resolve this is entirely up to you."

Augustine clenched his jaw, restrained himself from crushing the satellite phone in his fist. And said nothing.

"I'll tell you what," the disembodied voice said. "Why don't you think on it. I'll call you back in five minutes. You can give me your answer then."

The line went dead.

Red-hot anger boiled up in him like vomit. He hauled back and threw the phone at his aide, who howled with pain and dropped to the ground. Feet braced wide, he tipped his head to the sky, clenched his fists at his sides, and roared.

Roared until he was hoarse, until the veins throbbed on his neck. Until the rage inside him exploded like a secondary bomb.

"He thinks he can dictate terms to *me*?" He beat one fist on his chest and cursed toward the sky. "He thinks he can steal what is mine?"

His heart pounded like a drum of war; sweat poured down his face. Dizziness overtook him, finally making him realize he must regain control of his anger if he was to find a solution to the problem this pompous American had created.

He opened his mouth, sucked in a huge rush of air, slowly let it out. Then he repeated the process several times until his mind finally cleared. His heartbeat finally slowed.

He closed his eyes, lifted open palms to the sky, and drew deep within himself for wisdom.

When he opened his eyes, the shadow of an osprey drifted across the face of the mine shaft.

He instantly recognized it as a sign. The osprey was an intelligent, indiscriminate predator. It struck swiftly,

without mercy and without remorse, until it annihi-
lated its prey.

He now knew exactly what he had to do.

When Val came to, her hands were bound in front of
her. Her left wrist was swollen to twice its normal size, and
the slightest move made it throb with excruciating pain.
Each breath brought another stabbing knifelike slice just
below her breast. She couldn't move without generating
pain. She thought her head might be bleeding.

But the worst, the very worst, was the hood over her
head. And from the smell of the damp earth beneath
her cheek, and the sense of absolute darkness, she surmised she was lying on the floor of a cave.

Reliving her worst nightmare. Only it wasn't a nightmare; this was real.

A shudder ripped through her and she groaned at the
electrifying pain.

*Don't think about bugs, or rats or spiders or snakes.
It'll only give you bellyaches.*

Something moved near her feet, and she whimpered
like that helpless ten-year-old.

There was something in here with her.

Don't think about bugs or rats or spiders or snakes.

Momma . . .

Luke . . .

Oh, God, Luke . . .

Who thought she was tough.

She had to get it together. She had to figure out
where she . . .

A low moan of pain stalled her thoughts.

She whipped her head toward the sound and stars exploded behind her eyes.

She swallowed back her nausea. "Who's . . . here?"

A heartbeat of silence. A tentative "Val?"

Her heart stopped. "Marcus?"

"Oh, Val. Thank God."

She pushed herself painfully up on one elbow. "Santos? The others?"

"I don't know."

She heard male voices outside, then what sounded like canvas or a sheet being shoved aside. Hot, humid air, heavy with the scent of dust and sweat, rolled over her.

Someone grabbed her arm and jerked her to her feet. She bit back a cry of pain, struggling to keep pace as she was half-walked, half-dragged toward the source of the heat.

Another man grabbed her other arm, then someone wrenched the hood off her head.

She flinched and closed her eyes against the sudden, blinding light.

"Open your eyes." A hard hand grabbed her jaw and jerked her face forward again. "Open your eyes!"

She forced her eyes open, squinted and blinked against the brilliant light of the setting sun.

She tried to focus. A tall, thin African man dressed in a military uniform stood in front of her.

He pointed a satellite phone at her. "Smile," he said acidly and snapped a picture.

Then he turned away. "Throw her back in the mine. Bring the man out."

Seconds later, the men shoved her back inside and dragged Marcus out with them, leaving her in the dark once again.

30

Jesus Christ. Jesus fucking Christ—Augustine Sesay had Val.

Luke grabbed the SAT phone out of Nate's hand, hoping against hope that he was absolutely, positively wrong.

But there she was—bruised, bleeding, her wrists tied together, held up on her feet by two armed guards.

"She never should have come here!" he yelled and rounded on Nate. "This never should have happened! If she fucking dies it's on your head!"

He was barely aware that Gabe and Reed had moved in and were restraining him with a solid grip on each arm.

Only then did he realize how close he'd come to striking the man he had alwys looked up to—not just as his leader but as his friend.

"This isn't doing her any good," Nate said sharply. "Get it together, Colter. You can't help her if you can't push past your emotions."

He settled himself down.

The guys let go of his arms, and Luke listened with

dread as Nate spelled it out. Augustine Sesay had Val and Chamberlin. There had been no mention of Santos, Carlyle, or Waldrop. The assumption was that they were killed in a failed attempt to save their principals.

And the BOIs were no longer in charge of the negotiations.

Sesay had laid a new deal on the table. An exchange. One million American dollars and the delivery of his arms shipments for the Americans. A bargain, to his way of thinking, since the American mercenaries could parlay the hostages into ten times that amount.

Only for the sake of expediency, Sesay had taunted, was he willing to let them go for such a paltry sum of money.

"I don't have that kind of cash on me," Nate had said slowly, with just enough interest to suggest he thought he might be getting the better end of the bargain, but with enough hesitation that he didn't sound too eager.

"I don't know, though," he'd waffled, as if having second thoughts. "That's a lot of money for damaged goods."

"I can assure you, but for a few bumps and bruises, both are in excellent condition."

"If we do this," Nate had said thoughtfully. "I'll have to contact my bank."

"Then contact your bank."

"Let me think about it and get back to you," Nate had said and disconnected.

And Luke died a little inside, even though now that

he was thinking clearly, he knew that Nate had made all the right moves. If he'd acted too eager, Sesay would suspect a trap. And the only card they had to play to get Val and Chamberlin out alive was to stall until they came up with a plan.

"I want to talk to her. When you call him back, tell him to put her on the phone," Luke demanded.

"And let him know that we have a personal relationship with her? No." Nate shook his head. "They're both commodities and we're businessmen. You know that's what he has to think."

Yeah. He knew.

Over ten minutes passed before Nate lifted the phone and dialed. "I can't access my accounts until morning when the banks open in Zurich," he said when Sesay answered. "Switzerland is two hours ahead of Freetown. Give or take an hour to make the connection and complete the transaction, we can get this done over breakfast."

Sesay was silent for so long, Luke had to turn away to keep from grabbing the phone and threatening the psychotic bastard.

"Agreed," Sesay finally said, and the entire team breathed a sigh of relief. "Notify me when you have the cash in hand. We will then arrange for the exchange."

The phone went dead.

Luke felt helpless and useless and used up.

He saw Val's face in his mind, bruised, bloody, and valiant. He'd seen a cave or a mine shaft behind her, and his gut clenched with rage. The bastard was keeping her in a fucking cave.

Her worst nightmare.

He had to get her out of there.

But Nate was right—he had to get his emotions out of this or he wouldn't be any good to her.

A Zen-like calm came over him and clicked his mind into combat mode.

He looked to the man he respected, trusted, and admired, and would never make the mistake of turning on again.

"What's the plan?" he asked, and got back to the business of saving Val's life.

Two hours after Sesay ended the call, the sun had been long set. Their plan of attack had been set as well. Two trucks were loaded and ready to roll. The team was geared up in tactical-level body armor beneath their black shirts and pants. Face black covered their hands and faces. Black ball caps sat on their heads. It was hotter than hell beneath the armor, but they didn't bother with CamelBaks for hydration. They needed to travel fast and they'd already be weighed down with explosives and ordnance. And if all went as planned, they'd be in and out like fast-drying paint.

Though they were loaded with enough guns and ammo to take out a full company of combatants, phase one of their action plan was not about firepower. It was about silence and stealth. About close-quarters combat. About garrotes and blades.

"What about them?" Crystal hitched her chin toward the prisoners. They were bound together in the back of one of the transport trucks in a corner of the warehouse.

No one said a word but all eyes turned to Joe. Everyone knew his feelings about the RUF soldiers. His eyes were hard as he glared at the truck and absently fixed a sound suppressor on the barrel of his Glock.

This was Nate's call, no question, but their CO purposefully deferred to Joe to give him the chance to step up and do the right thing.

"Leave 'em," Joe said, after a tense moment. "We can send someone after them when this is over."

"Then let's roll," Nate said with an approving nod, and climbed behind the wheel of the lead truck.

Luke became one with the night. He felt the dark, throbbing beat of it thrumming through his blood. Tasted the rich, loamy essence of it on his tongue as he lay on his belly, hugging the dirt, keeping his profile low.

Beside him, the rest of the team had found their own zones. As a unit, they scanned Sesay's encampment through their night-vision goggles.

They'd established a position on a slight rise that overlooked the camp less than twenty yards away.

The trucks were parked within a quarter mile of the coordinates Sesay's baby recruits had provided. They couldn't risk the diesel motors announcing their arrival, so they'd loaded their packs with ordnance and humped the rest of the way in on foot.

It was now two a.m. When they'd arrived an hour

ago, the night had been eerily quiet. But for the distant rush of a small stream by the camp, it was alarmingly calm. Too calm to move in without being heard.

So they'd waited. Their patience finally paid off.

The weather finally changed. It was with them now—the wind and the rustling chatter it created in the cottonwoods added another layer of cover to the darkness. Fat gray clouds blew in from the west and rolled across the black sky. The air grew heavy and thick, teasing at the possibility of a storm to assuage this sun-parched corner of God's earth where godless men committed godless acts.

Crystal had spotted Carlyle and the other two, strung up by their wrists on ropes looped over the bough of a spreading cottonwood. Their heads hung heavily on their chests. Their feet barely skimmed the ground.

"Are they alive?" Nate's hushed tone was thick with the anger all of them felt but kept under control.

Crystal shouldered her sniper rifle, then adjusted the sights on the night-vision scope with a magnification factor so tight, she could see the lettering on Santos's tattoo. "Carlyle, maybe. Santos and Waldrop . . . I'm not sure."

They were all sure that if those men were dead, they had not died easily. Just as they were certain that when this night was over, they would not be left hanging from that fucking tree.

Leave no man behind wasn't just an edict. It was a promise.

Feeling his heartbeat slow as he mentally prepared

himself for the battle to come, Luke systematically scanned the encampment again. It was spread out over approximately two and a half acres. This small of an area was going to make it tough getting past the patrols without one of them sounding an alarm. The guards didn't even need radios; they could yell a warning.

Yeah, it would be tough. But not impossible.

Six Jeeps, three troop transport trucks, and an older-model Suburban were parked at the west end of a flat, open field. A crude latrine had been set up downwind at the opposite end of the camp. An open canvas mess tent, its roof flapping in the rising wind, was set up close to the stream, dead center in the middle of the camp beneath a copse of trees that encompassed an area of approximately four hundred square feet.

The smaller enclosed tent erected close by could only belong to Sesay. Surrounding him, fifteen men slept on pallets in the open, their rifles beside them.

According to the baby soldiers, thirty men were now bivouacked at the campsite along the river. The general liked to travel fast and light. He'd prepared for the possibility of a preemptive strike by posting several armed guards around the camp's perimeter—more in fixed positions at ten, two, four, and eight o'clock. One of them was asleep; another was fighting to keep his eyes open.

Four more guards patrolled in a random pattern. All were armed with AKs with iron sights. Another four were dug into shallow foxholes laid out in a semicircle facing the rise. Their sniper rifles were equipped with night-vision scopes; Ryang had supplied them well.

Between the vehicles and the mess tent, the terrain bumped up by a good six feet. Three men stood watch around a yawning opening; this was obviously where they were holding Val and Chamberlin.

Luke trained his field glasses on the mine shaft.

The three guards standing watch were already dead men.

"Commo check." Nate shimmied down the rise, a signal for all of them to follow suit.

They checked their earpieces and throat mics down the line. Everyone was "go."

"We clear on assignments?"

All heads nodded and they lowered their NV goggles into place.

Crystal had drawn sniper duty and would man a fixed position on the ridge. She'd cover B.J., who would go wide of the camp, disable the vehicles, then join Crystal with a second rifle. Both of them would cover the ground team, then wait for their Go to light things up when the field was set.

The rest of the team had predator patrol. They'd take out the guards, recover the hostages, and get the hell out.

Then they would deliver the surprise they had in store for the RUF leader. He wanted his weapons? He was going to get 'em, along with something that was guaranteed to blow the top of his head off.

"Let's do this." Nate gave B.J. a nod. "You've got five minutes, then we're heading down."

• • •

Every molecule in Luke's body wanted to head straight for that mine shaft and liberate Val. Every beat of his heart pulled him in her direction.

But that would jeopardize not only her life but the lives of the entire team. It was mission essential to stick with the plan: Take out the guards.

Extract Santos, Carlyle, and Waldrop, dead or alive.

Liberate Val and Chamberlin.

Blow this place sky-high.

The plan only worked if it was followed, and Luke would follow it to the letter.

He belly crawled down the rise, tactically but not visually aware of the rest of the BOIs spread out at thirty-yard intervals on parallel trajectories.

The ground was flat, the cover sparse. When he reached a clump of dry, brittle grass, he waited and listened. The first foxhole was no more than ten yards ahead now.

He reached into the drag bag attached to his belt, pulled out a pre-rigged Claymore, and set it behind the grass clump. When the time was right, B.J. and Crystal would set them off with remote detonators.

Then he moved on. Slow and steady, he altered course slightly to use a deadfall log for concealment. Once there, he set another block of explosives. Two yards away, the sniper in the foxhole hummed softly to keep himself awake.

Luke breathed quiet and deep, visualized the distance, envisioned the kill, slipped into his zone. Then he shot to his feet and launched himself on top of the guard.

Before the man could sound an alarm, Luke clamped a hand over his mouth, snapped his head back, and sliced his KA-BaR across the carotid artery. The guard convulsed twice, twitched jerkily, and went still. Luke waited thirty seconds, then removed his hand from the dying man's mouth.

Adrenaline mainlined into his system like rocket fuel, but his hand was rock-solid steady as he wiped the blood from his blade and peeked out of the hole.

Nothing moved but the flutter of the tent flaps. The sound of snoring, the rustle of leaves in the rising wind, and the absence of an alarm told him that the team had taken out their primary targets.

He crawled out and went back on the hunt, setting his final two Claymores on the way. Gabe, Rafe, Reed, Joe, and Nate had been setting similar charges in their wake.

Luke was standing behind a thick tree trunk when a perimeter guard strolled slowly by. He ducked out from behind the tree, looped his garrote around the guard's throat from behind, and jerked hard on both ends of the wire, simultaneously jamming his knee in the middle of the man's back. The guard was dead before he hit the ground.

Less than eight minutes had passed.

He reported into his mic, and heard exactly what he needed to hear.

Phase one accomplished. On to phase two.

He took off across the clearing at a crouching run.

He was a machine now. He had no feelings, no remorse. Only purpose.

He was eliminating enemy combatants; it was kill or be killed.

If he died, then Val died.

And Val was not going to die this night.

"Easy," Luke whispered as he sliced the thick rope cutting into Carlyle's wrists, then helped Joe steady him as he collapsed.

Joe clamped a hand over Carlyle's mouth to stifle any noise and pressed his lips against his ear. "Keep it down, buddy. We're getting you out of here."

"Ambush," Carlyle muttered. "Let you . . . down . . ."

"Yeah, we'll take it out of your pay," Joe said gently. "Can you walk?"

"Ankle's . . . broken."

That and a whole lot more, Luke thought grimly.

"No problem, I've humped heavier gear than you. Up you go."

Carlyle grabbed Luke's hand. "Santos? Waldrop?"

Luke looked over the kid's shoulder. He got a bleak nod from Nate, even though neither one appeared conscious.

"They'll be kickin' your ass tomorrow," Luke lied. "Get him outta here, Joe."

Tortured eyes that struggled to focus met his in the dark. "Valentina?"

"On the next bus," Joe assured him, hiked him onto his shoulder in a fireman's carry, and took off.

Silent as sleep, they eased the other men down. There was no time for triage. They'd been damn lucky—and damn good—to have made it this far without someone calling the alarm.

Fifteen minutes in. And Val was still captive in that mine.

Rafe took Waldrop's deadweight on his shoulder and headed out.

"It's your show now," Nate told Luke, as Gabe helped heft Santos over Nate's shoulder. "Meet you back on the ridge."

Luke nodded, then covered them as they disappeared into the trees with their heavy loads.

Then, with Reed and Gabe at his back, he headed for the mine shaft.

31

The mine entrance yawned open like the mouth of an angry dog. Broken timbers lanced into the dark like jagged teeth and caught on the stained, torn canvas that acted as a door.

Three guards stood with both hands on their rifles, bodies at rigid attention. No doubt Sesay had threatened to chop their hands off if they let the prisoners escape.

Luke crouched in the shadows ten yards away, waiting for Reed and Gabe to get into position. Once they'd both checked in, he gave them their assignments.

"L to R. Reed, take one. Gabe, take two. Number three is mine. Fire on my go."

Luke two-handed his SIG, sighted down the barrel, and drew a bead. He counted four heavy heartbeats. Gave the command. "Go."

Three muffled shots exploded through three sound suppressors in almost perfect unison.

Three kill shots to the head.

Luke jumped out from behind his cover and made

the opening of the mine shaft before the last body hit the ground.

He shoved aside the canvas tarp and rushed inside.

Right behind him, Gabe flicked on a flashlight with an infrared cover so it didn't blind them with their NVGs.

The eerie beam flashed around the cramped, sweltering shaft and landed on a body in the corner.

Val.

She was curled in a ball facing the wall. Her white slacks were filthy and torn. Her hair was matted with blood. She wasn't moving.

Luke dropped to his knees beside her.

She wasn't dead. She couldn't be dead!

His hand was shaking as he brushed her hair away from her neck. Breath stalled, he touched his index finger to her carotid artery . . . and almost wept with relief when it pulsed beneath his fingertip.

He leaned in close to her ear. "Val, it's Luke. I've come to get you out of here, Angelface."

She turned her head slowly, squinted up into the light, and gave him a weak, wobbly, absolutely beautiful smile. "Indy . . ."

He actually laughed. She could call him Ronald McDonald, for all he cared.

"Thank God you found us," Chamberlin said, rising painfully to his feet.

Luke spared a quick glance his way. He looked shaken up but ambulatory.

"We need to boogie," Reed said as he sliced through

the rope tying Chamberlin's wrists. "Chop chop. Beat feet and haul ass, people. I got a woman waitin' with an itchy trigger finger, and I don't want to be within a football field of this camp when she starts lighting the place up."

Reed was right. They'd pushed their luck beyond the limit. The rest of the camp could wake up any second.

Luke helped Val sit up and held her steady. "Can you walk?"

She nodded. "I think my wrist is broken."

Luke was sure of it after a quick look at the swollen and discolored joint.

"Brace yourself. This is going to hurt like hell." He quickly cut the cord binding her wrists together.

She sucked in a sharp breath, hunched her head into her shoulders, but otherwise didn't make a sound.

Kick-ass.

"We gotta go," Gabe said urgently.

"Get Chamberlin moving. We're right behind you, ten seconds tops."

He hadn't gotten this far to risk losing her by a bad decision, and wasn't moving her another inch without making a quick assessment. He skimmed his hands over her body, checking for more broken bones. He'd heard of men bleeding to death because a field medic had missed a broken femur. She bit back a cry when he touched her ribs.

Fuck. He was *so* not finished killing these bastards for putting her through this.

"Give me a deep breath."

She gave him enough. Badly bruised, maybe a couple broken ribs. But no lung puncture.

Satisfied he could move her, he helped her to her feet. "Let's go, Angelface."

Careful of her damaged ribs, he supported her against his side and followed the others outside. Gabe and Reed were already twenty yards ahead of them, halfway up the rise with Chamberlin. Like them, he skirted wide of the crossfire zone to avoid getting hit by friendly fire.

And that's when their luck ran out.

An AK-47 blasted from the camp behind them, and the ground by his feet exploded in flying divots of dirt.

Luke hauled ass, half-dragging, half-carrying Val along with him. Sweat ran into his eyes, blinding him. His night-vision goggles now distorted his depth perception rather than enhancing his vision, so he whipped them off, racing forward as the camp erupted in gunfire.

Answering fire cracked from the ridge. Gabe had broken out his M-4, Rafe and Nate were leaning on their MP5-Ks, while Crystal and B.J. laid down fire with their sniper rifles.

An explosion rocked the earth twenty or so yards behind Luke and he knew that one of the girls had set off one of the charges the guys had planted.

"Stay with me, babe," he urged Val—and stepped in a hole. He heard something pop; excruciating pain ripped through his leg, and he went down hard, letting go of Val so he didn't take her down with him.

He knew immediately that it was his hamstring.

Fuck and fuck again!

Reeling with pain, he dragged his SIG out of its holster and shoved it into Val's hand. "Go," he ground out.

She dropped to her knees beside him. "I'm not leaving you."

"You fucking *are* leaving me! Get your ass out of here! I'll radio for help."

Tears filled her eyes and she shook her head.

Goddamn it! If he didn't love her so much, he'd kick her ass with his good leg. He wanted her out of harm's way, and there was only one way he was going to get it done.

"You are not doing me any favors," he yelled through a blur of pain as the gunfire escalated and the decibel level shot off the charts. "Right now you're just a liability. So *go*, damn it!"

For a split second, he was afraid she wasn't going to buy it. Then she leaned in and kissed him hard. "Don't you dare die on me."

She rose to her feet and started sprinting up the hill.

He expelled a relieved breath and struggled to his feet. Pain screamed through his leg as he started hobbling after her.

He hadn't taken two steps when he knew someone was behind him. He whipped around—and stared straight into the muzzle of an AK.

In the split second when he knew he was about to die, he saw Val's face in his mind, and wished he'd had the chance to tell her—

Thunkthunkthunk

Three dark circles spread across the gunman's khaki

shirt, dead center in his chest. He dropped to his knees, then fell forward in the dust. Dead.

Luke whipped around . . . and there stood Val, the SIG extended, her broken wrist propping up her gun hand, the weapon rock-solid steady.

"Sonofabitch," he uttered in disbelief.

She seemed to come out of a daze, hurried to his side, and slung his arm over her shoulder. "We're leaving here together."

Two steps later, Reed and Joe came roaring out of the dark.

"You are such a grandstander, Colter," Reed said as they took Luke's weight off Val's shoulders.

"And you," Reed told Val with a grin as they all scrambled for cover, "are one kick-ass warrior woman."

"Keep 'em clustered together," Nate ordered as the team's gunfire pinned down what was left of Sesay's company. "Rafe's on his way with the truck."

Luke had set up a makeshift triage area out of the line of fire, and now worked frantically over Santos. He was pretty banged up, but Luke had pumped some IV fluids into him—all five hostages were dehydrated—and his vitals were starting to stabilize. He'd done all he could for Waldrop. They were dealing with a concussion at best, a brain bleed at worst. If he lasted until they got him to a hospital, Luke was going to throw a party. Carlyle was stable enough that Luke had been able to give him something for the pain and he was in the process of choking down an MRE.

Val—God, would you look at her—had insisted that
Luke tend to the men before she'd let him touch her
wrist. It had to be killing her, even though he'd splinted
and wrapped it, but she handled the pain in stoic
silence, even helping by holding Santos's IV bag.

Chamberlin was in a mild state of shock. He had a
nasty head lac and a bruised thigh, but other than that
he was in pretty good shape. He sat huddled beneath a
blanket, staring into space.

Headlights flashed behind them, the grind of a diesel
engine mixed into the sound of gunfire, and the transport truck pulled in.

Reed pushed to his feet. "Don't let it be said that we
didn't keep our end of the bargain," he said and jogged
over to help Gabe set the blasting caps and detonators.

Sesay wanted his weapons? No problem. The BOIs
were going to jam them down the bastard's throat and
then they were going to blow him into particles of red
mist.

With the exception of what they'd needed for the
assault, every last weapon, every last case of ammo
in Ryang's inventory had been stacked into the box
of one truck. Before they'd left the warehouse, they'd
wrapped det cord—plastic explosive in a flexible
tube—around strategically placed one-pound blocks
of C-4. Then they'd fed the cord through the ejection
ports and ammo crates, essentially wrapping the weapons in explosives.

Reed and Gabe jumped down from the back of the
truck. "All set."

Rafe climbed up onto the running board and got behind the wheel of the idling truck. He hammered down on the brake and shifted into gear, then he wedged a block of wood between the steering wheel and the dash so the truck wouldn't turn off course.

This was it.

He eased off the brake, gave it a little gas, rode it until it got a little momentum, then jumped clear.

He hit the ground, rolled, then crab scrambled back up the rise and dove behind the ridge onto his belly with the rest of them.

Luke watched the truck bounce across the rough terrain and slowly pick up speed. It was halfway down the hill.

"Duck and cover!" Nate shouted. "Plug your ears!"

Luke huddled over Val, covering her head and shoulders to protect her from the possibility of flying shrapnel.

Any second now, Joe would hit the detonator and Sesay's world would light up like the fires of hell. Anything within thirty yards of that vehicle would be a memory.

"Fuck! It stopped."

Luke jerked his head up to see what Joe was talking about.

Double fuck. The truck had hit a rut. The left front tire was buried up to the wheel hub fifteen yards from the designated kill zone. The engine had died.

"Plan B," Nate said, regrouping. "Gabe, Jones, Mendoza, and Reed. Keep a steady stream of fire on the camp. B.J. and Crystal. Pop off a few of the perimeter Claymores to make sure Sesay and his thugs stay put. We need to keep them pinned right where they are, before they figure out what's going on and beat the hell out of there."

"You are not running down there and starting that truck," Crystal said, reading Nate's face and realizing what he had in mind.

"Someone's got to do it," he said.

"Jesus," Luke said, not believing what he was seeing. "Someone already is."

A lone figure ran full out down the hill, heading straight toward the truck.

It was Chamberlin.

Val gasped. "Oh, my God. What's he doing?"

"The right thing," Luke said grimly, feeling respect for this man who had done so many wrong things to this woman but was finally doing something right.

"Give him cover!" Luke shouldered an M-4 and, like everyone on the hill, emptied his magazine.

"Son of a bitch," Reed whispered in awe. "He made it."

Luke lifted his eye off his rifle sights and watched as Chamberlin crawled up into the truck.

"Careful, careful, don't flood it," Rafe muttered as Chamberlin ground on the starter.

The engine turned and rumbled to life.

They all watched, dumbfounded, as the big truck rocked forward, rocked back, then lurched out of the rut and barreled straight into the belly of the Sesay beast.

The door swung open, and Chamberlin burst outside and started running back up the rise.

"Head down!" Luke shouted out in warning.

Their M-4s and MP5-Ks opened up and every team member laid down cover as Sesay's camp returned fire.

"Come on, come on, come on!" Luke yelled, urging him on.

Chamberlin was within fifteen yards—he was going to make it!

The gunfire was deafening. They never heard the shot that hit him. His legs just stopped moving, his arms flew wide in the air, his head snapped back. His body jerked spasmodically as an AK riddled him with bullets, and he fell face first to the ground.

Val screamed. Luke pulled her close to his side, covered her head with his hand.

"Fry those suckers," Nate yelled on a savage roar and Joe hit the detonator switch.

The truck exploded in a monstrous fireball that lit up the sky like a shuttle launch. Luke ducked his head against the lightning flash brightness. Then came the roar, like God's own hand smashing down on the earth; louder than every thunderstorm he'd ever heard all compressed into one violent millisecond. It felt like every molecule of air was sucked from his lungs. Beneath him, Val gasped for breath as shrapnel whistled overhead.

Then there was nothing left but the fire and the sound of ammo cooking off.

And the silent weeping of the woman he held in his arms.

The fire was still blazing when they heard the *whump whump whump* of a chopper.

"That would be our ride," Nate said. "Let's get these casualties ready to load."

Luke leaned over Santos, protecting him from the prop-wash as the chopper hovered above them, then slowly settled down close by.

By the time the bird landed, Luke recognized it as an Mi-8—a big old Russian transport bird. As the main rotor blades wound down, Mike Brown jumped out of the aircraft and, ducking low, ran toward them.

"Jesus, Nate," he said as the fire from the explosion continued to blaze, "I know I asked you to leave a light on, but this is overkill, don't ya think?"

"Glad you could make it." Nate extended his hand. "We've got casualties. We need to rock and roll."

Brown sobered and without another word started helping with the transport.

Val's eyes were filled with sorrow as she watched Gabe and Rafe walk by carrying a plastic tarp that contained Chamberlin's body.

"There was good in him," she said, leaning into Luke when he wrapped an arm around her shoulders.

"Yes," he agreed, pressing his lips against her hair. "There was good."

32

BBC news report, Macau.

"We interrupt this regularly scheduled financial report to bring you breaking news from Freetown, Sierra Leone. Government sources have confirmed that Augustine Sesay, the grandson of convicted war criminal and former leader of the Revolutionary United Front, Issa Sesay, is dead.

"Recent speculation on the international terror watch front had raised concerns that for the past several months, Sesay had been gathering support from sympathizers of his RUF reunification movement, and had plans in the works to stage a military coup on the now democratic Sierra Leone government, a country still recovering from a brutal civil war that ended less than twelve years ago. Our sources also implicate Ryang Wong Jeong, a North Korean official, as the primary facilitator of numerous illegal weapons transactions involving Sesay, which are in clear violation of international gun control treaties. Wong Jeong is rumored to have been highly regarded by Kim Jong-il prior to the abdication of his leadership to his younger son, Kim Jong-chul, late last year. The North Koreans have remained silent on the incident, but unofficial reports are that they disavow any association with Wong Jeong.

"Our sources further state—"

Ryang flicked off the TV with his remote. He had DVR'd the original report and replayed it several times since he had closed himself in his office an hour ago, when the story first broke.

He had brought disgrace upon himself. Unacceptable media attention to his government. Forgiveness was a weakness of Western culture; Kim Jong-chul would not tolerate this horrific mistake.

He had prepared for this possibility long ago. The moment he recovered from the shock of the newscast, he had initiated his plan. Under assumed names, his wife and daughter were now on a flight to the British Virgin Islands, where he maintained a safe house. No one knew of its existence. They would be safe there.

The stealthy footsteps outside his office were expected. And when the door behind his desk swung quietly open, he did not turn around.

There was no need. He knew he was already a dead man.

Aboard Africa Mercy, *Port of Freetown, Sierra Leone*
Luke hadn't realized he'd dozed off until he damn near fell sideways off the chair at the side of Val's hospital

bed. He set himself straight, dragged his hands over his face, and rubbed his bleary eyes. Dim light fell softly in the room; the scent of antiseptic filled the air. From out in the hallway he could hear the sound of monitors, soft voices, and the swish of crepe soles on polished tile floors.

Inside this small berth aboard the *Mercy* fleet's largest charity hospital ship, there was only the sound of Val's soft breathing and the tick of the wall clock.

It was 11:48 p.m. Val was asleep. Finally. Except for the angry purplish bruise on her cheek, her face was pale. Reed had been the first to scrawl his name and his phone number—wink, wink—on her white fiberglass cast. Primetime Brown, of course, had crossed out Reed's number and replaced it with his own.

The entire team had added their John Henrys and their good wishes before they'd caught their flight back to B.A.

They'd been damn lucky that the *Africa Mercy* had chosen Freetown for its port of call this year—and that Primetime had connections that had cleared the way for them to set the Mi-8 down on her deck. The floating medical facility was well equipped and staffed by some of the most dedicated medical personnel in the world.

Carlyle was resting comfortably after surgery; they'd had to pin his ankle. Waldrop and Santos were still in ICU but they were stable. If there were no setbacks, Santos might be upgraded from critical to guarded condition in the morning. Waldrop had a little tougher row to hoe, but the reports were promising and Josh was a fighter.

Luke rolled his head on his shoulders to work out the kinks and forced himself to stand up. His leg throbbed like a bitch but other than that, and a little residual ringing in his ears from the explosion, he was fine. Forgoing the crutches, he hobbled over to the small portal—the only window in the berth—and stared out over the lights of the harbor.

Val had ten stitches in the back of her head and two badly bruised ribs in addition to her broken wrist. Physically, she would heal within a couple of months. Emotionally . . . recovering from her captivity and from Chamberlin's death was going to take a while longer. The horror of watching him die would stay with her for a long time.

Nate had personally accompanied the senator's body back to the States. Just as he'd made certain the team's anonymity remained secure, Nate had ensured that the press was aware of Chamberlin's heroics in the operation. Right or wrong, at this point it didn't matter. The man was dead. The press would be all over the story and yeah, the whole truth about his dealings with Ryang would eventually come out. For now, though, he would return home a patriot—because in the end, that's what he'd been.

"You should be sleeping."

He whipped his head around to see Val watching him.

"Hey," he said softly and limped back to the side of her bed.

"Why aren't you using your crutches?"

"What do you take me for, a sissy?" He grinned when he got the eye roll he'd expected, and eased down on the chair.

"How you feelin'?" He touched a hand to her fore-head, gently brushed back a fall of dark, silky hair.

"I think I might feel better than you look." One cor-ner of her mouth tipped up in a brave smile. "You don't need to sit with me."

"Got noplace else to be, Angelface. Noplace else I want to be." Though he hadn't needed to be admitted, the staff had taken pity on him and told him he could hang around. Like a few rules would have stopped him.

He carefully lifted her casted hand to his lips, kissed her swollen fingers. He'd come so close to losing her. "I was so scared. When I saw that picture of you on Sesay's SAT phone . . ."

He choked up; lowered his head and pressed it lightly against her curled fingers.

"It's okay," she murmured, lifting her other hand to his hair. "It's okay."

His heart felt huge; he ached with feelings for this woman. And he couldn't keep them in any longer. She was hurting and emotionally drained, and this was the *worst* possible time to have this discussion—but he couldn't stop himself. "I love you, Val."

Tears pooled in her eyes and he realized she was still afraid of this. "How can you know that? You don't even know me."

"Val . . . I've known you all my life."

She shook her head. "You know 'Valentina'. You know a face in a magazine. A sound bite. A commer-cial. You fell in love with a media image."

"I fell in *lust* with an image. But I fell in love

with the woman. A strong, compassionate woman. A woman who's been through hell and came through it like a warrior."

She gave him a sad smile. "Why do you have to be so good at that? At making me want to believe?"

It hurt that she was fighting this. Fighting against believing not only in him, but in herself. He thought he knew why, but he asked anyway. "So what's stopping you?"

She turned her head away and stared at the ceiling. "I've made so many mistakes in my life, Luke."

The turmoil in her voice broke his heart. "And you think I'm a mistake?"

"No," she said quickly and turned back to him, her eyes searching. "But if I let myself love you and you end up walking away, I don't think I'll be able to recover this time."

His heart beat wildly with a rush of tenderness and relief and optimism. Her admission was as close to a profession of love as he could wish for.

"Then problem solved—because I'm not walking anywhere.

"Look," he said as the doubt in her eyes fought the transition to hope, "as little as seven days ago, I was ready to walk away from everything. The job. Who I was . . . hell, who I wasn't and what I'd become. And then you came into my life—and life had meaning again.

"You're my heartbeat, Val. You're my reason for being the man I need to be. With you, anything's possible. Without you . . . without you, I'm not the man I want to be."

Her tears fell freely now.

"I'm not saying it's going to be easy. I can't tell you that your schedule and my job aren't going to give us some problems. But I *am* telling you, with everything that I am, that I will never, *ever* walk away from you."

He lowered the side rail so he could get closer.

"Look in my eyes, Val. My heart is there. My promise is there. Let yourself believe."

"I do," she finally whispered, and with her smile, he saw the tension drain out of her body and the trust slip in. "God help me, I do."

His own eyes burned as he crawled carefully into bed beside her. "God help us both, Angelface." He settled against her warmth and drew her against him. "Because I've got a feeling we're going to be in for one helluva ride."

Epilogue

Val stood behind Luke watching him deal cards around the poker table in the Tompkinses' game room. He'd clamped an unlit cigar between his teeth; a green dealer's visor sat jauntily on his forehead. She'd watched Crystal, Johnny, Rafe, Gabe, and Gabe's wife, Jenna's, stacks of poker chips dwindle substantially over the past hour, while Luke's now spilled onto the table in front of him.

She shook her head and glanced around the table. "You all know he's cheating, right?"

Rafe tossed his cards facedown onto the green felt. "It's his thing. He gets real pouty if we don't let him beat us. I fold, by the way."

Completely unruffled, Luke flipped a five-dollar chip into the pot. "One, I'm right here and I can hear every word you say. Two, I don't have to cheat to beat you amateurs. And three"—he grinned across the table at Val—"whatever happened to 'stand by your man'?"

"Look at him," Reed said, "all cocky and smug now that he's got his own woman."

"In or out, people?" Luke fanned his index finger impatiently over the edge of the deck. "I'm growing roots here, waiting for you all to decide to stay or fold."

"In." Jenna Jones counted out three chips and shoved them toward the growing pot. "I'll call your bet and raise you ten bucks. Baby needs a new pair of shoes."

"Too rich for my blood." Gabe tossed his cards on top of Rafe's and pushed away from the table. He leaned down and pressed his lips against the gentle rise of his wife's abdomen. "Don't let Mommy gamble away your college fund."

The beautiful redhead reached up absently and caressed her husband's cheek. "Come on, Tink. Let's take this chump to the cleaners."

"Disrespect," Luke lamented. "All I ever get from these people is disrespect."

"So how are you adjusting to life in the circus?"

Val smiled at Ann Tompkins when she walked up beside her. "Ringling Brothers has nothing on this crew."

Val had liked Ann and Robert Tompkins immediately when Luke had introduced them. Val's celebrity generally garnered one of two reactions from people who, like the Tompkinses, were in power positions: They either groveled or they postured, and both made her uncomfortable.

The Tompkinses had done neither. They'd simply made her feel at home in their lovely Virginia home.

They were sincere, open, and clearly loved the entire team they'd welcomed into their hearts and home after their son Bryan had died.

The reasons for gathering them all together this Labor Day weekend were many, babies being the recurring theme.

The gentle affection that tough Gabe Jones showed Jenna, who was due in December, brought tears to Val's eyes. She was completely taken with the beautiful redheaded journalist, and they'd already talked about the possibility of Jenna doing a piece on the bush wives of Sierra Leone—a project that would bring renewed attention to Val's cause.

Sophie and Wyatt "Papa Bear" Savage were an interesting couple. The soft-spoken Georgian had struck Val immediately as a gentleman. She still had difficulty reconciling the combat stories Luke had told her about Wyatt with the man bouncing his six-month-old daughter, Mariah, on his knee and with his loving acceptance of his adopted daughter, Hope. The same could be said for Sam Lang. He was a dark, intense man whose face transitioned to light and indulgence when he looked at his wife, Abbie, and their children, Thomas, almost a year old, and two-year-old Bryan, named after their fallen brother.

Yes, she thought again, the BOIs were quite a crew. Even Nate had come, although his wife, Juliana, had not been able to join them, disappointing everyone. Val had heard so much about Juliana, she was looking forward to meeting her.

The only BOI absent from the party was Joe. And his absence had thrown a bit of a pall on the otherwise festive gathering. She glanced toward the open French doors that led to the patio. Nate was out there, deep in conversation with Ann and Robert's daughter, Stephanie.

"Steph and Joe kind of have a thing going," Luke had confided when she'd asked him what was going on. "But since Sierra Leone, he's pretty much dropped out of sight. No one knows what's going on with him. It's working on her."

It was working on all of them. Val could tell that all the guys were concerned about Joe. Something had happened to him in Sierra Leone. Something cold and dark that was clearly eating at his soul.

"Hey, Tink," Reed called to his wife. He'd given up on the poker game and was cradling the little pink bundle that was Mariah Savage in his arms. "Look how cute she is. I think I want one. S'pose we can stop by Walmart and pick up one just like her?"

Crystal glanced up from her cards and gave her husband a look. "Three o'clock feedings. Smelly diapers. Responsibility."

"Oh. Right," Johnny said with a thoughtful look. "I'd have to grow up." He kissed the baby's little pink cheek and handed her back to her mother. "So . . . who wants a beer?"

"How much did you take them for?" Val asked as Luke sank down on the sofa beside her a little while later.

The game had just broken up. She was keeping an eye on little Thomas while Sam and Abbie put Bryan to bed.

"Fifty and change," he said, looking put out. "Crystal rallied or it would have been closer to a hundred."

"You're a shameless hustler," she said with a grin.

"I'm also incredibly horny," he said as if he was announcing that he was hungry or thirsty or tired. "What do you suppose we ought to do about that?"

She laughed. "Not in front of the children."

"He's a cute little pork chop, isn't he?" Luke stroked his big hand over Thomas's curling brown hair as he toddled by, dragging a tattered blue blanket and leaving little handprints all over Ann's glass-topped coffee table. "You ever think about making one of these?"

His question was light, but the look in his eyes told her that her answer was very important to him. And the fact was, she *had* been thinking about it lately. She'd been thinking about it a lot.

"Might be nice if we were married first."

His eyes warmed and he lifted her hand to study the pearl engagement ring he'd given her last week. Because of her abhorrence of the Sierra Leone diamond trade, he'd known better than to buy her diamonds. "You say the word, I'm there, Angelface. My mom's been waiting a long time for some woman to make an honest man out of me."

As men went, they didn't get more honest than Luke Colter. Val smiled. "Then let's work on that."

Just as Luke leaned in to kiss her, little Thomas let out a squeal.

Luke laughed and picked him up. "Hey, little man. Not cool to ruin the moment when a guy's putting a move on his best girl."

A flood of tenderness and love swamped her as she watched this big, strong man hold that precious little boy with such gentle care.

"Oh, man. Now *I'm* horny," she whispered.

Luke grinned and baby high-fived Thomas. "I take back what I just said to you, Thomas. You are now officially my wingman."

Luke had sprung for a five-star hotel for their last night in the States. Tomorrow morning they would say their final good-byes to the Tompkinses. He'd head back to B.A. with the team, and Val had a late flight for a photo shoot in L.A. He planned to meet up with her there later in the week and take her to meet his parents. His mom was already baking. His dad, well, he had no doubt that Val would win over his father.

In the meantime, tonight was all about them. The hotel room was dark and cool. The bedding was sumptuous and lush—like the naked woman catching her breath beside him.

"I have so missed that fedora," she said stretching her arms above her head and arching her back like a satisfied cat. "Thank you for that."

"My pleasure."

She'd reminded him a couple of days ago how sexy she thought he looked in that hat, so he'd dug it out. When she'd walked out of the bathroom after getting ready for bed, he'd been waiting for her, stretched out on the sheets wearing nothing but the fedora and a smile.

After she stopped laughing, he'd gotten lucky. Real lucky.

He propped himself up on an elbow and looked at the source of all that good luck.

She was so freaking beautiful. Her dark hair spilled across the pillow, a long tangle of silk. Her eyes were slumberous and a deep, melting brown as he trailed a fingertip slowly between her breasts, where her heartbeat thrummed in the aftermath of their lovemaking.

He leaned in and kissed her there, where her skin was hot and salty and damp, and knew that he would love her with his dying breath.

"Think we'll ever get tired of this?" he whispered against her breast, then smiled when a shiver of arousal rippled through her body.

"Not a chance," she said on a husky laugh. "As long as you keep the fedora, we're golden."

Turn the page for
a sneak preview of
the final novel in the
exciting Black Ops., Inc. series!

Last Man Standing

by

Cindy Gerard

Coming in early 2012

Joe Green was as good as dead. He'd known it the moment he'd started digging for answers to questions no one wanted asked.

What he hadn't known was the magnitude of the havoc his hunt would create.

What he hadn't wanted was for the priest to die.

The teenage boy standing beside him was frozen in horror.

"No, man. Oh, man. You—"

"Quiet," Joe snapped.

Pale candlelight cast his and Suah's shadows in tall, wavy relief along the far wall of Sacred Heart Cathedral.

On the stone altar floor in front of them, crimson blood pooled beneath the priest's head and crept around the base of the chancel rail before spilling down the single step that elevated the altar.

The barrel of Joe's SIG was still hot as he tucked

it into his waistband at the small of his back. He dropped to a knee and pressed his fingers to the cleric's neck.

There was no pulse.

Just as there was no life in the eyes that stared at the ornate stained-glass windows depicting the Stations of the Cross in bold, saturated colors.

"Is he—?"

Joe swallowed heavily. "Dead."

Penitence, self-disgust, and defeat pounded through his veins, reminding him that what he had started would come to no good end.

Jesus. Ends don't come much worse than this.

He glanced up, beyond ornate gold candlesticks placed on the white cloth draping the high altar, above the yards of maroon velvet cascading beneath an alcove that held a life-size statue of a benevolent Christ cloaked in white robes and surrounded by a sunset sky.

God help me . . . what have I done?

The thick wooden doors at the front of the cathedral swung open with an echoing thud. He whipped his head around. Several uniformed officers stormed into the nave. The police—Freetown's bastion of corrupt law enforcement—had arrived in force, ending any hope of a quick search of the cleric's body.

"Hide before they spot you," he whispered urgently when Suah stood petrified in fear. "Duck under the high altar. Now!"

He shot to his feet and gave the boy a shove as the

gunmen raced down the center aisle between the worn wooden pews. Satisfied that the kid was well hidden beneath the altar cloth, Joe made certain the men got a glimpse of him, then sprinted for the sacristy, leading them away from Suah.

He got as far as the epistle door. It swung open and the rattle of rifles being shouldered and the *snick-click* of a dozen safeties switching to off position greeted him. The beams of as many flashlights temporarily blinded him.

He was surrounded.

"Hands in the air," a voice shouted from behind him.

Slowly, he did as he was told. Slower still, he turned around and stared into the dark, angry faces of the officers who had passed the priest's body to get to him.

Without warning, the butt end of an assault rifle swung around hard and slammed into his temple.

He fell to all fours, fighting screaming pain and the hard pull of unconsciousness. Yeah — he was as good as dead.

Then darkness sucked him under.

The last thing Stephanie Tompkins needed was for him to show up tonight. Joe knew that. Yet here he was, drawn like a storm-battered ship to the welcome waters of a calm homeport.

It was so not fair to her, but he just couldn't leave without seeing her one last time. Possibly the *very* last time, if this high-stakes game ended the way he suspected it would.

He walked slowly along the third-floor hallway, then stopped in front of her apartment door. It was going on midnight. She'd be asleep. And he was going to wake her to tell her something that was going to kill her.

Hell, just thinking about it was killing him. But he couldn't check out on her without saying good-bye. And lie through his teeth while he did it.

Swallowing the rock of guilt lodged in his throat, he shoved his fingertips into his hip pockets and stared down at his boots while he screwed up some courage. Melting snow clung to his soles; he'd left slushy tracks on the tiled hallway. Like he was going to leave tracks all over her heart.

His hand was cold when he finally lifted it and, after a heart-thumping hesitation, gave the door a soft rap.

Maybe she'd be lucky and wouldn't be home. Maybe she'd gone to visit her parents in Virginia for the weekend and would escape dealing with the shitstorm he was about to dump on her. Maybe he should just turn the hell around and crawl back into his hole.

His heart kicked up when he heard movement inside the apartment. The soft whisper of footsteps. A tentative turn of the doorknob before she slowly opened up as far as the safety chain allowed and peered into the hall.

"Hi," he said with a clipped nod when he met the surprise in her soft brown eyes.

Everything about Steph was soft. Her lush, curvy body. Her generous smile. Her nature, which made a hard man like him want to play white knight and save her from the dragons of the world that could hurt her.

But tonight he was the dragon. A fire-breathing, breath-stealing, soul-defeating dragon. And he was going to hurt her bad.

Someone should knock him senseless for doing it. If Bryan was alive, he'd damn sure kick his sorry ass from here to the next zip code. Her brother wouldn't even let him within shouting distance of his kid sister.

But Bry was dead. A lump welled up in his throat. Even fifteen years later, Bry's death was the reason Joe didn't sleep most nights. It was also the reason he had to tell Stephanie good-bye.

"Joe." Relief, happiness, and concern colored her tone. "Hold on."

She shut the door, unhooked the chain, then swung it open again.

Her long sable hair, bed-mussed and fragrant, tumbled around her face and fell softly on shoulders. She'd hastily wrapped up in her short blue robe. The loose folds of silk exposed warm, sleep-flushed skin, the generous curve of a breast. She was gorgeous, sexy, spellbinding. Yet as beautiful as she was, it was her eyes that always got to him. Those soulful, deep brown eyes were open windows to her heart as she stood searching his face.

So many emotions. So little guile. And no defenses at all against the pain he was about to lay on her.

"Come in." She stood back, opening the door wider so he could step inside. "It's cold out there."

Another woman would have laid into him. Another woman would have slapped him hard, demanded to know where the hell he'd been for the past four weeks, then cursed him out before slamming the door in his face.

But she wasn't another woman. She was Steph. Giving. Forgiving. Vulnerable.

"You've got to be freezing." She headed for the kitchen on bare feet. "I'll make coffee."

"Don't," he said with a stiffness in his tone that made her stop abruptly.

A man who loved a woman didn't treat her the way he'd treated Steph during the past month. He didn't just clam up, and not call for a solid month, didn't not explain himself.

And he sure didn't show up unannounced in the middle of the night and expect coffee before he sliced open a vein.

When she just stood there, her back to him, her silence and the rigid set of her shoulders giving away how uncertain she was, he almost lost it.

"You don't have to make coffee for me," he said inanely.

Her chin dropped to her chest. Her shoulders sagged. *Aw, hell.*

In two steps he was behind her, pulling her back against him. He wrapped one arm around her waist, another around her chest so his forearm was sandwiched between her breasts.

"I'm sorry," he whispered as he lowered his head and pressed his lips against the silk of her hair. "Steph . . . I'm . . ." Hell. Sorry didn't begin to cut it.

She turned in his embrace, lifted her arms around his neck, and, with a desperation as sharp as the hurt in her eyes, drew his head down to hers.

"Don't talk," she murmured against his mouth. "I've missed you. I've been so worried."

He tasted the salt of her tears on her lips, and it was all over for him. He had no defense against this. No resistance. No restraint.

He slammed his mouth over hers and took what he'd

been missing but had no right to claim. Not anymore. But the instant her body pressed against his, he stopped thinking about right and wrong and just reacted. Like he always reacted when surrounded by the feel and the taste of her.

"Joe," she whispered.

No anger, no censure. Only welcome.

Only giving.

Only love as he scooped her up and carried her into her bedroom, where soft lamplight gave the room a warm, yellow glow.

He laid her down on the bed that still held the sweet scent and lingering warmth of her body and kissed her deeply. Then he wrenched himself away and started shucking his clothes.

His pulse slammed like crazy as he shrugged out of his jacket and tossed it on the floor. Her gaze followed every move as he whipped his black sweater over his head, then reached for the snap on his jeans.

Hunger flamed in her eyes as he stripped off his pants and boots and finally, naked, knelt beside her hip.

"I've missed you," she whispered again, her fingers skimming slowly up the length of his thigh, then circling over his hip before trailing across the tightly clenched muscles of his belly.

"Missed you," she repeated on a breathy sigh, and finally brushed her fingertips along the throbbing length of his erection.

He groaned and she sat up; her robe slid off one shoulder to reveal a creamy, round breast as she slowly pressed her mouth to all the places her fingers had been. Her lips trailed fire along his thigh, his hip, and the taut, quivering muscles of his belly.

He was one live electric nerve, one raging sexual urge, when she finally caressed the tip of his penis with a slow stroke of her tongue . . . and damn near blinded him.

He sucked in a harsh breath, let his head fall back, and knotted his hands in the silk of her hair. Then he lost himself in the sweet, wet caress of her lips. Let her enfold him in sensation with the delicate tip of her tongue and the hot, fluid suction of her mouth.

She always drove him out of his mind with the self-lessness of her giving, and tonight was no exception. She humbled and thrilled him with the passion of her sighs and her touch, until mindless pleasure gradually transitioned to a dawning understanding.

He didn't know what finally triggered his synapses to connect and make him realize that her fervor had evolved to desperation. That her desire had become a plea.

Don't leave me. Don't leave me. Don't leave me.

She didn't say the words. She didn't have to. But it was clear that she knew he'd come to say good-bye. With every kiss, every wild and reckless caress, she told him she knew and that she was begging him not to go . . . bargaining with him to stay.

Regret and guilt finally brought him back to his senses.

He couldn't let her do this.

"Steph," he whispered. "Steph, don't." He tipped her head back so he could look at her.

At the tears trailing down her face.

At those beautiful brown eyes so burdened with pain.

He hated himself for doing this to her. He'd made her beg, and he was so far from being worth it.

He gently laid her down on her bed and brushed his fingers across her cheek. "I'm sor—"

"Don't." She caught his face in her hands, dragged his mouth down to hers. "Don't talk. Just love me. Please . . . just love me now."

A better man would have resisted.

A better man would have done the right thing.

But he'd stopped being a better man when he'd chosen the course that was going to take him away from her and everything he'd ever stood for.

Helpless to deny her, he lowered his body over hers and captured her mouth with his. And when she wrapped her ankles around his hips and opened herself for him, he drove deep. And kept on driving, gratefully accepting the one good thing he'd ever had, for what could be the last time ever.

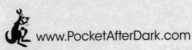